For my children,
Nadine, Earl and Bryan

For while the tale of how we suffer, and how we are delighted and how we may triumph is never new, it always must be heard.

James Baldwin

BRENDA FLANAGAN

YOU ALONE ARE DANCING

PEEPAL TREE PRESS

First published in Great Britain in 1990
Peepal Tree Press
53, Grove Farm Crescent
Leeds LS16 6BZ
Yorkshire
England

ISBN 0 94883 33 5

Note: In 1985 this novel won the Avery and Julie Hopwood
Award for Major Fiction at the University of Michigan, Ann
Arbor.

PART ONE

Santabella is a small island in the Caribbean. Some maps don't even include it, and on others you might have to use a microscope to find it. But I know it's there. Some tourists also know it but not like I do because I lived there for a long time. I know Santabella like the back of my hand. I'm not like them tourists who just come for two three nights, stay in a hotel, swim once in the sea, buy a straw hat and a coconut shack-shack, and then go back to their homelands boasting to everybody that they've been to the islands and know the natives. But what they know? What they see? They see smiling 'natives' selling embroidered baskets in the market, calypso singers with their shack-shacks moving to the rhythm of the island music in between tables of tanned women sipping rum punches and pineapple daiquiris. They see white beaches with surly waves lapping at their heels as they take their early morning strolls in search of sea shells, and later, they sit at tables on the verandas overlooking gardens of purple bougainvillaea bracts and pink hibiscus blossoms, and they write postcards about the orange glow of the setting sun and of coconut trees swaying in salt sea breezes. But if they would leave their plastic pool chairs, cross the road, walk away from the smooth tarred streets and climb the hill, they would find another world, a vibrant world; the real Santabella, and they would write home a different story, one that would need more than a postcard.

Beyond the beach, a steep quarry road leads up through Rosehill village. It winds past one and two room tapia houses that sit on pillar trees cut from sturdy two by four pine logs, and every now and then it tapers to the left or to the right to confront a larger house made from poured cement, with glass louvers for windows and lacy curtains that say to the neighbours 'we have a little more than you.' The houses, even the tapia ones, are washed in bright bright pinks or greens or blues that match the deepness of the water in the Gulf. Through the years, these houses have weathered hurricanes and storms, hot hot sun, and several earthquakes. Some have slipped in the weakened dirt but few have fallen. They remain as steadfast as the hill on which they were built, and as sturdy as the people who live in them. And perhaps in tribute to their resiliency, the people, their houses, the hill itself receives in June and July and August perfumed baths of roses. Roses—red, deep rookoo red, darker than blood—escort the light rain that comes in June, and by late August when thunder and lightning shout and flash at each other in the sky, pink rosebuds drink in the mornings and wait to usher out the rain in the afternoon.

Rosehill looks over the Gulf of Paria. Unlike many of the villages in Santabella named after the Spanish, the French, and the British who came from overseas to claim the land, Rosehill is one of the few that is named after something local—the roses that bloom on the hillside. There was a time, though, when it had a different name, one belonging to the La Romain family. The La Romains used to live in Haiti where they had enslaved many African people. When the revolution came, they managed to escape to Santabella where the French were also in power. The French government gave them land to open a cocoa plantation,

8

and supplied them with black people to work it. Naturally, they called the place La Romain estate. The place thrived for years, but after emancipation, it started to suffer. The La Romains couldn't get anyone to cut the cocoa and prepare it for market for the less than nothing wages they used to give people. By that time too, Brazilian cocoa was selling cheap cheap and the La Romains just couldn't compete on the world market. The estate started to lose big money and the family tried to sell out, but their asking price was so high, they couldn't get anybody to buy.

The estate began to fall apart, and old Mister La Romain couldn't stand the strain. They found him one evening hanging from a cocoa branch. His wife went mad after that. People used to see her walking the estate mumbling to herself two three o'clock in the morning. She died in the mad house and the last remaining great granddaughter married an Englishman and went to live in England. The bungalow went to pieces after that: bush and weeds took over the land, and snakes crawled all up in the rafters of the sheds where the cocoa beans used to dry.

The land lay abandoned for more than twenty years until Mister Pashouel, an old old fellar who had worked the cocoa in his young days, came back up the hill. He hacked down some trees and put up a one-room shack. He planted a garden, and after he had sold the first crop, he went back down to town and brought back his wife and children. They carried stones up from the ravine and laid a foundation for the first concrete house on the hill. After that, more people came up from town where a lot of them had been catching hell in the backyards, and they cut away the undergrowth, turned over the soil, and claimed a lot or two for themselves, depending on how big their family was. After they had put up a little house, they cleared another piece of land to plant short crops, but they always left the rose bushes. The roses made a natural flower garden. After a while, everybody had a rose garden, and nobody called the place La Romain estate any more.

They called it Rosehill.

About sixty families settled on the hill. Most of the men and women worked garden, but not all of them had good hands to plant, so some of them cut trees, built boats, and went out fishing in the Gulf waters around the Dragon's Mouth. Some of them continued with the trades—carpentry, painting, shoe-making—they had practised in town. But whereas in town they would work day in and day out with nothing to put away, on Rosehill they had a piece of land to call their own.

From the beginning, Rosehill didn't have life easy. Because Santabella is right in the path of the hurricane line, and Rosehill faces the Gulf, hardly a wet season would pass without a few houses on the hill falling. And during the dry season, if the ravine dried up, Rosehill wouldn't have water for days. The crops suffered, and when the crops couldn't be harvested, a lot of people on Rosehill didn't have money, but that never dampened their spirits.

Individual families had tragedies but Rosehill liked to boast about how they could hold strain even in the face of hard times. Take Miss Ann, the lady who owns the parlour by the street lamp. She liked to tell how her great grandmother died on Rosehill from pleurisy after she got soaked in the rain. The old lady had been ironing all morning, and before her body could cool down, she went to work in the garden. She just had to work in the garden every day as God send. Rain started to fall, but she had to finish putting in the plants. She caught a fever. They rubbed her down with tiger balm and soft candle to sweat out the fever but she never recovered. Hard work killed her, Miss Ann liked to say.

Miss Ann's husband, Willy, would give you the story about his grandfather—he came from Saint Vincent—and the fight he had had with a big snake on the hill. He had been clearing some old wood from the property, and had sat down to rest for a while, and before he knew it, he had fallen asleep. When he woke up, a big big snake had wrapped tightly around his leg. Willy swore the old man had to cut off his own leg with his machete to get away from the snake. 'You talk bout bravery,' Willy would boast. 'That was bravery father.'

And Oya, the old woman who lived near the Ledge, could have told you how her three children died when the coalpot she was cooking on toppled over and set her little ajoupa on fire. They couldn't put out the fire in time–it was the dry season–and Oya's two little boys and her one girl child got burned up. Oya was never right after that, and mothers warned their children to stay out of her yard.

Ling Chung, the shop owner, listened to these stories, and came to admire the people who bought goods from his grocery and liquor from his rumshop. He especially liked Jestina, young, fresh, ripe like the mango julies in his backyard. All the men loved Jestina for she was wild. She had no husband but hardly a year went by that she didn't have a child. Rosehill would have been surprised if she didn't make a baby each year, and nobody ever asked who the father was. Jestina and Melda were riding partners, going to all the clubs in town on Friday nights, dancing calypso and wining down the steelbands on Carnival days until Melda met Roy. Roy was so strict, he wouldn't even let Melda go to the market in town by herself and Miss Ann told every-body that Melda was too stupid to let man tie up her foot so. 'Not me, nuh,' Miss Ann told Jestina and Miss Roberts, her next door neighbour, as they washed clothes by the ravine. 'No man in this world could get me under control. Not even Willy.'

'Especially not Willy,' Miss Roberts laughed, and Jestina whispered to her that probably Willy didn't even want to try. 'Ann think she so smart, if she only knew what I know.' And despite Melda's insistence, Jestina refused to say more. The whole of Rosehill knew about the frequent rows between Willy and Miss Ann, and they knew too that their quarrels were no worse than any other man and his wife had. Rosehill took these things in stride.

With the exception of the roses, Rosehill could pass for any other village in Santabella. It has a government elementary school, a community centre, a Catholic church, and a Baptist church clustered at the foot of the wide road that leads up from the junction past Ling Chung's grocery and rum shop. Of the four narrow tracks branching off to wind up and around the hill, one leads straight into Ann's parlour. Another ends at the Ledge, a flat piece of land jutting out with a sharp, dangerous drop.

Just by looking at them you could tell who on Rosehill has a little money, and who's still fighting life. The poorest families live in the tapia houses, and as they get a little money, they add a concrete room or two from the back, until they could build a gallery up front. Every concrete house has a gallery. It's a sign of prestige to be able to sit in your gallery, look down on what your neighbours doing, and talk them bad. That is not to say, though, that Rosehill people don't live good together as most country people do, but every now and then a little bacchanal might break out if somebody lose a fowl suspiciously.

For years, Rosehill had only one murder, and that was a crime of passion. The postman, Mister Graves, found Tyrone, Miss Melda's son, in his bed with his wife, and he chopped off Tyrone's head. People said Tyrone got what he deserved. If you want to sleep with a woman, you don't insult the husband by doing it in his house, they said. And besides, they reminded each other, Tyrone's mother had warned him time and time again to stop friending with the postman's wife because Mister Graves had a bad bad temper. He used to beat up his wife all the time, and people said he was the one who poisoned Mister Roberts' goat with paraquat just because the goat ate a few of his bodie plants. But Tyrone didn't listen. And when children don't hear, they must feel.

In the late sixties, an American company bought the rights to drill for oil in Talparo, the village next to Rosehill. Talk soon spread through the villages that the company had also bought all the land from Rosehill to Speyside. Rosehill people were squatters, the rumour went, and the Americans were going to bring down bulldozers to clear them off the land.

The Rosehill Village Council sent officers to talk to a solicitor in town. Legally, the solicitor told them, they were

12

squatters, but if they could prove they had lived on the land for more than twenty-five years, the law said they had to be given first rights to buy or lease.

'Buy?' Miss Ann asked him, 'Buy what? My grandfather sweat blood on this land. When he come the whole hill was bush. He work day and night to clear it. Snake bite him and he didn't stop. He work this land till he dead, I tell you, and you come to tell me I have to buy land? Yuh making joke, man!'

'I'm only explaining the law, madam,' the solicitor told her.

'Is no sense quarrelling with the lawyer, Ann,' Willy said. 'He's not responsible. What I want to know is when the Company coming.'

'These things take years sometimes,' the solicitor told them. 'From what I hear, they intend to drill Talparo first. If they find oil, then certainly, they will expand. I advise all you to use that time to raise some money. You don't have to buy the land. You can lease for a while.'

'But lease from who?' Willy asked him. 'The old time owner dead in England long time. Is not today we on the land, man.'

'The government acquired the land from the estate owner, and subsequently sold most to a private corporation,' the solicitor said. 'So some of you are squatting on private land, and some on government's.' He raised his shoulders and dropped them, and Miss Ann, Willy, and the rest of them went back to Rosehill to tell the people that it looked like they had a hard row to hoe.

At the next Council meeting, Willy explained the position. 'Is all for one and one for all,' he told then. 'We have to stick together. If one family give up and these people get their hands on the land, we can't stop them. We have to remain united. All you hear me? We have to remain united. I want a vote on that right now. Nobody giving up. We pulling through this thing together.' The people voted, swearing that the government and the Company would have to kill them first to get them off the

13

land. But some of them, despite their brave talk, went away wondering how much time they had left before the bulldozers would come to sweep them off the hill.

That year rain fell as if it was going out of style and wanted to make a big impression. Water washed away a lot of good top soil, making the dirt heavy and hard to turn. Then, as if to compound the misery, a crazy kind of wind came pelting in over the Gulf, blowing down trees and uprooting most of the corn and banana trees Rosehill had planted. The weatherman on the radio said a hurricane was sure to come before Christmas. So Rosehill had plenty trouble to look out for. But, as Miss Ann told Jestina, 'Girl, God don't give you more than you could handle.'

The American oil company set up headquarters near the Talparo, Rosehill boundary line, and hired men from town to clear the land. Rosehill watched them as they cut down trees and piled them up on the side. Then they brought two bulldozers to push the logs into the ravine. As soon as they did that, trouble started.

There was only one standpipe in the village, and that was usually dry, so Rosehill depended on the ravine for water. The logs blocked the flow, and people like Sammy, who lived near the boundary line between Talparo and Rosehill, couldn't get any water for their gardens. Their short crops started to dry up. On top of that, the bulldozers were flinging mud wild wild all over the place, and Sammy's yard was like a mud hole every day.

He complained to the foreman but the foreman said he was only doing his job. The very next day, as if for spite, the bulldozers flung more dirt on Sammy's yard, hitting the children, and dirtying up all the clean clothes his wife had put out on the line to dry. That same week, the Company rolled more logs into the ravine and stopped the trickle of water that had been coming through.

Willy and Roberts went with Sammy to the Company's headquarters in Talparo, but a man there told them the supervisor was in town and might not come back for a fortnight.

14

Sammy could see he was getting the runaround so he went down town to complain to the Lands and Development Ministry. A clerk in the Ministry told him there was nothing the Ministry could do. The drilling was under private development. Yankee people's business. Government didn't have anything to do with that.

The next week rain fell hard again but the men in the bulldozers didn't stop working. They loosened the dirt above Sammy's house and the land began to break up in small wet pieces. By the end of that week, most of it had slipped down, taking Sammy's crops along. Sammy and his wife came out to watch all their bodie plants, their cassava, their chives, tomatoes, lettuce, and cucumbers sliding into the ravine.

'We lose everything,' Sammy said, and his wife put her hands on her head and squeezed it tight to keep from bawling.

The Village Council's officials went to survey the damage and console the family. 'We have to make a representation to the Ministry,' Miss Ann told them. 'The government have to compensate you.'

'It's not me alone who lose,' Sammy said. 'Roberts lose too. All his zabocca plants root out. Pepper, bodie, string beans, all his short crops gone. What we going to sell in the market?'

'The Ministry *have* to do something,' Willy told him. But he and Sammy spent two weeks in the Agriculture Ministry before they could talk to a field officer.

'A lot of farmers lose crops,' the officer said. 'You think is Rosehill alone! That Company doing a lot of damage to the farmers up there. But we can't do much about it. It's private development. All I could do is have all you fill out these forms. Put down what you think the crops worth.'

'We do that already, man,' Willy told him. 'Forms done fill long time.'

The officer went to search his files. Hours later he came back to say that he couldn't find the forms anywhere. 'All I could tell you is to fill out some more. But I'm not making any promises about compensation.'

'Is not just rain cause this,' Willy explained. 'The Company digging down the hill and causing dirt to shift. The water just making things worse. But is the Company at fault.'

'You have to take that up with Lands and Development Ministry, man,' the field officer said. 'I can't help you there.'

'We try man,' Willy said. 'We went down there three times. They say is private development. But how they could let these Yankees just waltz in and take over like that, eh? Tell me that, nuh?'

'Money is power, man,' the field officer said, 'Besides, all you don't have much grounds to stand on. You squatting.'

'But how you could call that squatting, man?' Sammy asked him. 'Is years now we on that land. Years. That don't count for anything?'

'You have land deed?' the officer asked him. 'You have paper giving you title to the land?'

Sammy had to shake his head.

'Well, you see what I mean, padner? I really wish I could help, but my hands tied, man. All I could do is take the forms, but if government say they not giving squatters compensation, is not one damn thing all you could do.'

Weeks passed and the Government didn't send anybody to check out the damage. The Company finished clearing the land and started to dig wells.

Frustration was ripe on Rosehill. Down in the shop, in Miss Ann's parlour, everywhere one or two Rosehill people met, they couldn't talk about anything else but the problem.

Miss Ann told Willy, 'We shoulda gone to Wilfred Smalls. He and some of them Ministers is good friends.'

'What Wilfred Smalls could do?' Willy asked her. 'Wilfred Smalls is small potatoes. We need somebody higher up.'

'What about that Syrian man you do some carpenter work for last year, Roberts?' Sammy asked. 'Elias. He's right up there with the big shots. You can't go and talk to him?'

'Elias didn't even pay me for the work I do for him,' Roberts told them. 'Every time I go down there, the wife say he's in America; next time he's in Venezuela; he's in Aruba. Finally I tell she, look, Miss Lady, if I put meh eyes on that man, he go find heself in the cemetery, yuh know.'

'If Cudjoe was still in the government, he coulda help, He is one man who never forget where he come from,' Willy said.

'Cudjoe and them opposition fellars trying, but this country lock up tight tight. Opposition can't do a thing,' Roberts told them.

'Even if we go to Cudjoe and the opposition make a big noise, how's that going to help?' Sammy asked. 'Government will say we against them and is then we dogs dead in truth.'

But all that talk didn't help to solve the problem. Every day that passed, the Company went about its business, digging wells, running pipes, piling more and more logs in the ravine, making life harder for Rosehill. Rosehill finally had to face the facts: if the government hadn't stopped the Company from closing up the ravine, or damaging their crops, it wouldn't prevent the Company from taking over the whole hill.

Willy called a meeting of the Village Council's Officers and they talked things over. They decided to pull together two hundred dollars to bribe somebody in the government. Roberts was the only one not in favour of the bribe. He had gotten burned once before when he had bribed a government man to approve a contract. The man had turned right around and given the job to his own nephew, and Roberts couldn't do anything. So he refused to take part, but he promised to assist the treasurer in holding a susu for the whole village so people could start putting aside a few dollars for the leases.

While all this was going on, Rosehill got some good news.

Miss Ann, as usual, claimed she was the first one on Rosehill to hear the news. She said she was listening to the twelve o'clock broadcast on Radiofusion, and just as she was about to cut a block of ice to put in the box to cool some sweet drinks, the announcer made the report.

17

'I almost stab meh hand with the icepick,' she told Jestina. 'I know Sonny has a lot of brains, but I didn't know the boy so bright to get scholarship.'

'Well, I'm not surprised, yuh know,' Jestina answered. 'I always know Sonny was bound for greatness. I used to watch him when he was a small boy. He was always quiet quiet. When the other children playing football and cricket, Sonny reading book. Is only when he start wearing long pants that he start blossomin'.'

'You only *think* he was quiet,' Miss Ann told her. 'I used to watch him too, and I see a lot of things other people didn't see.'

'So what you see so?' Jestina asked her.

'What I see?' Miss Ann shook her head. 'Girl, you know I don't like to talk people's business.'

'So okay,' Jestina said. 'If you want to keep it to yuhself, keep it. I have to go ketch the sun anyway. Since ten o'clock I washing.' And she made a move to leave Miss Ann's parlour.

Miss Ann raised her hand. Jestina hesitated. 'You know I don't like to put people's business in the road, Jestina,' Miss Ann said. 'So if I hear this from anybody, I will know it come from you.'

'My lips glue down with laglie, girl,' Jestina laughed, and she kissed God's cross.

'I used to see them all the time,' Miss Ann said.

'Sonny and somebody?' Jestina asked, 'Who?'

'Reme's young daughter,' Miss Ann told her. 'She and Sonny used to be down by the ravine holding hands and thing. Many nights when they think Rosehill sleeping, they down there. So don't think Sonny so quiet quiet, nuh. Is only sly he sly, oui. And I learn never to trust sly people.'

'If Reme ever hear that!' Jestina said. 'That woman don't make joke with her one girl child, nuh.'

'You telling me?' Miss Ann said. 'Reme think that girl could walk on water self.'

'Well at least it ent affect Sonny's brains,' Jestina said. 'He still win the scholarship. First time anybody in Rosehill do that.'

'I not denying that,' Miss Ann told her. 'And if things wasn't so bad with me, I woulda throw a big time fete for him.'

'I feel the same way,' Jestina said. 'Sonny make me proud, girl.'

'Not you alone,' Miss Ann said. 'He really make everybody on Rosehill proud.'

'I think the Village Council should sponsor a fete,' Jestina told her. 'You's the secretary, Ann. Bring that up at the next meeting.'

Before Jestina left, they had worked out the details for the fete, and Miss Ann promised to make a motion on it at the next Village Council meeting.

Miss Ann's husband, Willy, was mending his old fishing net when his youngest son brought him the news. He sent the boy further down the beach to tell his Uncle Clive, and as the news spread, the fishermen dropped their nets and beached their boats, and went up to Ling Chung's rumshop to meet Willy. Uncle Clive called for a quart of rum, and Ling Chung put the bottle and some glasses on the counter. Uncle Clive opened the bottle and poured a few drops for the ancestors. Then he filled everybody's glass. Willy made a toast for Sonny. Then another fellar made a toast for Moko, Sonny's father. Then somebody made a toast for Rosehill, and before you knew it, the bottle was empty.

'Ling Chung!' Willy called out. 'Like you not glad we boy win or what? How come you don't stand the fellars a round, man?'

Ling Chung laughed.

'Yes man, Ling,' Uncle Clive told him. 'You is one of we now, yuh know. Show we the feeling, man.'

Ling Chung laughed a little bit again but he could see the boys were serious. They watched him. Ling Chung made a few turns about the bar, trying to ignore them. The fellars waited. After a little while, Ling Chung couldn't stand the tension, and he reached under the counter and came up with a bottle of rum.

'Is good. Is good,' he grinned.

'But how you stingy so, Ling?' Willy told him. 'This is cheap rum, man. Here we boy get this fine scholarship and you want we to toast him with white rum? You making joke or what?'

Ling Chung shook his head as if he was trying to get rid of a fly bothering him, and went over to the sink to wash some glasses. The fellars heckled him but Ling ignored them. After a while the fellars gave up, and Willy poured the rum. They drank the bitter white rum slow, and to help drown out the taste, they began to tell stories.

'All you used to argue with me,' Willy told them. 'I is the one who always say that Sonny would be Prime Minister one day. All you doubt me. Me! I could read Sonny like a book.'

'But how you so two-tongue, Willy?' Sammy said. 'Is you self stand right on this very spot and say that Sonny going to make himself mad with all that book learning. Now you change yuh tune.'

'I say that? Me? I never say that!' Willy swore.

'But is true, man,' Roberts said. 'Book learning could send you mad mad, oui. It happen to a fellar over in Macayreap. He read so much book, he went crazy. Now he walking all over town barefoot. Every time I see him, he ask me, "You be or you not be?" So one day I ask him, well, what is the question? He take out a dirty piece of paper like he had it long time, and he read it to me. He say, "De wall... of China... is greatly... curved." I tell yuh, that man mad for so.'

The men laughed, and Willy told them, 'Cecil was mad to begin with, man. Half his family in the madhouse. Madness rampant in their blood.'

'But Sonny is sound like a shilling, man,' Roberts told them, 'And I observe him from small, yuh know. He has a pointy kinda forehead. People with that kinda forehead does be bright bright.'

'That is ole talk, man,' Sammy argued. 'Sonny just make up his mind from small that he was going to be something big. The boy has ambition. You think he want to turn out like

Moko?'

'Is true, yuh know,' Willy agreed. 'After Angelina leave, Moko break down, man. He loved the dirt that woman walk on...'

'Wait a minute, Willy,' Valmon put up his hand. 'Angelina is Sonny's mother? She leave Moko?'

'I forget you just move up here, oui,' Willy answered him. 'Everybody up here know that story, man. About six months after Angelina make Sonny, she drop the child and run of with some taxi driver. Moko like he get totolbay. Tabanka hit him so hard, he couldn't work. He used to work in Doctor Chow's office delivering medicine but he start drinking so bad, the doctor had to fire him. Everyday Moko in this rum shop, morning till night. But you know what? The man was a true gentleman. You never see him without jacket and tie. Every morning as God send he wake up and put on his clothes as if he going to work. Then brisk brisk he walking down the hill. Children playing under the standpipe calling 'Morning Mister Moko, Morning Mister Moko,' and Moko not answering them. He walking fast fast like jumbie running behind him. Bap! He reach the rumshop. He come in. Then he stand there quiet quiet. Ling Chung pass him a bottle and a glass. Fellars come up to him and he offer them a drink but he ent carrying on no long conversation. All morning he sit there, nursing the petit quart. When the bottle done, he thank Ling Chung and go back up the hill. But he never cuss, yuh know. Not like some fellars when their head full of rum they cuss everybody and their mother. I never hear Moko say one bad word, not even about Angelina.'

'He used to sing about she though,' Sammy said. 'He had a little song he used to sing all the time.' And Sammy started to imitate Moko: 'I want you to know, Angelina, I want you to know...'

'That's him,' Willy laughed. 'That was Moko self.'

'I used to feel sorry for Sonny,' Roberts shook his head sadly. 'Sometimes he coming home from school with the boys and he see Moko sitting by the road side singing "Angelina, I

21

want you to know I love you..." and Sonny wouldn't say nothing. Yuh could see he want to die from shame, yuh know, but he wouldn't even shout at Moko. He just lift up Moko and walk up Rosehill one today, one tomorrow, like Bajan molasses.'

'That boy stand a lot of grind,' Sammy agreed.

'Year after year it went like that, oui,' Willy continued the story. 'Then, when Sonny was about thirteen, motor car knock down Moko right outside the rumshop. The funny thing about it was that he wasn't even drunk that day. Sonny had a pot hound he used to keep tied up under the house. The dog get away and Moko went pelting behind him. The dog run him quite down by the Main Road. Bam! Car hit him. When he come out the hospital, he have only one foot.'

'He changed after that,' Roberts said. 'Yes man, it looked like that accident knock some sense into him. He stopped drinking all together. He start planting corn and chives and hot pepper. Then he and Sonny put up that stand in the front yard and Moko start to sell boil corn in the evening.'

'But people used to say Moko wasn't even Sonny's real father,' Sammy reminded them. 'Yes man, that talk make the rounds a long time.'

'Then how come she leave the boy child with Moko then?' Valmon wanted to know.

'You know how woman's mind does work, boy?' Sammy asked him. And Valmon had to shake his head.

The Solo clock on the wall chimed and Roberts said he had to hit the breeze. He had left some tar boiling on the beach and he didn't want it to overflow. Ling Chung, when he saw the men getting ready to leave, gathered up all the glasses.

Before the fellars walked out, Willy called to them: 'But how all you could leave so? What about throwing something in for Moko. Come, Clive, drop that change on the counter.'

'But I thought you say the man don't drink any more?' Valmon asked.

'He does drink stout, man,' Willy told him. 'For strengthening purposes. We could get him a six pack. Here, Ling, take this five.'

Ling Chung counted the money. 'Dollar fifty more,' he said to Willy.

'That's your contribution,' Willy told him.

Ling Chung glanced at the men watching him, and without another word, he put the six pack of stout on the counter.

Willy told the fellars he would drop it off for Moko, and the fishermen went back down to their boats and nets on the beach.

Rosehill wasn't the only place proud of Sonny. Down on the wharf the stevedores stopped loading cargo and crouched around Joseph as he read the news in the *Santabella Guardian*. 'Is a big time scholarship he get, yuh know,' Joseph told them. 'Not no small thing. Sonny getting to go to America.'

'How much money he getting?' Cyril asked.

'But how your mind always on money so, Cyril?' Sharky told him. 'Is not a matter of money, man. That will come. Is the fact that Sonny is the first black man to get this scholarship. Is history he make, man.'

'You have a good point there, Sharky,' Leroy agreed. 'But what one man and one scholarship could do? All the money this government have, don't tell me they can't give fifty, a hundred black people scholarships. Is only one brains in this country?'

'Indian fellar get one too,' Joseph told them.

'Them Indians all for theyself man,' Leroy said. 'But I really glad for Sonny. He's we own boy.'

Sonny used to work down on the wharf right after he had finished secondary school and was waiting to hear his examination results. Sharky and Leroy and the rest of the fellars got to like him because he could take fatigue without getting vexed, and they could trust him. They let him hold the bank when they played whappie and all fours, and he always went down to the Union Hall to lime with them on Fridays after work. And he wasn't pretentious just because he had a good education. After the fellars learned he could speak foreign languages, they pestered him to teach them to cuss in Spanish, French, and Portuguese, and when the foreign sailors came to shore, they heard bad words they had never heard in Santabella before.

'We have to show appreciation,' Leroy told them, and they agreed. Just then, the twelve o'clock horn blew, and Sharky passed his felt hat. The fellars pitched in their small change and Sharky promised to buy a present for Sonny.

Moko was probably the last person from Rosehill to hear the news. Miss Ann had sent one of her children to find him but the child had come back complaining that she had looked and looked and couldn't find Mister Moko anywhere.

'One foot man can't hide!' Miss Ann screamed at the child. But Melda, passing by the house at the same time, said she had seen Moko out by the Main Road early that morning waiting for a taxi.

Moko had gone into town early that morning to see Dr. Chow to help him get Sonny a visa. The doctor was an important man with friends in high places. When Moko had heard that Sonny had received three grade A passes in his A level examinations, he was so proud, he decided to try to send the boy away to study. He quietly began to throw susu hands, and he had saved just about enough to pay Sonny's passage to America. But he needed a visa. A good word from the doctor and the boy would have no trouble when he went up to the embassy.

So while Miss Ann was looking all over Rosehill for Moko, he was waiting patiently in the doctor's office. It was after one before Dr. Chow had time to see him, and when Moko explained why he had come, the doctor was sceptical.

How Sonny would live, he wanted to know. 'It costs a lot to study in America,' he told Moko. 'Where you going to get that kind of money, Moko?' He went on about regulations, and restrictions. 'America isn't letting just any and everybody into their country anymore, Moko.'

'But Sonny is not just any and everybody, Doc,' Moko

24

said. 'He has a lot of brains. He....'

The doctor cut him off. 'I thought you promised to have him come work for me when he finished school, Moko? Remember when you came and asked for that letter of recommendation, eh? Remember? You promised then.'

'I didn't forget, Doc,' Moko said. 'But Sonny want to be a barrister real bad.'

'Everybody and their brother want to go to America these days, Moko. Everybody thinks American is paradise. It's not as easy as people think.'

'Is a chance the boy want, Doc. Just a chance.' Moko pleaded and he heard the whine, the begging in his own voice, and he was feeling ashamed, but this was for Sonny.

A nurse called the doctor and he left Moko for a few minutes. Moko looked around at the doctor's office, at the desk piled with important looking forms and papers, the brass lamp with green glass shade; the leather chair on coasters; the glass-encased certificates on the walls; and he saw Sonny there, shaking hands with important clients.

The doctor came back and Moko put away the dream.

'I can't promise anything, you know,' Dr. Chow said, 'but I'll see what I could do. But tell the boy to stop by. I have some things he could do for me. You have taxi fare, Moko?' And without waiting for Moko to answer, he called to the nurse and told her to give Moko two dollars. Then he went into another room.

Moko smiled at the nurse and refused the money. 'Tell him I say thanks anyway,' he told her. Then he leaned on the banister and went slowly down the stairs, racking his brains for some other way to get Sonny the visa. He suddenly remembered that Paul, Sonny's godfather, had many connections, and he hopped on his old homemade crutch all the way over to Nelson Street to Paul's tailor shop. Paul is a 'town' man, Moko thought, and he always in some scheme. He know plenty people, and if he couldn't help Sonny, nobody could.

Moko found his friend pinning two pants legs together,

straight pins stuck in his mouth.

'So what's happening, padner?' Paul said, pins still in his mouth.

'Come see, come sah,' Moko dusted lint off a chair before he sat down. 'You know the old boy struggling.'

'How's Sonny doing?' Paul asked. He liked Sonny. Every year, just before school opened, he used to make two pairs of pants for him, and the boy never failed to come by to say thank you. He would gladly have taught Sonny the trade, he told Moko, but the boy was bright. His godson deserved better.

'He's doing okay. You hear how he pass?' Pride overflowed Moko's voice.

'Yeah, he came by here when he get the results. I wasn't surprised you know.'

'He tell you he want to go away?' Moko asked.

'Nah. But you mentioned it last time you came. Is the best thing for him, man. This country don't have future for young people.'

'Well, is that self I say,' Moko told him. 'That's why I trying so hard to get him a visa. That's why I come to you. You does still see that fellar who does give bank statement? He still around?'

'You mean Selwyn? He still running bobol for so, man. Making money like peas.'

'Is him self,' Moko said. 'How much you think he'll charge to give Sonny a bank statement? Embassy say anybody who want visa has to have big money in the bank. I don't have that kinda money. I was hoping Selwyn could put up some for Sonny, the boy could have a good bank statement and he's certain to get the visa.'

'Don't be so sure, man,' Paul said. 'I hear them Embassy people wising up. They see people coming up there with bank statement saying they have five, ten thousand. When the consul ask them how they get so much money, they saying they throw susu hand. Ent no susu hand in this whole island worth more than five hundred dollars. Embassy not stupid. They getting suspicious. Now they say people who want a visa must have old account, they must show a saving history. Some people was just opening account two three days before they go to the Embassy. Selwyn and them fellars lend them money, they get a statement, and they run to the Embassy. It bound to look fishy.'

'Desperate people will do anything, man,' Moko agreed. 'But Sonny not going to have that problem. He has a bank account long time. Yeah, is years he saving the pennies.'

'Embassy know how to tie people foot too, man,' Paul warned. He had finished pinning the pants, and was checking the measurements with a tape measure.

'So is how much Selwyn charging now?' Moko asked him.

'Selwyn's more for higher now, padner. When he first start, he used to charge fifty, sixty dollars. Now he charging a hundred plus. But he's my good padner, you know. Lemme talk to him. How soon you need to know?'

'Soon, man, soon. The boy just wasting time in the pharmacy. If I check you on Friday, you think you'll know by then?'

Paul promised that he would try his best, and after Moko had taken a soft drink with him, he went down to the taxi stand. Although rain had begun to drizzle, and workers were crowding the streets, he managed to get a taxi quickly.

It was on the way back to Rosehill that he heard the news about Sonny on the taxi's radio. He heard the name but wasn't sure he had heard right. He asked the driver to turn up the radio a little louder please and the man obliged but it was too late: the announcement had passed.

The taxi driver said, 'Is about a fellar up in Rosehill. He win some big time scholarship.'

'You heard the name?' Moko asked.

The passenger in the front seat said, 'Sonny something. It sound like Allan or Allen.'

'Is Allen,' the driver said. 'Sonny Allen. You know him?'

And Moko, with a strange wonder in his voice, said, 'But that is my son. Is only one Sonny Allen in Rosehill.'

The driver turned to congratulate him and the passengers began to talk as if they knew Sonny well. The woman sitting next to Moko in the back seat introduced herself as Mistress Brathwaithe and asked Moko to tell the boy how pleased she was to hear the news.

'Is nice to hear we people doing these things,' she said. 'Long time when we was growing up you not hearing we people winning no scholarship. No. Only white people and backra johnny. Creole people didn't stand a chance!'

'You don't see how things change since we get indepen-dence?' the driver asked. 'England not running this show, nuh. Is we running we own thing now.'

'I not so sure about that, padner,' the front seat passenger said. 'Is two years now since we have independence. Party people come round and say everybody getting job. Look me. Two whole years now I going down by that Public Works office every day as God send and every day I hearing the same ting. 'No work today.' Is best we was still under the Union Jack. At least then I used to do a few days work in St. Clair. Now all them white people run back to England like they 'fraid we now we independent.'

'All of them not gone, man,' the driver said. 'They only laying low, you know, till they see which way corbeaux flying. And them who gone playing smart. They not selling their prop-erty, nuh. They holding on to their big houses in St. Clair until things quiet down. They just cooling it in England, man. Soon you'll see them back down here.'

'But that is one of the problems self,' the passenger in front argued. 'The Prime Minister say what is in this island is we own. But who is this *we* he talking about? Not you or me or the man in the street. Nah padner, he not meaning we at all. Is all them big shots he meaning. They're the ones who getting jobs and big houses and scholarship...'

'But I ent no big shot,' Moko cut in. 'Is years now I self not working.'

'Well, who you know, man?' the man asked, 'because I'm

telling you, is only big name or big money talking in this country these days.'

'But I don't know any big shots,' Moko protested. 'Sonny was always bright. Moon don't hide behind cloud forever, man.'

'I hear if you join the Party you getting anything you want,' the driver said. 'Look at Beausejeu Village. All of them vote for the Party. Right after election, Prime Minister went up there and tell them they getting water and lights and community centre. These days, Beausejeu light up like Christmas tree, and they have two standpipes. Prime Minister opening community centre up there next week. I tell you, one hand don't clap, you know.'

'This government only know bobol,' the front seat passenger wiped away the argument. 'Is curry favour all the way with them.'

'But why you don't join the Party?' Mistress Brathwaite insisted. 'I living up in Marabella. A lot of us up there didn't vote for the Party, but when we see how things going, we open a Party Group quick quick. We invite the Minister to come up, and now things flourishing in Marabella. Is true the street lights still to come but the Minister say he sending surveyors soon and we getting lights before this year up. Is only so you could get through, man.'

'You telling me I must join the Party to get what is rightfully mine?' The front seat passenger was getting vexed. 'I rather dead first! Is blackmail this government doing!'

'But is just a formality, man,' the driver spoke like a man with experience. 'Join the Party. Election time nobody know who you voting for. How they go know how you vote behind a closed curtain?'

'This government? This government know everything!' the man said. 'I hear they have some fellars acting as if they is police. Mongoose squad, people calling them. You think I want them to burn down my house? If I say I voting Party and don't do it they bound to hear. Poor people have no hope in this country, I tell you.'

'I don't believe that,' Moko argued. 'Look at my son. All he has is the brain God give him.'

'You know why yuh son get that scholarship, man?' the passenger told him. 'Eh? Lemme open yuh eye. This is just another scheme to fool people. The government say we'll give two scholarships to some poor people. Then they can't say we not doing anything bout education for them. In the meanwhile, look by the back door and see how many Minister's sons and daughters getting free schooling. You think they fooling me? Not me, man!'

'That is ole talk, man,' the driver said. 'But how all you people so? When the white man was in power, you had to go to school barefoot. Now we in power and you have new school and community centre and water and paved roads, you still complaining. But how all you creole people so?'

'Is true, man,' Moko agreed. 'The day we take over this country was a blessed day. Everything can't happen at once. We have to give government a chance. Have patience.'

'I not asking them to do everything one time,' the passenger said. 'But how long I must wait to feed my children? Prime Minister's children belly full, you know. Mine still belching gas.'

'His children not even over here.' Mistress Brathwaite declared. 'They up in England in private school. So I hear.'

The driver laughed, 'All you could hear things in truth, oui. The man don't have chick nor child. He's a lone ranger, man.'

'So what he do with that Chinese woman he marry?' Mistress Brathwaite wanted to know. 'Creole woman wasn't good enough?'

'Give the man a break,' the driver laughed. 'If he like a little Chinese tail and ting, what wrong with that? All ah we is one. That's the motto.'

'The motto is a blasted lie,' the front seat passenger snapped.

The driver swerved to avoid a branch that had fallen onto the road and when the car was straight again Moko tapped him on the shoulder.

'Take your fare, please driver,' he said.

'You hold on to that, man,' the driver waved Moko's hand away. 'Tell your boy I wish him plenty good luck.'

'And tell him when he come back here don't forget who he is!' said the front seat passenger.

Moko thanked them and the driver pulled up at Rosehill junction. As he got out of the taxi, some fellars liming on the bridge shouted congratulations to him, and Moko asked them if they had seen Sonny go by. He hadn't passed yet, they said, and he shook their hands and went up the hill to his front steps where Willy sat waiting for him.

'We thought you leave we and gone, Moko,' Willy joked. 'You know how we people does play social when we is big pappy. I say now Sonny win, Moko gone clean from Rosehill.'

'Where I going, boy?' Moko laughed. 'Sonny is the brains in this family. My grave done pick out in Laparouse cemetery.'

Willy shook his hand and gave him the envelope of money Sharky had left for Sonny, and the pack of stout. Then the two men went into the house where Moko opened a can of condensed milk and poured it into a plastic pitcher. He added two stouts, wrapped a chunk of ice in a cloth, hit it twice with a hammer, and dropped the crushed pieces into two glasses. Then he filled the glasses with the stout mixture and offered Willy one.

Willy sipped, savouring the sweet blend, and then asked, 'But where the boy gone? He hiding or what? He only work half day today. I look but I didn't see him all afternoon.'

'I don't know where that young fellar gone,' Moko said. 'When boys put on long pants, you can't ask them where they going, you know. They is man. Sonny make twenty next month.'

'I sure he gone Bagatelle,' Willy said.

'For what?' Moko asked him.

'Don't play sly with me, man,' Willy challenged him. 'You know he has his girl up there.'

'Beatrice you mean?' Moko asked.

31

'Don't play you don't know what going on, Moko. You know how tight Beatrice and Sonny been all these years.'

'The only thing Sonny's tight with these day is book, man,' Moko said. 'He ent have time with girl friends.'

'Man always have time for woman,' Willy laughed.

Moko tried to sidestep the taunt. 'The girl pass all she exams and Reme tell me she going to send her up to New York.'

'Ah har! What I tell you man?' Willy exclaimed. 'Them two young people have something cooking or crapaud smoke meh pipe.'

Moko turned to the ice box for a bottle of goat's milk. He poured it into the pitcher and added another bottle of stout and offered Willy another glass.

'Nah,' Willy said, waving it away. 'Save it for Sonny. He going to need strength when he come back from seeing that girl,' and he got up from the Morris chair laughing.

Moko wrapped some corn in a sheet of gazette paper and handed it to Willy. 'Give the madam, that, nuh.'

'Thanks man.' Willy went to the front door to look out. 'Rain still drizzling. Gimme a piece of newspaper.' He folded the paper into a buccaneer's hat and put it on. Then he tucked the corn under his arm. As he went toward the door he remembered to tell Moko about the fete the fellars on the wharf were planning for Sonny. 'We inviting everybody, man,' he said expansively.

'I only coming if you going to have plenty rum,' Moko joked.

'Man, what you talking? Is fete for so! Is fete for so! We buying out Ling Chung rum shop! We going down by Angostura and we telling them is we own boy who get scholarship and if they want we to buy rum for Christmas, they better donate a whole case for Sonny.'

'You better not let Sonny hear that, nuh. You know how he is with all this drinking business.'

'We having sweet drink for Sonny, man,' Willy laughed. 'Ketch you later.' And with the newspaper hat on his head, he ran down the hill to hold a late lime with the boys in Ling

Chung's rum shop.

For a long time after Willy left Moko sat still, listening to the drizzle hit the roof and thinking. He remembered Angelina's stinging words, shouting to him that the boy was a blight; that he, Moko was blighted too. He had believed that for a long time after she had left, but it wasn't true, it wasn't true. Sonny had proved it wasn't true, and he wished with all his heart that he could tell her how Sonny had turned out.

He felt suddenly that he should do something grand for Sonny to show him how proud he was, but he could think of nothing. Then he remembered that Sonny's pigeons had not been fed since the evening before, so he scooped up a pan of corn and went out to the pigeon coop, and as he sprinkled the corn he talked to the pigeons, calling them by name, telling them about Sonny. After he had watched them eat, he went back into the kitchen, filled a pot with water and placed it on the coalpot to boil. Then he sat down with a pan between his knees and began to peel ground provisions to make Sonny some soup.

He could hear the rain falling harder, beating pan on the roof and soon water began to slip through the holes in the galvanize so he put cups and pans around the room. The water for the soup began to hiss, and he rinsed the provisions and dropped them in the pot. When the water started to bubble again he added salt and onions. Then he mixed some cornmeal dumplings and stirred them slowly into the pot. When the dumplings were hard enough, he took them out and put them in a bowl on the side. Then he lit the lamp and waited in the half dark for his son to come home.

Beatrice, Sonny's girlfriend, had moved to Bagatelle village, about ten miles away from Rosehill, after she had finished secondary school. She had grown up on Rosehill with her Tante Vivian but not long after she had taken her General Certificate of Examinations, she had had to return to her mother's house in Bagatelle. Her mother, Reme, was sick with a complaint that baffled the best doctors in Santabella. Her belly had swollen slowly and surely over nine months and Reme thought she was making a baby. But nine months went, and then ten, and then twelve, and no baby came. The midwife had said it was a baby; Dr. Chow had said it was a baby, but no baby came, and Reme's belly remained hard. People whispered that somebody had put something on Reme, and they went further to say that that somebody was the wife of a man with whom Reme had been 'friending' for years. 'It going to take strong obeah to make Reme's belly go down, oui,' people said. And when they heard that Tante Vivian, known all over Santabella for her cures, couldn't find anything to help Reme either, people shook their heads sadly and said, 'Well papayo, when you see Tante Vivian can't help Reme, you have to leave it in God's hands, oui.' But Reme refused to give up the ghost. She began to talk about going to America for medical help, and Beatrice went to work half days at the peas factory in Bagatelle to try to help her mother raise the cost of the trip.

Beatrice had just come from washing a basket of clothes in the river and was hanging them on the line to dry when Miss Jonnah, the next door neighbour, came across the backyard to tell her the news about Sonny.

'I just hear it on the radio, child,' Jonnah beamed. 'Your Sonnyboy self.'

She pinched Beatrice's arm. 'You getting married before he leave the country? Tell me right now, you know. I have to set the wedding cake.'

Beatrice shook her head and continued hanging clothes. Without turning around, she asked, 'Is only Sonny's name they call?'

'They called some Indian fellar too, but I can't remember that.'

Beatrice moved away from her with the empty basket under her arm, and Miss Jonnah asked her, 'Beatrice, like you not happy for Sonny or what? How your face swell up so?'

'What you want me to do, Miss Jonnah? Jump up and down?' she stupesed. Then she turned her back to Miss Jonnah, hung the clothes basket on a nail beside the back door, and went up the steps. Miss Jonnah followed her inside.

Beatrice said, 'Miss Jonnah, I thank you for bringing the news, okay? But I really don't have time to talk now. I have to finish a dress for Claudette by five o'clock.' To make the point, she sat down at her sewing machine and began threading a bobbin. Miss Jonnah didn't move.

'But how you so vexed up, Beatrice?' she persisted. 'I say, well, you and Sonny friendly, your mother even tell me Sonny talking marriage. I thought you would be glad for the news.'

Beatrice pressed the pedal harder and the bobbin spun off the machine. She bent to pick it up before she replied, 'I didn't say it wasn't good news, Miss Jonnah. Is just that I really have to finish this dress for Claudette. So excuse me, please?'

Miss Jonnah, feeling insulted, left through the back door and went on across to another neighbour to tell her how rude young people were these days, even when they had big education.

After Miss Jonnah left, Beatrice sat at the machine for a few minutes, staring at it, not really seeing it. Then she got up to turn on the radio. The announcer, in his imitation American accent, was introducing a tune by Aretha Franklin. Beatrice turned up the volume but turned it down again when the dejay kept cutting into the song with 'Hey baby, respect yuhself, uh huh...'

She went back to the machine but couldn't sew. She kept wishing the news would come on so she could hear the announcement about Sonny for herself. But news was read only on the hour, and the clock on the sideboard told her she had eight more minutes to wait. She pulled a piece of fabric from a box near the machine, laid it out on the ironing board, and tried to cut but soon gave it up. She sat back down at the sewing machine and couldn't keep her thoughts from overflowing.

So only two names were called. No Beatrice Salandy. No Beatrice Salandy. Why should she be so surprised? She had known she wouldn't get it. Who ever heard of a girl getting a scholarship? She had told Tante Vivian that, but Tante had insisted that she should try anyway. 'There's a first time for everything, child,' Tante had said. People in the Ministry had told her rules were changing. So she had made Beatrice study night and day, day and night. All that money Tante had invested in her education, what was it worth? Sonny had won. So what now? What now? Reme, Tante, everybody had depended on her to get big scholarship, to go away, to help Reme, to build big house, to give them a chance to boast that she was in America. What they would do now? What she would do now? Become a seamstress? Reme would say it was a good thing she had insisted on her learning the trade. 'You need to have a backup, girl.' But she hadn't wanted to learn to sew. She'd wanted other things, big things, things that young Santabellan girls didn't even dream about because they seemed impossible. And Sonny. Sonny had said over and over that he didn't want to go away. He was going to stay at Mister Maxwell's pharmacy and work his way up. Lies. He'd been lying to her all the time, and she'd been a damn fool to listen to him.

Sound from the radio floated toward her and she heard the names. Sonny's and the Indian boy's names and sour bitterness seeped into her mouth and wrapped around her tongue like laglie and she wanted to spit it out, to keep it from choking her. He could have said something. He could have told her. He should have told her.... They were friends, some people said girl friend and boy friend, and that was supposed to mean something. They had made plans together and she had believed him.

And although Beatrice didn't want to cry, water came into her eyes. It welled up and flowed out, and she wasn't sure why she was crying. Was it because Sonny had deceived her, or because she hadn't won? She didn't know. She wasn't even sure that she understood herself anymore. She got up and looked at her face in the mirror behind the door. Who was this person who looked back at her? This girl with the thick eyebrows, the flared nostrils, the thick lips. This dark-skinned, dark haired girl with water dripping down her cheeks. 'I'm nineteen years old,' she told the face in the mirror. 'What I doing with my life? I don't

36

want to spend the rest of my days in this damn place! I want to go away, I want to see the world. Oh God! I not asking too much. I don't want to be picking peas in a factory. I don't want to be no seamstress. God help me!' She heard her voice cry out and realised suddenly that she had been talking aloud. Ashamed, she reached for her hem, wiped her eyes, and sat back down at the sewing machine determined to finish the dress for Claudette to wear to the wedding.

Usually on a Thursday when the drugstore closed, Sonny could ride to Bagatelle on a friend's truck. But on the day his scholarship news was broadcast, his friend's truck was broken down, so Sonny had to take a taxi. That wasn't so easy because sometimes when heavy rain fell, as it was doing that day, Bagatelle Road, because it doesn't have any drain pipes, would flood, and traffic would have a hard time getting out. Sonny was determined, however, to visit Beatrice. He hurried his last minute duties at the drugstore and just as he reached the taxi stand, a fellar called out to him that Jeddoo, Indian fellar with a private car, was taking off for Bagatelle from the court house soon. Sonny told him thanks, and ran round the square in time to catch Jeddoo.

'Is a three dollar trip,' Jeddoo told him.

'When it rains it pours, eh?' Sonny laughed. He knew Jeddoo was overcharging him.

'You ent bound to take my car, nuh,' Jeddoo answered. But Sonny gave him the money and climbed into the back seat.

'I hope yuh sleeping in Bagatelle oui, padner,' Jeddoo said 'You can't get ants to crawl out of there tonight.'

'Is okay, man,' Sonny said, and he rolled down the window.

Jeddoo told him to roll the glass back up. 'It costs like hell to get anything fix in this country, man,' he grumbled. And he took out his handkerchief, leaned over the front seat, and wiped two little drops of water from inside the back door.

He told Sonny that he had to wait for his daughter and son-in-law, and after they came out of the courthouse, he turned on the ignition and they took off. The son-in-law asked him to turn on the radio. Jeddoo fiddled with the knobs, turning them right and left but static was too loud and he finally turned the radio off.

The drive through the rain was slow, and inside the car was stifling. It was only after they had passed the botanical gardens that the rain cooled down enough to allow Sonny to ask Jeddoo if he could open the window for a little fresh air please.

Jeddoo told him okay, and Sonny rolled the glass down a little bit. Then the son-in-law asked Jeddoo to try the radio again. Jeddoo fiddled around with the knobs and turned the volume up so high that when he came to the station, the noise burst out. He turned it down quick quick but Sonny could still hear. 'Indian Talent on Parade' was on, and the announcer was giving news about Indian happenings in and around Santabella.

He announced that he was pleased that Boysie Ramkesoon, son of Lal Ramkesoon of Manzanilla, was the winner of an Independence Scholarship. Sonny Allen of Rosehill, he announced, was also a winner.

'Boysie is Lal's son, man,' Jeddoo said. 'I know him good good. Thin thin fellar. Legs like two cokeyea stick but he have big brain on he shoulders, boy. Is New York he going, yuh know. Dentist, nuh. First Indian dentist in dis island, oui.'

'But you talking as if de man gone and come back already,' the son-in-law told him. 'He ent even gone yet. And suppose he do like Ramjohn and marry white woman and stay up there? When them fellars down here they does say a lot of things. When they go up, is a different story altogether.'

'He have to come back, man,' Jeddoo said. 'Government making him sign paper to say he coming back.'

'So what the government going to do if he don't come back? Send police for him?' the son-in-law asked.

'You think is freeness or what?' Jeddoo said. 'This government playing tough, boy. Them fellars have to sign bond. Is their parents' house and land on the line, oui. You think Ramke-soon go make he father lose land? No way! If he don't come back, government taking everything the family have. You think it easy?'

All this time Sonny was sitting quietly in the back. He wasn't surprised at the announcement because a letter had come to the pharmacy early that morning telling him the news. He had stayed out of the conversation deliberately, smiling inwardly sometimes at the comments. As Jeddoo mentioned the bond, however, Sonny got serious. His letter had mentioned nothing about a bond, and if that was true...

The only property Moko owned was the old board house. Wood lice had eaten through the board. Moko had tried to burn the nests with a flambeau but before he could turn around, the woodlice had built them up again. Sonny thought about the leaky roof. Every few days, during the rainy season, he had to paste tar over the holes because Moko couldn't afford new galvanize. Even then, when he lay down on his cot at night, water dropped on him. The latrine pit in the backyard was overflowing and no matter how much lime Moko threw in the hole, it still stank. A man charged them sixty dollars to dig a new hole and put a drum down, but they couldn't afford to pay, so he and Moko had tried to dig the hole themselves. The ground was hard as a quarry. Days upon days he and Moko scraped away dirt, and dug out rocks, only to find more rock below. After a month, the hole was only two feet deep. They gave up.

Sonny closed his eyes tightly to shut out the picture of the house and the latrine, but it wouldn't go away. Then the picture got all mixed up in his head with Moko in it standing on one foot trying to prop up the house with his crutch. He opened his eyes and tried to concentrate on the movement of the car as Jeddoo sped through the wet streets. All of a sudden, the car swerved, Sonny hit the door, and Jeddoo's daughter bawled out. Jeddoo just laughed. 'I know this road like the palm of meh hand, girl. We ent going over no precipice. Don't worry.'

He skidded round a sharp curve, swung around a big

boulder, and tooted his horn at every animal they passed. Sonny wondered if he was going to end up in the hospital. But gradually, Jeddoo slowed down as the showers eased, and the drive continued quietly. Sonny closed his eyes again and tried to block the thoughts out of his mind. He must have dozed off because he had not realised they had come to a stop. He awoke to hear Jeddoo calling him, 'Boy! Hey boy! You dreaming or what? Here's de junction.'

Sonny got out of the car, put his jacket over his head, and ran up the dirt track to Reme's house.

'Afternoon,' he called out, pushing open the front door. Beatrice answered him from the kitchen and he went toward her voice.

'What's happening, girl?' He tried to kiss her on her neck but she moved out of his way.

'So you hear?' he asked her, hanging his jacket on a nail.

'Who ent hear, don't have ears,' she said, and coming from the kitchen she handed him a towel. Then she went back to the stove.

He stood in the kitchen doorway drying his hair and face, watching her.

'So that's all you have to say?'

She shrugged.

He put the towel on the table and pulled out a bench. 'So how come you so vex?'

'I vex?' she stupesed.

He went over and tried to stop her from turning the pot spoon. She pulled her arm away, spattering his shirt with rice grains. 'You want to burn me with hot food, eh?' he tried to get her to laugh but Beatrice ignored him. He opened the fridge. 'You have any juice?' he asked. She pushed him aside, took out a bottle of lime juice, and poured some in a glass for him. Then she covered the pot and went into the living room. He followed her. She sat down at the sewing machine and began to pin the hem of Claudette's dress. He sipped his juice, waiting for her to say something.

Finally, she asked him, 'So what Moko say?'

'I never tell him. I came straight here from the pharmacy.'

'You shoulda go home first,' Beatrice said.

'I feel kinda funny to face him, to tell you the truth. I didn't tell him I was applying for it.'

'Well, Moko is not the only one get a surprise today,' Beatrice said.

'I never believed I had a chance, girl,' Sonny tried to pretend not to notice her tone. 'So what was the point in saying anything? Besides, it was a last minute thing. I decided late late to take the exam.'

'So when you leaving?' Beatrice asked him, and her voice was cold, distant, as if she really didn't care to hear the answer.

Sonny shook his head, 'I tell you, this thing take me by surprise. I have to go down to the Ministry to find out. I still can't believe it.' He smiled a little nervously and stroked the wet glass.

'I was thinking about how Moko would take it,' Beatrice said.

'Don't worry your head about Moko, girl,' Sonny told her. 'How *you* feeling about it?'

'I happy for you, Sonny,' she said.

'You still planning to go up, right? We could probably go up together,' he said.

'I not going anywhere, Sonny,' she said softly.

'What you mean you not going anywhere? Last week you say Reme was going to borrow the money. She changed her mind?'

'No,' Beatrice said.

'You changed your mind?'

'Is not a matter of changing my mind, Sonny. You think I could walk on water?'

'You mean Miss Ames refuse to lend Reme the money?'

Beatrice nodded.

'I'm not surprised, nuh.' Beatrice could hear the anger boiling.

41

'All these years Reme work for them. I tell you Beatrice, them people ent have a good bone in their body. You slave your backside for them night and day, and when time come for them to give you a little something in return, they shove you out the door. Is just like Moko. All them years with Doctor! What he get?'

'Chow is Chinese, Sonny,' Beatrice said.

'That is a difference?' he shouted. 'What the hell difference that make? Moko work for him for seventeen years and what he has to show for it? Chow kick him out on his arse as soon as he had a little trouble. I went one day and ask him, you know. I never tell you this. But I went to his office. I asked him how he could just throw Moko down like that. No pension, nothing. You know what he tell me? He say if I come to work for him, after I finish school, he will fix up something for Moko. I wanted to tell that man kiss my arse, but the nurse was standing right there. That man? I will never forget that man!'

'I learned long time ago not to depend on anybody but mehself,' Beatrice said.

'Girl, I really wish I had the money to give you to go,' Sonny said. 'I have a little bit saved but I might have to leave that with Pa.'

'Well, maybe I wasn't supposed to go away. Tante Vivian always say whatever happens happens for the best.'

'You always believe that damn stupidness,' Sonny's voice rose again. 'Not me. You tell me how it could be better for you to stay down here? What you going to do? You done pass all the exams; you want to go to college. Where you going to get money for that? And Reme. Poor Reme has her heart set on you going away. You telling me this is for the best?'

'Sonny, the world not ending next week. I could still go next year. I could throw a susu hand....'

'You not working for anything much now, girl. It could be three four years before you get up enough.'

'Nothing don't happen before its time, Sonny.'

'I wish you would stop talking this shit, Beatrice. You

42

could go this year. You plan to go. We could go together. You forget how we used to talk about going away together? If Miss Ames wasn't such a stingy bitch she could lend Reme the money.'

'For God's sake, Sonny!' Beatrice shouted. 'I never really expected Miss Ames to lend Ma the money!'

'You're right!' he snapped. 'She should *give* Reme the damn money!'

'Mama gets her pay.'

'What pay?' Sonny asked her. 'You see you, Beatrice? The nuns full your head. They tell you we does get what we deserve! Jesus loves all the children!'

Beatrice got up, grabbed his jacket off the nail, and threw it at him. 'And what Saint Mary's priests tell you, Sonny? They tell you you is Moses?'

'I ent saving nobody but myself girl. You...!' The look on Beatrice's face stopped his words.

'I didn't really mean...,' he began, but she turned away from him.

'Rain stop,' she said quietly. 'You better try to get out before it start up again.'

'So what you going to do now?'

'That's my business, Sonny,' she went and stood by the door, forcing him to leave. He took a step toward her, then stopped.

'You could take the civil service exam,' he said. 'Next year.'

'What you think?' her eyes blazed at him. 'You think I going to rust away? I don't need you to tell me what to do. Look, Reme's coming home just now. Go, okay.'

He went out. On the steps he turned as if he wanted to say something to her, but changed his mind, walked quickly down the dark track, and made his way to the Main Road.

When she knew he couldn't see her clearly if he turned around, Beatrice came to the door and watched him. He looked taller, his stride longer even in the muddy trace. She watched

43

him until he had turned the bend in the road and even as she was angry with him, she still hoped he would not have to wait long for transportation back to Rosehill.

Then she closed the door and lit the lamp. Mosquitoes and sand flies had floated into the room as she had stood in the doorway, and she had to get rid of them. From a pile in the corner of the kitchen she took a few bundles of bush and placed them in an aluminium bucket. Then she added a small piece of brown paper and struck a match. Smoke crept out of the bucket and she pushed it with her foot to the centre of the room. Mosquitoes began to sing and dance around her head, trying to escape the smoke, and she went outside, closed the back door and sat down on the steps. Around her, candleflies played hide and seek, flitting from bush to bush, and crapauds croaked together in the wet grass. The steps were damp but she didn't mind. The coolness reminded her of the concrete bridge on Rosehill where she and Sonny used to sit at nights when she still lived there. She remembered it was there she had seen him for the first time. She had just moved to Rosehill and he had come up to her by the bridge.

'I never see your face before on Rosehill, girl,' he had said.

'And I never see yours either, boy. You see me dying from fright?'

'Humm... you have pepper sauce on your tongue?' he had asked her. 'Move over on that bridge, girl. This is mine, you know.' She had slid off the concrete and had run her hand over the whole bridge.

'I don't see your name mixed in the cement,' she said.

'Girl, you really freshup!' he laughed. 'You always talk this way to big people?'

She looked around and past him. 'You see a big person here?' Her eyes opened wide.

'What your name is?' he demanded.

She got off the bridge again and flounced away without answering. He threw a small stone at her. She felt it fall at her heel but didn't turn around. She remembered thinking he was

44

fresh, and hoped she would see him soon again.

The next afternoon Tante Vivian called her in from the backyard to meet somebody. It was him. 'Sonny coming to give you lessons, Beatrice.' Tante Vivian told her. 'He passed through all your books so pay attention to what he tell you.'

He came three afternoons to give her private lessons and to cut wood, carry water from the stand pipe on the Main Road, and at Christmas time, to varnish Tante's Morris chairs. In the evenings he and Beatrice fell into the habit of going for walks. He would break a stick and strip its leaves and as they walked toward the bridge, he would hit the Tee Marie grass and watch them fold, closing themselves off from the lash. The neighbours would watch them walk down the hill and they would shake their heads and tell each other, 'Dat girl will get big belly soon. Mark my words. Why she have to hang out wid boys so?'

Beatrice knew what they were saying. She knew too, why she liked Sonny's company. Sonny shared her dreams, he wanted to go away, to explore the world, to make something of himself. When he spoke to her about these things, he put lyrics to the melodies she held in her heart, the ones she couldn't bring herself to say even to him because she knew, deep down, that young women did not dream such dreams. Why was she different from the young women on the hill, she often wondered. Why couldn't she settle for being a seamstress, or for planting garden besides a husband? Years later she would think that maybe she had been foolish to dream of a life beyond Rosehill, beyond Santabella. Maybe she would have been happier, safer within the limited boundaries that life had set for her. But on those nights that she and Sonny walked and talked, she had no such doubts. In Sonny's words her dreams came alive, and the verse of a poem she had read somewhere came back to her:

> *The woods are lovely, dark and deep*
> *And I have promises to keep*
> *And miles to go before I sleep.*

She could not recall the poet's name, but she held onto the words for dear life, just as she held unto Sonny's words. But the time came when Sonny's talk had changed, when he'd lost hope in a future that would take him beyond Santabella's boundaries.

'Is Moko,' he told her. 'How I could leave him? He depending on me to take care of him. I thinking about staying with Mister Maxwell in the pharmacy.'

Beatrice wanted to scream at him; she wanted to demand that he not give up because if he did, what would she have?

'Moko wouldn't stand in your way,' she told him.

'But who going to look after him? I not ungrateful, girl.'

'But that's not what you want, Sonny.'

'We always talking 'bout what I want,' he said. 'What you want to do with your life? What you going to do after you sit exams?'

She wanted to tell him then: she wanted to tell him about the poems and stories she wrote in copybooks that she hid in a box under her bed because whoever heard about a Santabella girl being a writer?

'Girl, you gone Toco, or what?' Sonny laughed. 'I ask you a question. How come you never want to tell me what you want to do? Tante spending all this money on education for you; I know she want you to be a nurse.'

'I hate hospitals,' she laughed. 'And I can't stand the sight of blood.'

'So what use you going to put your education to?'

She hesitated. 'If I tell you, you have to promise not to laugh at me,' she said.

Sonny put his index fingers together to make a cross and kissed it. 'If I lie, meh mother die,' he swore and Beatrice, still not quite believing him, said quietly, 'I want to be a...a..wr....a reporter.'

Sonny watched her seriously. 'For newspapers?'

She nodded. 'Sort of.'

Sonny got up and walked away from her. She watched him, angry with herself for telling him, wondering if he was laughing, but when he came back to sit beside her on the bridge, he was serious.

46

'Uh...hummm,' he nodded. 'So that's why you always writing in those copybooks. What you reporting on so much, girl?' And then she heard the laughter in his question and it made her angry.

'I never laugh at you Sonny! I listen to you all these years. You ever hear me laugh?'

'Is not laugh I laughing, girl,' he tried to apologise. 'Is just that reporters have to be all over the place, night and day. How you going to have children.'

'You have my life plan out for me, Sonny? You have me married and settle down on this hill?'

'Sometime I feel as if I don't know you, Beatrice,' he said, shaking his head. 'All these years I talking to you, and I still feel as if I don't know you. You so quiet...'

'I not quiet, Sonny,' she said. 'You just never have time to listen to anybody but yourself. You think you is the only one with big dreams?' And she got up and walked away from him.

In the house, smoke curled up into the celotex and the mosquitoes had stopped singing. Beatrice went back inside and sprinkled water on the smoking bush. Then she set the bucket on the back steps and went to turn down Reme's bed. She wondered if Sonny had gotten a ride. If he had, he should be nearing Rosehill and Moko. He hadn't even told his own father. So why should she have expected him to tell her? Reme had always said she was too stupid, too trusting. She tried to banish her mother's voice from her head. No. Sonny deserved to win. He did win, and she was happy for him. She was glad, though, that she hadn't told him that she had applied for the scholarship too.

Sonny got off the bus when it reached the city, and decided to walk to Rosehill. Rain drizzled onto his uncovered head and he could hear Moko's voice warning him about pneumonia and whooping cough, but he went on, slipping in the mud once or twice as he tried to avoid the pools of water that had settled in the streets.

Once a car passed him and the driver, recognising him,

tooted his horn and slowed but Sonny waved him on. He wanted to walk, to think about what had happened with Beatrice; to plan what he would say to Moko. But as he walked other thoughts kept pushing out Beatrice and Moko, thoughts about America, about going away, far from Rosehill, from Santabella, and although he was alone in the quiet, wet streets, he began to feel a little bit ashamed, as if somebody was watching him, reading his mind, telling him how ungrateful, how selfish he was. So he forced himself to look around, to think about where he was instead of where he would be going in a short while. And he noticed, as if for the first time, the stores and offices around him. Their dingy showcases were almost empty. Through one window a few pairs of shoes with bold 'for sale' signs above them rested alone on top of a bed of torn yellowing newspaper, and Sonny turned away. Shut out the present, he told himself. Think about how it used to be, and he remembered the nights when he was a small boy and just before Christmas Miss Ann would bring him and all her children down town to window shop. Everything was new and fresh then. Now it all seemed old, rusty, and he wanted to escape. He hurried out of town and made his way quickly to Belmont Point where he stopped to look over the city.

Below him, a few car lights danced in the wet streets, and in between the narrow lanes he saw the red tin roofs of the backyard shanties. A sudden urge enveloped him and he wanted to stretch his legs, to leap over those roofs, to fly high above them until he reached the sea. 'I going mad,' he whispered, and he remembered Mister Maxwell telling him that afternoon that he shouldn't let the scholarship business go to his head. He shook his head to clear it, and took a deep breath to try to calm himself. He focused on the sea beyond the roofs, where he could see the outline of three ships at anchor. One of them, he knew, was the *Scarlet Ibis*. It had come in earlier from Trinidad with a cargo of market women.

He had seen the women that afternoon toting their bags of rice and sugar and flour from the wharf to the market, and from the darkness around him the sound of the women's voices seemed to float up to him from the harbour. He heard their high laughter as they gathered up their baskets. They were glad to get back to Santabella, they said. That Trinidad bad too bad, and prices too high. But he knew that the next week they would be on the boat again, heading back to bad Trinidad, their heads tied, their bellies banned.

Sonny jumped as a breadfruit dropped suddenly from a tree nearby and rolled down beside him. He took it up by the stem and pelted it toward the beach that snaked around Point Lisas. As the breadfruit disappeared in the darkness, landing, he hoped, on the beach, he thought about the times he had climbed the coconut trees on the beach, and how he had ridden on the branches of the almond trees, daring the wind to throw him off. 'I must take a sea bath before I leave,' he told himself. He would take Beatrice to Black Water Beach early one Sunday morning, he decided. She would like that. He remembered how she had told him a story about the beach, about how it was connected with Rosehill. She had said it was a sacred place.

Point Lisas and Rosehill used to be part of cocoa estate, she had told him, and ships used to come from France and England to collect the beans. The people who worked on the estate were from Africa. Enslaved people, Beatrice told him. They had to work the cocoa every day from morning until night. Some of them ran away but the estate owners always caught them and brought them back and beat them for days. Then one day the people heard the English sailors say freedom had come.

Come? they asked. Where? Not here.

But yes. The sailors said. People would be free to go wherever they could go.

Some people believed the talk was true. The sailors had told them so. But others said the sailors were lying, playing jokes on them. So they asked the man in charge of the estate. He said it was a black lie.

That year the cocoa was plentiful. The man in charge made the people work harder. Every hand on the estate had to cut the cocoa. In the evening, when they should have been getting some rest, they had to work in the sheds, cutting open the pods, setting them out to dry, and the slime from the cocoa stayed on their hands and their skins so that when they tried to wash themselves, the soap couldn't get off the layers of slime. They rubbed down with leaves and cold rain water but day in and day out they smelled like cocoa, until it seemed cocoa slime was in their blood.

One of the women was making a baby, and it was near time for the child to come. One morning she started bawling in the field and the overseer came over to see what was going on. He said she was only pretending to be sick and sent her out with the others. The baby dropped in the field and an old lady cut the navel string with a machete. They buried the navel string underneath a cocoa tree as the man in charge watched from a distance. Then the women banned the baby's belly with cocoa leaves and set him in the cool until night came and his mother could take him to her room. That night the baby died. The mother screamed and she ran to the big house and threatened to kill the overseer. The other women had to catch her and tie her to the bed to save her life.

Old men came with sticks and pans that night to beat the child's spirit back home. They danced the stick fight, and the bongo, and the women rubbed the small body with blue and sang soft songs, trying to console the mother because she was afraid the child would be a douen. Early the next morning, the father took the child outside to wait for the sun to rise because it had died before it could be blessed. Before the people went to the fields that day, they buried the baby in a blanket of cocoa leaves. The child's mother became sick and never recovered. People said she died from grief. They buried her next to the baby and they promised they wouldn't forget.

Freedom talk swelled from estate to estate, and the owners cleaned their guns on their verandas so the people could see them. In the night they lit flambeaux by the roadside leading toward the house and set the dogs free. The people watched all of this, and talked quietly between themselves, biding their time.

The cocoa beans dried, and the ships came to collect them. Every man, woman and child on the estate had to tote the bags down to the beach, and that's when the people made their stand.

They stayed in their houses and refused to work. The overseers sent men to crush the houses and when the people tried to escape, the men blocked the tracks into the hills. The people didn't have anywhere else to run so they ran down into the sea, and the men followed them on horses, flinging whips at them, trying to force them to turn back, but they wouldn't. After that the sea turned black. That is why the beach is sacred, Beatrice had said. Sonny remembered laughing and asking her if she had made up that story but she swore that Tante Vivian had told her, and whatever Tante said was true.

From where he was standing, Sonny could see Fort George on his right, with its four cannons pointing toward the bay and he remembered reading how the British had fought to capture the fort from the Spanish, and how the Spanish ships had sunk under the weight of the British fire balls.

Darkness was covering Rosehill and Sonny's shirt was soaking wet but he still lingered on the road, looking at Santabella as if he hadn't seen it before, as if he would never see it again. He walked slowly by Oya's yard with its huge immortelle hanging over the road and he jumped up to break off a piece of branch. Then he stood underneath the tree for a while, remembering the nights when he was small and had sped past it in fright. A phantom lived in the tree, people used to say, and at night it stretched its legs across the road and blocked people from passing. Sonny stripped the leaves from the branch and swung it around him, passing it from his left to right hand, daring the phantom to appear, feeling silly and brave at the same time. He continued up the hill stopping at the Ledge to look back to the sea again to the Dragon's Mouth. He remembered how he had searched his history books to find information about the Dragon's Mouth, but he could never find any. Tante Vivian had told him, though, that long time ago, a volcano had erupted under

51

the great salt waters in the Gulf, and the whole island had trembled for days as if it had fever and ague. Part broke off, and the rest of the north coast land that jutted into the sea was shaped like a dragon's mouth, and that's how it was named.

The moon was out, big like a shining circle above him, and suddenly Sonny broke out in a cold sweat. He felt a chill up his spine and his head felt as if somebody had thrown ice water on him and he took off running, pushing thoughts out of his mind, stumbling over roots and stones, running as if Oya's phantom was behind him. A ball of light flashed across the sky and he thought of Beatrice and her soucouyants and zombies and douens, and he flung himself against the wind that was trying its best to push him down.

He didn't stop until he had reached his front yard. Exhausted, water running down his cheeks, he stood panting by the gate, and when he looked up, Moko was standing in the doorway holding up the oil lamp. Sonny went past him quietly and Moko set down the lamp on the sideboard.

'You want someting to eat?' Moko asked him.

'Let me get out these wet clothes first,' Sonny said, and stripped down slowly to his underwear. He put his damp clothes on the back of a chair, pulled on his old grey pants and stood in front of the coalpot of blazing coals to dry off. Moko waited, watching him, wondering. When Sonny wouldn't say anything for a while, Moko, to break the silence, asked him about Beatrice.

'She okay.' Sonny's tone wasn't rude, but Moko could tell he didn't want to answer any questions. Sonny picked up a bowl and started to dip out soup.

'I could do that for you,' Moko offered. 'You sit down and rest.' He tried to take the soup spoon from Sonny but Sonny moved his hand away. Moko sat back down, watching him. Sonny remained near the coalpot, holding his head down, eating the soup slowly. When he finished, he rinsed the bowl and spoon in the bucket of water and put them in the rack. Then he went to his cot and sat down.

Moko couldn't stand the quiet any longer. 'So why you not talking tonight, Sonny? I do something to you?'

'I don't know what you talking 'bout, Pa,' Sonny answered. 'I can't come home and go to sleep in peace? Sometimes I just don't have anything to say.' He unfolded the coverlet, and pulled it up to his shoulders as he lay back on the cot with his eyes closed. Moko waited, watching him. After a few minutes Sonny opened his eyes and asked if the postman had brought any letters for him.

'He didn't come today,' Moko said. 'Too much rain.'

'It fall hard in town too,' Sonny said.

'I know,' Moko told him. 'I was downtown today. I went by Doctor Chow.'

'I don't know why you still go there, Pa,' Sonny said. 'If I was you I would never paytay on that man.'

'He want you to work for him,' Moko watched him closely.

'You asked him for job for me?' Sonny propped himself up on his elbow.

'I didn't ask him, boy. I know you working. I went to ask him to talk to the people in the embassy.'

'What he say?'

'He say the man he used to know up there gone back to America. Then he tell me to tell you he want you to work for him.'

Sonny threw off the coverlet and swung off the cot vexed vexed. 'You expected something different, Pa?' he asked. 'You really expect that man to help you out? But why we people so stupid? You and Beatrice is the same thing, oui.'

'The man never do anything to me.' Moko said, but Sonny cut him off.

'He fire you, Pa! He fire you and never give you a pension for all them years you work for him!'

'I work for the man. I wasn't no slave, Sonny,' Moko said.

'No! You wasn't no slave. You was a big office boy!'

'So that make you shame, Sonny? You woulda prefer me

53

to beg in the street instead?'

'What I know bout shame, Pa?' Sonny shouted. 'I is your son. Remember? The great Moko Allen! Doctor Chow's office boy. What I know bout shame? You forget I is Angelina's son too? Well I don't forget, Pa. I don't forget. When people make calypso on you, how you going to forget, eh? You forget? Well, not me. I hearing the words right now, Pa. "Where your Mammy gone, Sonnyboy? Where you Mammy gone? She run down Venezuela. She leave your one-foot father. Pam pa lam!"'

'So you shame.' Moko said sadly. But Sonny was still reciting. '"Your father have just one foot! He crawling on the ground. The woman send him crazy. Motor car knock him down!" What I know bout shame, Pa!' He sat down abruptly and the springs in the cot shook.

'But you win scholarship,' Moko said.

'I win de consolation prize!' Sonny shouted, and he rolled over onto his belly and put his hands over his head.

Moko sat in the Morris chair quiet quiet not knowing what to say. He wanted to say something, to tell the boy he was sorry, to say anything to make Sonny feel better but he didn't know what was right. So he stayed quiet, hoping Sonny's shoulders would stop shaking. After a while, Sonny wiped his face with the coverlet and Moko asked him, 'What you going to do with the pigeons?'

'I letting them go,' Sonny said, and rolled over on the cot, turning his face to the wall.

'I could take care of them, you know. Till you come back from America.'

'Is best you let them go,' Sonny said.

'But they is homing pigeons, Sonny. They'll come back home.'

'Them pigeons glad to fly away, Pa. They cage up too long.'

'I going to miss them, boy. I get to like them, yuh know.'

'Is best to let them go. Seed cost gone up. Is a long time now I've been thinking bout letting them go.'

54

'But suppose they come back, Sonny. You mind if I look out for them? You don't mind, eh?'

'I don't mind, Pa,' Sonny said wearily. 'But don't look for them to come back.' Then he pulled the coverlet over his head.

Moko sat for a while watching the wick in the lamp flutter and hearing the light rain beating music like a tenor pan on the roof. He remembered suddenly that he had not covered the water barrels after he had fed the pigeons. Soon, they would overflow with cold, brackish rain water. He shook his head again, trying to remember if he had closed the pigeon coop. Sometimes he forgot. But he told himself not to worry. Sonny had trained the pigeons well. Even if they left, they would come back. He looked over at his son's back, wrapped hard and tight under the coverlet and he wanted to touch him, but he couldn't. Instead, he called his name softly. 'Sonny? Sonny, you sleep?' Sonny didn't answer. Moko waited a little, hoping Sonny would turn and face him, but Sonny didn't stir, and after a while Moko reached out and turned down the wick. The light went out slowly and darkness came between them.

Miss Ann brought the matter of the farewell party for Sonny before the Village Council, and they agreed to fund it despite the shortage of money in the treasury. The Council hadn't found anyone effective to bribe yet, and they didn't want to spend the money in case somebody turned up, but each member volunteered to make a personal contribution to Sonny's party and Miss Ann went ahead with the arrangements. In the meantime, Rosehill was fighting for life. With his garden gone, and only a small parcel of land with grass left nearby, Sammy sold his goats and bought some Italian bees. He painted 'Sammy's Sweet Honey For Sale' in red on a piece of pitchpine and nailed the sign onto the mango tree in his front yard.

'That is a ketch arse business, man,' Roberts warned him. 'I know a fellar in Grenville say he minding bee's two years now. He ent get one good gallon of honey yet.'

'A man have to try something,' Sammy said. 'I have five

mouths to feed.'

'Is best you did buy a boat, man,' Roberts advised him. 'Bees is a lot of trouble.'

'Who say so?' Sammy wanted to know. 'These bees ent no trouble, man. That fellar in Grenville just didn't know what he was doing. These is Italian bees. Best in the business.'

'So since when you talking Italian, Sammy?' Roberts asked him.

'They understand we talk, man,' Sammy said. 'These is international bees.'

And to demonstrate, he pressed his face to the wire netting and mumbled a few words. A bee flew up against the wire and tried to sting him in the face. Sammy jerked out of the way and almost toppled the hive.

'He think you cussing him, man,' Roberts laughed, as he helped him set the hive upright again, and he continued laughing all the way down the hill to the rumshop where he told the fellars the joke. Soon, the whole village had heard, and the nine days' wonder on the hill was Sammy and his mad Italian bees.

If Rosehill wasn't talking about Sammy and his bees or about Sonny's going away, they were talking about the weather. Every day more rain fell and more crops washed away. Red water rushed down the hillsides, sweeping away rocks and boulders, and Melda and Jestina and Miss Ann warned their children not to play in the road or they might get swept down into the sea.

The sea itself was dry. The fishermen came back with empty nets each day. Willy said it was as if the fish had heard that a hurricane was coming and they all had run away to hide. Uncle Clive, who had been a fisherman since he was a small boy, said no fish could outsmart him, and he went further out in the Gulf each day, searching. One morning he and Valmon left early. They said they would go only as far as the Dragon's Mouth because the wind was blowing strong, but even after it had gotten dark they hadn't come back. The wind grew stronger and the water blasted the beach. Willy shook his head and said he couldn't see how on the face of the earth Uncle Clive's old boat could withstand the crush of those waves. 'Look for broken pieces of the boat on the beach,' he said. And it looked as if he was right, because stars came out and the men still didn't come in. Rosehill went down on the beach to wait.

Mother Dinah, Uncle Clive's wife, lit two flambeaux and knelt in the sand to pray. Her Baptist followers, dressed in white, walked up and down the beach singing hymns. Tante Vivian came down and joined them, and tried to console Mother Dinah. 'They all right, girl. They coming home. They coming home.'

But the sun came up that morning and although the wind had died down, Uncle Clive and Valmon didn't return. Beatrice went into town to ask the Red Cross to call the Coast Guard on the Mainland to see if they could spot the boat and waited all day to see if there were any messages. In the meanwhile, the Baptists sang and prayed and Mother Dinah said she wasn't going to leave the beach until she heard something, good or bad.

Miss Ann, ever watchful to make a penny, brought a case of sweet drinks and a tray of sugar cakes down to the beach to sell. Jestina sat next to her on a coconut branch. Miss Ann said, 'I know something bad was going to happen after I had that dream, girl. My dreams don't lie, especially if I dream early early in the morning. Was a lot of confusion I see.'

'Tante say they're all right,' Jestina told her, 'and Tante could see things.'

'Tante getting old, girl. It ent like long time when she could see all kinda things. I tell you is best we all go back up the hill and make some wreaths.'

But despite her talk, she wouldn't leave the beach, not even when Willy asked her why she wasn't going home to cook his food. She told him to eat the half of roast breadfruit she had left on the fire. Willy argued that he had eaten breadfruit that morning, but Miss Ann told him he could either eat it again or lie down close to it. Willy left her on the beach and went up to Ling Chung's rumshop.

'Rain rain go away, come again another day,' the children on the beach sang as Rosehill waited. But no sign or word came about Uncle Clive or Valmon that day. In the evening the men put up some bamboo poles under the coconut trees and covered them with a tarpaulin, and Mother Dinah stayed under the tent all night.

Five o'clock next day, Beatrice brought the message. Venezuelan fishermen had found the boat adrift and had taken the men down the Main. Uncle Clive and Valmon would come home in a day or so. Mother Dinah, exhausted, knelt in the sand to give thanks. Then she rang the bell, and invited everybody to her church for a thanksgiving feast. Before they left the beach, her followers made a circle and prayed while the little children danced boatay in the sand.

The Coast Guard brought Uncle Clive and Valmon home two days later and warned them to stay out of the high sea. But Uncle Clive and Valmon told the fellars in the rumshop that they would never run from bad winds. 'We is riders of de storm, man,' Valmon boasted, remembering some words he had read in a play in school. This bravado, this 'we ent fraid nothing at all, man,' attitude sustained them, and while Mother Dinah prayed day and night for them to be safe, God willing, they went out with their nets every day, storm or no storm, sometimes way past the Dragon's Mouth despite the daily warnings that a big hurricane could hit at any time.

The *Santabella Guardian* published a story about the farmers on Rosehill who had lost their crops. The paper blamed the Company and asked how it was that foreign nationals could come in to the country and mistreat Santabellans and the government did nothing. WHO PAYING OFF WHO? the paper asked.

The next day, Cudjoe and a group of men came to Rosehill. They had come, they said, to see for themselves how the government was taking advantage of poor people. A photographer took pictures and the next day a snap shot of Sammy

58

pointing to the Company tractor that had damaged his land, was on the front page of the *Guardian*.

'Well, is now we arse in trouble,' Jestina groaned. 'Who the hell tell Sammy to take picture? What Cudjoe and them opposition could do? Not one blasted thing. We shouldn't get the government vexed. Is punish they going to punish we, you know.'

Rosehill waited anxiously to see what the government would do but nothing happened. The Company continued to lay pipes and dig wells.

Every day the *Guardian* printed a story about villagers in trouble. It said several prominent local businessmen were part of the scheme to throw people off the land. The paper called on the government to answer the voice of the people, and finally, the Prime Minister made a radio broadcast.

He said the news reports were false. His government's hands were clean and no member of his Party was involved in the Americans' efforts to drill for oil. The opposition, he said, or those who called themselves the opposition, were power hungry, avaricious rumour-mongers who went about the country trying to fool poor people with their lies. He asked the people to check out who owned the *Guardian*. It was owned, he told them, by forces who would stop at nothing to destroy his government's credibility.

He asked the people to pray. Good words always turn wrath away, he said, and one whole good day of prayer would wipe out those deceitful words that were being spread all over the country. On this special day of prayer, he said, the churches should stay open day and night. He named the following Tuesday 'Prayer Day'.

'Is madness we hearing, oui,' Miss Ann told Tante. 'People starving and this man talking bout national day for prayers. Why he ent tell the people what he doing with all that money the Yankees pay for the land, eh? Why he ent go and confess that?'

'That man not mad. Mad what?' Jestina said. 'He know good and well what he doing. He think the people stupid. He think he could dazzle them with old talk and they going to forget their belly empty.'

'He not fooling me!' Miss Ann declared. 'I watching all the moves he making.'

'But plenty people still can't see him for what he is, girl.' Jestina said. 'Is like a flambeau shining in they face, but the glare so strong, it blinding them.'

'That glitter don't blind my eyes!' Miss Ann told her. 'All this running here, running there he doing, he ent fooling me one bit. Every minute he opening community centre and next morning the buildings leaking and walls caving in. The contractors stealing all the money and building the centres weak weak. I watching them.'

'Is he own Party people doing that, you know!' Jestina said. 'Is only them getting work. All of dem is a bunch of fowl thiefs!'

'Let them go in the church and pray,' Miss Ann said. 'I ent going no way!'

The day of national prayer came and more than three-quarters of the churches stayed empty. The *Guardian* printed a front page spread the next day, denouncing the government, and leaving one whole page black to signify the darkness it said the people were being led into. In the night, a fire burned the *Guardian* offices to the ground.

Cudjoe called for a mass rally in the town square and brought bus loads of people in from the country districts. He led the marchers through the town from the square to the burned building, and in the glow of candles lit throughout the crowd, he declared the site a national monument. Then he made a speech.

The voice of the people, he said, could not be stilled by fire. He told them he would continue to speak against the injustices the so-called government was perpetuating on the masses, and he questioned the police report on the cause of the fire. 'They say lightning caused the fire. Big bolt! But I ask you, since when lightning does fall and thunder don't roll, eh? Since when? Now, we not saying the police lie, you know. The police is sworn to

60

tell the truth, right? All we wondering is how come, on the night in question, nobody hear thunder roll after the bolt of lightning fall?'

Then he asked the people to blow out their candles. Jestina, who was right in front watching, said it was a dramatic moment. All the candles went out except one – Cudjoe's. And then he asked for silence. Everybody got quiet and Cudjoe raised a conch shell to his lips and blew two slow slow notes. And while the notes were echoing back to him, he put the conch shell aside and shouted, 'This is a new beginning for all of we. With the conch we herald the start of a new day for Santabella!' The crowd roared.

For days afterwards, Rosehill talked about the rally. They almost forgot about strong winds and heavy rains. When hurricane Flora hit, she caught a number of people by surprise.

Flora devastated Santabella. She blasted in from the Gulf, laughed in the Touton mountains face, slammed into houses on the hills and in the valleys and by the time she left, thousands of people were homeless and at least twenty were dead.

Rosehill was hit hard. The village, set so near to the Gulf, caught the full fury of the wind. Nearly all the homes above the Ledge were blown down. Oya's immortelle cracked in two and fell on her house. They found her dead. A small boy, pitching marbles in his yard, tried to fight the wind when it came but a piece of flying galvanize hit him in his head and he died too.

Moko's house fell and Sonny's pigeon coop rose with the wind and landed in the next door neighbour's yard. Moko said later that when the wind started, something had told him to go to the latrine even though he didn't want to use it. He had sat there, feeling the wood shake, wondering what he had done so bad in his life to cause him to die like a bat in a latrine hole. But the latrine didn't shift. Tante Vivian laughed and told him that was because Miss Lezama, the old soucouyant who used to live in the house, used to fly off at night from the roof of the latrine and her spirit was still in it. All up the hill, kitchen sheds had

61

fallen, trees blocked the tracks, and water flooded the houses down below. Miss Ann's parlour fell and she blamed Willy.

'Every day as God send, I beg this lazy man to nail down the roof, nail down the roof,' she told everybody. 'But no! He never had time. He had all the time in the world to go and lime in the rumshop but he never had time to nail down the galvanize. You know what he do? He put two big stones on the roof instead. Now look what happen! Meh parlour fall. All the hops bread gone! All the sweet drinks roll away! All the sweety bottles break! He telling me I shoulda bring them inside when I hear hurricane coming. But you ever hear asshole foolishness like this?'

Willy got cut on his forehead. Jestina said Miss Ann had hit him with a bottle but Willy told everybody that a piece of sharp galvanize had cut him. Miss Ann, grumbling, said she hoped he could bleed to death so she could get his lodge money to build back a parlour. Jestina felt sorry for Willy and put a poultice she made of grated aloes on the cut.

A portion of Mister Roberts' gallery fell, and looking at the mess, he said, 'Well, let me see if the government not going to do something now.' And he and Rosehill waited for the Prime Minister to make a stop in the village during his island inspection tour.

A few days after the hurricane, a newspaper, put out by the Prime Minister's Party, said the Prime Minister had sent a special mission to a meeting of the heads of Commonwealth nations to ask for hurricane relief. In the meanwhile, the paper said, the Prime Minister would personally tour each devastated area and check the damage himself.

Rosehill hoped he would make a stop in their village, but in the meanwhile, they didn't sit on their hands. They gathered together to rebuild their houses that had fallen, and to clear debris from the hill. Their biggest problem was drinking water. At the foot of the hill the central water main had burst so the standpipe in the street was empty, and the ravine was still blocked since the Company had never removed the logs. Willy and Roberts decided to take matters into their own hands. They took a group of Rosehill men to clear the ravine themselves, but the men from the Company were waiting for them with shovels and machetes. Sammy wanted to fight but Roberts said it was no use getting into trouble, and he pulled Sammy away.

Roberts borrowed a truck and took three barrels into town and filled them up with water. When he came back, he distributed the water and everybody got at least one full pan. But they knew they couldn't continue like that. They had to have fresh water.

One night, in desperation, Sammy and Willy went far up to the waterfall and made a small dam so Rosehill could get water. Next morning the Company said the dam was on its land and moved the boulders to the side. Then they put up a tiger wire fence with broken bottles on top of it all along the side of the waterfall, and a no trespassing sign. 'They trying to make life hard so we'll run off the hill,' Miss Ann said, 'but they have to come a lot harder than that.' She sent Willy down to the Ministry to complain about the Company and the Minister promised to send somebody to look into the matter, but nobody came.

Very little rain fell in Santabella in the weeks after Flora. It seemed to the people as if the hurricane had delivered a whole rainy season one time, and they wondered what they had done to deserve such treatment.

'Is blight on this country,' Miss Ann pronounced. 'All the badness this government doing, the hurricane is a warning. Let them go on. They ent see nothing yet. When God get mad, he don't joke, you know.'

'So you saying God spiteful?' Melda asked her.

'And what I do so for him to punish me and my children?' Jestina wanted to know.

'Is only one thing I have to say,' Miss Ann told them. 'When God turn his back on you, look out for thunder to roll.'

'What you know bout God?' Melda asked her. 'When last you put your foot in a church, Ann?'

But Miss Ann refused to allow Jestina and Melda to get her

defensive. She left them throwing words at her from the yard, and went into her house to make tea.

A few days before Sonny was due to leave Santabella for America, Rosehill began to make final preparations for his farewell fete. Each evening the steelband fellars gathered in the panyard to practice, and as that sweet sweet music resounded through the hills, Rosehill danced. Miss Ann shook her waist and hummed as she dug sugar-sweet white meat from the dried coconuts her small children and Jestina's and Melda's had gathered from the beach. As secretary of the Village Council, Miss Ann had taken charge of refreshments. She was also in charge of invitations. On the day she was grating coconuts to make pay-mee and bread and sugar cakes, she was also waiting anxiously for Clyde, her oldest son, to return from town where she had sent him to deliver invitations by hand to the Prime Minister and several other dignitaries because she did not trust the mail. Clyde breezed in as she was spooning coconut mixture into the hot pan for sugar cakes, and dipped his finger into the bowl. Miss Ann knocked his hand aside and demanded to know why he had taken so long to return.

'All this time you gone,' she fretted, 'you coulda reached Grenada and come back. I only hope you give that invitation to the Prime Minister's personal secretary, you know.' She shook a swizzle stick in his face.

Clyde stepped quickly out of her reach. 'How you expect me to see the man's personal secretary, Ma,' he complained. 'I had to leave it with the guard at the gate.'

'Boy!' Miss Ann shouted. 'I tell you to give anything to any guard? But how children so hard ears these days? Eh eh?'

'Is not any and everybody they letting in, Ma,' Clyde tried to explain. 'The man promised me he'll give it to them today. What you want me to do?'

'So what bout the other invitations,' Miss Ann demanded. 'What you do with them? You give them to the guards at the other ministries too?'

64

Clyde inched further to the back door, all the while keeping a close eye on the swizzle stick she was holding. 'Well... to tell the truth...' he stammered, 'By the time I reached down there, the office was closed so...'

'What you mean closed,' Miss Ann shouted, advancing on Clyde. 'Since morning you leave here. What you been doing, Clyde? Eh? You went in the ravine gambling again?'

Clyde was nearly to the back door when Miss Ann reached for the long handled broom. She lashed out at him and a lick caught him on his head before he fled through the door shouting, 'When I get inflammation in meh head and dead I want to see who's going to mind you in your old age!' He went fuming down to the panyard and didn't come back for tea that evening.

Willy, as Village Council chairman, delegated Jestina to collect donations from various merchants and Jestina welcomed the assignment. She would like nothing better, she said, but Willy expressed some concern. Jestina was a real saga girl, and a dancer too. She danced in the Sapphire Club on Friday and Saturday nights, and all who saw her spoke – some in envy – of the way she swayed and rolled her behind on the stage, and how she tantalised the men so much that some of them wanted to pee right there in ecstasy.

Willy told her, 'Look, Jestina. Don't go shaking your backside in front of them men, eh. You never know if the wives might be looking on, and is some of these women who control the cash registers. So behave yourself, okay? And wear a dress, not pedal pushers. Since Flora things hard hard and them merchants might not want to give. Don't make things worse with your bad behaviour.'

Jestina laughed, 'You want me to dress up like a nun?' she asked him. 'You think is carnival or what? What you worrying about, eh? Trust me.'

But Willy went away still a bit worried. Later that day he caught sight of her getting into a taxi at the Main Road. She was wearing a white strapless bodice on top of a hot pink mini skirt. Willy shook his head and wondered for a minute what man could ever control Jestina.

Sammy killed three chickens and gave most of the meat to his wife to put in roti that she and her sisters had spent a whole afternoon making. Melda was to make the souse, and when Mister Roberts brought pig's feet and tail from a little one that he had killed, she seasoned the meat down with fresh black pepper, salt and limes, and then sent her daughter to get some cucumbers from Miss Ann. When the child returned she said Miss Ann had told her to tell her Mammy that she was to put all the cucumbers in the souse. Melda understood. Miss Ann was warning her not to make a salad with any of the cucumbers for Roy, her husband. She knew how much Roy liked cucumber salad. Miss Ann didn't like Roy because he hadn't helped the other men to build back her parlour after the hurricane. On top of that, she had heard that Roy had said that he would never buy anything in her shop because she was a bad-minded woman.

That afternoon, after she was done with the souse, Melda took a plate full for Miss Ann to taste, and as Miss Ann ate, Melda praised the quality of the cucumbers and then casually mentioned that Roy really liked the big salad she had made with two of them for him lunch time. Miss Ann's cut eye could have melted a stone.

Ling Chung donated two cases of sweet drinks and Willy asked him if he was mad or what. Two cases of sweet drinks, Willy told him, wouldn't even be enough for the little children, far less for the big people. 'Come on, man Ling. Throw in some cream sodas at least.'

Ling Chung gave him a case of cream soda. 'Is all, eh?' he said hopefully.

But Willy wasn't satisfied. 'So what about the rum, Ling?' he demanded. 'You mean you not going to donate two three bottles of Old Oak, man? But how all you Chinese people chinky so? I have to tell everybody bout this, oui.' And he turned to call to some fellars who were liming outside the rumshop.

'Okay, okay,' Ling Chung grumbled. 'You want to bust meh shop. You want to bust it. I could see that, Willy.' But he went into the storeroom and returned with a case of rum. 'Don't come for Christmas,' Ling warned. 'No more, no more!'

Willy laughed as he took the case. 'All of we is one, man. And I hope you bringing the madam to the fete, eh. But where she is, man? Why you hiding the woman so?'

Ling shooed him out the shop and Willy called, 'Bring she, man. Bring all the children too.' He put the case of drinks in a wheelbarrow and pushed it up the hill. On his way, he met Jestina coming back from town, her arms loaded with paperbags of goods. The men, Willy could tell, had obviously been generous. He laughed with Jestina, and together, both of them went on up Rosehill to make the last minute preparations for the farewell party.

The day before the fete, Beatrice came by Miss Ann's house to drop off the present she had purchased for Sonny with donations the Village Council had collected. She found Miss Ann and her daughters shelling pigeon peas in the kitchen. On the table behind them were loaves of sweet breads and several sponge cakes.

'I could smell your cake from the foot of the hill,' Beatrice greeted Miss Ann.

'Is the vanilla essence, child,' Miss Ann beamed. 'I put two extra pints. Here, taste a piece,' and she cut a thin thin slice from one of the smallest cakes.

Beatrice tasted the cake and coughed and held her throat as she swallowed. 'Whew!' she said, when she could speak. 'Tell Uncle Willy we don't need no rum, Miss Ann. Everybody getting drunk from this cake.'

'I put a whole bottle of Scotch in there, girl,' Miss Ann laughed. 'It give the sponge a nice zing, eh? Joycelyn, give Miss Beatrice a glass of ginger beer.'

The child fetched the ginger beer and Miss Ann put some ice in the glass and gave it to Beatrice.

'Prime Minister coming, girl,' Miss Ann glowed. 'Two three other ministers too. Everybody who is anybody coming. I

67

invite them, you know. Sonny going to get a big send off.'

'This is fete father, Miss Ann,' Beatrice agreed.

'When I plan party,' Miss Ann declared, 'it ent no pappyshow, you know. Everything have to be just right. By the way, you write the farewell speech yet? How it sounding?'

'What farewell speech?' Beatrice asked her. 'Who tell you I'm making any farewell speech?'

'But who else you expect to give it?' Miss Ann said. 'I already tell everybody you making a nice speech, so people looking forward to it, girl.'

'But why you always do this to me, Miss Ann?' Beatrice protested. 'You always telling people I will do something before you even check with me. I don't even like to give speeches.'

'But what's wrong with you, girl?' Miss Ann asked. 'We want some intelligence here. You prefer for Willy to get up there and embarrass everybody? Not in my party, dou dou!'

'But Uncle Willy is the chairman,' Beatrice argued. 'He is the rightful one to give the speech.'

'Beatrice,' Miss Ann said, 'is big shot people I having here, you know. We have to make a good impression. Besides, people expecting you to do it. And on top of that, you is Sonny's girl friend and...'

'Who say that?' Beatrice demanded. 'Sonny and I is only friends. What right people have talking about me and Sonny? People can't have a friend now?'

'No need to get so hot up, girl,' Miss Ann tried to get back on Beatrice's good side. 'Just do a little speech to please me, okay?'

Beatrice gathered up her purse, 'I have to go now,' she said. 'It's getting late and I still have to deliver this laundry to Doctor Chow.'

'Reme still doing his office laundry?' Miss Ann asked. 'I thought she give that up.'

'I'm helping her with it for now,' Beatrice said. 'Just until I get something better.' She got up to leave.

'Every penny counts these days, child,' Miss Ann nodded.

'I know how it is. So don't forget to write something nice for the speech, eh,' and Beatrice shook her head in resignation as she went out to the yard and down the road.

It was a while before she caught a taxi, and by the time she arrived in town it was after five. She hurried up Parker Street to the doctor's office, and when she pushed open the door that led up to his office on the second floor, she almost bumped into the nurse leaving.

'Doctor's getting ready to leave,' the nurse told her. 'You'd better go fast.'

'Can you wait a minute, Miss Sung?' she asked the nurse. 'I don't want to bother him.'

'I have to catch Ramesar's taxi, girl,' the nurse said. 'It's too hard to get transportation at this hour.' And she left Beatrice standing on the steps while she hurried out.

Beatrice stood there for a minute trying to decide what to do. She hated being alone with Doctor Chow. The way he stared at her always made her uncomfortable. She thought of leaving and telling Reme that she had gotten to the office too late, but Reme had said that morning that she needed the laundry money. Someone had told her about a medicine she could buy from down the Main that would help her belly go down. Yet Beatrice knew that if she went up the stairs and into the doctor's office, she might have to face his advances. He had tried, on several occasions in the months since she had been bringing his office laundry, to touch her breasts and to kiss her. The touch was always light, friendly, fleeting, and the first time it had happened she hadn't wanted to accept that it had been something he shouldn't do. He had been her doctor since she was a small girl, and he had always been friendly. Everybody on Rosehill knew him. He had grown up on the Main road in Rosehill with his family, working in his father's grocery until the old man later sold out to Ling Chung. His family had moved out of Rosehill but came back often to the small citrus grove they still owned in the valley near to Sammy's place.

The Chow family was a part of Rosehill, as far as everybody was concerned, so when the son came back from studying overseas and opened a doctor's clinic, Rosehill went to him. They had only stopped recently when word had spread that he was in league with the Company to throw them off the land. Reme had been doing his office laundry for years and she wanted to stop, but she needed the money.

Beatrice hadn't wanted to believe that the doctor's slight touches were anything but accidental. But it had happened again when she had delivered the laundry one afternoon. He had made her wait until all the patients and the nurse had left. Then, he had called her into his office, and when she walked in she was shocked to see him standing in front of his desk, his pants down about his calves, hands wrapped around his penis, jerking it up and down. For a minute Beatrice was too horrified to move. She stared at the man she had grown up to respect, and a curious fascination overwhelmed her. As she watched, breakwater came spurting out of his penis and suddenly, in fear, she dropped the bag of laundry and fled.

The memory of that evening flooded her as she stood on the steps wishing that she had told Reme. But what good would that have done? Reme might not have believed her. Who would believe her? A doctor? And where would she find the words to describe what he had done? Anyway, Beatrice told herself, he had just done that thing to himself... but maybe... Just as she had decided to leave, to tell Reme the office had closed early, she heard the doctor calling her from the top of the stairs. She turned and went slowly up.

'Bring the laundry into my office,' he told her, and she followed him out of the waiting room, but hesitated at the door of his office. He went over to a file cabinet.

'Come in, Beatrice,' he said, in his usual friendly voice. 'Close the door, eh. Somebody always coming late. They'll see the sign on the door with the office hours but you think they care? "Doctor will see me, man." As if I don't have to get some rest too, eh?'

He closed the file drawer and turned to see Beatrice still

standing in the doorway. 'Why are you still standing there, Beatrice? Put the laundry in the back room.'

He was casual, friendly and she went past him hoping that whatever madness had made him do what he had done before, had passed. She bent to put the laundry into the linen closet as he closed his office door that opened into the reception area. 'Why'd you come so late?' he called to her.

'I had to stop off in Rosehill,' she answered, trying to keep her voice light.

'Ah,' he nodded. 'Sonny's farewell party. I got an invitation the other day. Too bad I can't make it. Don't forget to take the dirty sheets off the cot in the examination room.'

She went into the examination room, and he called out, 'There are some dirty towels in the other cupboard, too.' She bent to gather them, and when she raised up, he was standing in the doorway. 'So how's Sonny doing?' he asked her. 'Excited about leaving?'

'I suppose so,' she said, keeping her voice formal.

'You're sorry he's leaving?' he asked.

'No,' she said straightening up. 'You want me to put the clean towels in here?'

'Don't bother,' he said. 'Just leave them on the bed. Miss Sung will divide them up.'

'Well, I'm finished.' She closed the cupboard doors.

'How much I owe you?' he asked.

'Reme say it's ten-fifty.' She folded the bag she had brought the laundry in.

'Okay,' he said, but he didn't move. He smiled. 'You getting to be a big woman, eh Beatrice. I remember when you used to come to me little little. You remember?' He came toward her still smiling. 'You remember how I used to touch your breasts and examine you down there, eh? You liked that, didn't you, Beatrice?'

Beatrice backed away, her body rigid against the cot. She looked anywhere but at him. There was no other way out of the small room, not even a window.

71

'Why you so frighten, Beatrice? I ever hurt you? Eh? When was the last time you see your menses?' He started to unbutton his white coat.

Beatrice tried to slip by him but she got only as far as his office door. He came up behind her and put his hand over hers as she tried the knob and found it locked. 'Open this door!' she shook the knob.

'You know wh, you come so late, Beatrice?' he taunted her.

'I was late because I went to Rosehill,' she snapped.

'You came late because you wanted to meet me alone.'

'You're crazy.' Beatrice shook the door. 'You're a sick man. You should see a doctor bout your head.'

He laughed. 'Everybody's gone, Beatrice. And you knew that.' He spun her around. 'Take off your clothes.'

'You're a nasty man!' she hissed, forcing him off.

'Why you trying to fight me?' he reached for her again. 'You want to give it to Sonny alone, eh? You tell him about us, eh? I watching you a long time Beatrice.'

'You'd better leave me alone,' she shouted, pushing him away and reaching for the door. 'Let me go!'

He hit her hard in the face. The blow stung her cheek, and as she pressed her hands to her face he pushed her back on the floor and straddled her. She kicked and grabbed at his face. With one hand he pulled down her skirt, and with the other he un-buckled his belt. She screamed and twisted, and kicked and beat her fists on his head, but he had a steel grip and as he jammed himself into her she felt her insides sear painfully. She deliber-ately slipped into a pain-filled daze, forcing the sight of him from her mind, feeling only rage swelling up in her. When he was done, he left her folded on the floor, got up, and pulled on his pants. Then he took a clean towel from the set she had brought, threw it on her, unlocked the door, and went out of the room. She got up unsteadily, staring down at the globs of slime on her skin. Disgusted, she grabbed the towel and scrubbed her thigh hard but the more she scrubbed, the more she felt the slime on

72

her skin. She flung the towel aside and put on her skirt. She looked around for her underwear. He had torn her panty. She took it up and put it down in her skirt pocket, praying that nothing would happen to her in the street. She would die of shame if anyone saw her without a panty in the street.

He came into the room again and stood by the now open door, his outstretched hand holding some money. Beatrice moved slowly toward the door, her head down. She paused in front of him, took the money, folded it, and slipped it into her pocket. Then she raised her face to look at him. He smiled. And Beatrice gathered all the mucous she could hawk up from her lungs and spat violently into his face. He lashed out at her, missing her head by an inch, and she ran out and down the steps and into the dark street.

Her head ached and she felt dizzy. She wanted to throw up. She moved closer to the side of a building but when she retched, nothing but saliva came up, and she tried to hurry on. Her mind told her to run but she couldn't make her legs move faster, and the water in her eyes made her steps uncertain. When she finally reached the taxi stand, she raised her hand to hail one but suddenly changed her mind. She could not stand the thought of sitting close to anyone. The bus station, she thought, would be nearly empty now, and she would be able to get a seat to herself.

She caught the bus, paid the driver quickly, and went to the back to sit alone. The driver looked back at her but she slipped low into the seat and ignored him.

At the Carenage stop she got off and walked down the muddy path to the beach. The sea was calm at Carenage. A reef broke the force of the waves several yards out, and the shallow water that came up to the sand was a safe place for small children to bathe. She slipped twice as she made her way toward the water. The second time her shoes stuck in the mud so she took them both off. On the beach she dropped the shoes and walked straight into the sea to where the water came up to her hem. Then she raised her skirt above her waist and stooped so the water came up to her hips.

73

Gritting her chattering teeth against the cold she stayed in the water feeling the numbness creep up her thighs, and forcing back the urge to lie down, to give in, to float until dark blue water covered her. The cramps made her legs heavy, and her shoulders trembled. She slipped deeper into the water, wanting the numbness to envelope her heart, her mind. She turned to face the beach, a part of her forcing consciousness upon the numbness, forcing her to think rationally, to gauge how far she had come from the shore, to anticipate going back. Then, out of the dark, she saw a light and heard voices, and knew that night fishermen were coming along the shore. She stumbled back to the beach where she rubbed her legs to get rid of the cramp. As the light and the voices got nearer, she quickly dug a hole in the sand, reached into her pocket, took out her torn panty, and buried it. Then she got up and walked the half mile to her mother's house.

On the evening of the farewell party a white Cadillac with a small Santabella national flag on the bonnet purred up the hill. Children ran alongside the car and the man in the back seat smiled and waved and wished he had thought to bring a bag of sweeties. When the car reached the community centre, the driver swung it around so that the front was facing down the hill. Then he came round to the side and opened the back door. The man inside alighted, straightened his jacket, and went toward the building.

Inside, all Rosehill waited, dressed to kill: Miss Ann in her pink taffeta with a red rose at the waistline; Willy, in the blue serge suit he saved for funerals and weddings; Moko, in the black pinstripe he hadn't worn since he had lost his leg, sat next to Tante Vivian, her hair plastered with black kiwi polish to hide the gray. She fanned herself with a neatly folded newspaper and Willy told her he didn't know how she was able to lift the fan with those two thick gold bangles weighing down her tiny wrists.

Near to them, the two local county councillors, Wilfred Smalls and George Padmore, were seated. Smalls and Padmore had come early and Miss Ann, after escorting them to their seats, had whispered to Jestina to keep her eyes on Padmore because he would drink all the rum before the party started. Mister Peters, the Headmaster, Mister Maxwell, the pharmacist, Mother Dinah and Uncle Clive sat in the second row.

The man from the white Cadillac stood in the door waiting to be acknowledged and escorted to his seat. All eyes in the room had turned toward him but no one moved. No one recognised him. A small boy came to the door and asked him to move so he could pass, and the man walked down the centre aisle. When he had gotten about three feet from the front, Wilfred Smalls whispered to Padmore, 'A..a..but I hardly recognise the man. He's the Permanent Secretary in the Ministry of Education.' And he rose and extended his hand. Miss Ann, coming from the back room where she had gone to check on the food, introduced herself, and it wasn't hard for the man to see her disappointment when he explained that the Prime Minister had sent his regrets.

'I can't stay too long either,' the man said. 'Another engagement, nuh.' Then he asked to meet the 'scholarship boy.' He said he had a envelope for him.

Miss Ann looked around for Sonny but didn't see him. Roberts suggested that he might be outside and volunteered to go and find him. But he came back a few minutes later to say that Sonny was nowhere outside. Miss Ann got vexed. She had reminded Sonny only that morning that the 'occasion' was to start promptly at six. 'Where the hell Sonny gone?' she asked Moko, but he shook his head. Miss Ann looked around her to find Beatrice. Beatrice wasn't there. The Prime Minister hadn't come – Miss Ann swore under her breath that she would never vote for the bastard again – Sonny was nowhere to be found, and Beatrice hadn't had the decency to turn up. 'My people? My people?' Miss Ann swore. 'You think you could ever trust my people to do anything right?' And she stupesed so hard, Tante Vivian's blood began to crawl.

Tante Vivian said she had not seen Beatrice since the after-noon before, but Reme, coming in just then, told them that Beatrice had come down with a sudden sickness. The girl could hardly walk, Reme said, and all night she had had roasting fever. She had asked Reme to come and tell Miss Ann that she was sorry.

'So what I going to do now?' Miss Ann asked, realising that her reputation was at stake. '*Somebody* has to give a speech.'

'Don't worry your head bout that, girl,' Jestina consoled her. 'People not coming to hear a lot of ole talk anyway.'

But Miss Ann was frantic. The occasion wouldn't be an occasion without a speech. She ran down a quick mental list of speechgivers. Willy could give a good speech when he was sober, but he had been drinking since early that afternoon and she couldn't risk him going on and on and embarrassing her. She decided she would just have to give the speech herself. 'If you want anything do right in this damn world, you better do it yourself,' she complained to Jestina.

The Rosehill crowd was too large for the tent the steelband boys had put up in the back yard. The lucky ones, who had come early in the evening, laughed and waved at their neighbours standing outside. Roberts searched among them again but he couldn't find Sonny, and Miss Ann stupesed again in disgust when Moko said Sonny had dressed and left home long before him. 'I thought the boy would be here, man,' he said, admitting he was worried.

'I don't care, nuh,' Miss Ann said. 'Is *my* fete and I starting it without Sonny!' But as she made her way through the crowd to the front table to announce the opening of the proceedings, someone shouted that Sonny was coming up the hill.

Sonny, dressed in a dark brown suit, white tie with brown polka dots, and shiny new shoes, came through the crowd of well-wishers with a cardboard box under his arm, and as he neared the table, people began to clap. Reme pulled him over and whispered in his ear before Miss Ann grabbed his arm and led him to the front.

76

Jestina, meanwhile, put some ice in a pan and took that, some paper cups, and a bottle of rum to the steelband fellars. She told them to hold some strain with that until the fete started.

Back inside, Willy banged on the table and called for order. Small children cried loudly, and above the noise, Miss Ann rose to sing 'Bless This House,' accappella. Her voice was shrill and she held the notes too long as she asked God to bless all the sinners there within. The crowd tried hard not to laugh but some rude boys didn't pinch themselves.

When she was finished, a fellow in the back shouted. 'Bravo! Bravo!' and Willy prevented the crowd from heckling by introducing the dignitaries. Next, he said, the Permanent Secretary would give a speech on behalf of the government. The man rose and said that on behalf of the Prime Minister, who regretted he couldn't be with them, he wanted to extend warm greetings to all the people and especially to the fortunate young man. He shook Sonny's hand, gave him a brown envelope, and told the crowd that he had another pressing engagement and would have to leave. Willy thanked him, gave him a shot of rum which the man swallowed in one gulp, and escorted him to the door.

Jestina whispered to Melda, 'But that was speech too? The man say two little words. These people can't talk, nuh. I wonder if is money he give to Sonny?' But Melda shushed her and pointed to Willy who was at the podium again, trying to continue above the noise.

'On this auspicious occasion,' Willy was saying, 'we, the people of Rosehill, come together to honour a man born and bred among us, a son of the soil, Sonny Allen!'

The crowd whistled and clapped. Willy continued.

'As you know, Beatrice, Sonny's good friend, was supposed to deliver some special words on behalf of this community, but unfortunately, Beatrice sick and can't make it. I will now ask Miss Ann to make a presentation to Sonny on behalf of Rosehill. Miss Ann.'

Miss Ann nudged him. 'Not yet, not yet. I have to give a

speech first.'

Willy whispered, 'Forget speech, Ann. You can't see how people sweating? Let we give this boy the gift and start the fete.'

The crowd was clapping. Miss Ann shot Willy a cut eye, and the Headmaster looked at them curiously, so Miss Ann yielded. But Willy knew he could expect trouble later. Miss Ann motioned to Sammy and he brought up a large package wrapped in newspaper which he ripped off. He handed the gift over the table to Miss Ann and she, planting a kiss on Sonny's cheek, presented him with a brown suitcase. The people clapped and hooted and called 'Speech! Speech!' and Sonny kissed Miss Ann's cheeks and shook Willy's hand.

Then, putting the suitcase aside, he began to speak.

'First, I want to thank everybody here tonight for this present. How all you know I want a grip?'

The crowd laughed with him.

'...And I want to say a special thanks to Miss Ann and to the officers of the Village Council who put this occasion together. I thank all the dignitaries for taking time to come quite up here on the hill. Well, is not much I have to say. Everybody here know me. I just want you to know that I will never forget how kind everybody was to me from the time I was small. I know you all want to start the fete so I'm not going to say much more. I just want to give special thanks to my father, and I have a present for Rosehill.'

He took the box he had rested in Moko's lap, opened it, and took out a silver cup. He held it up. 'This is the silver cup they gave me for winning the scholarship. I went down earlier today and asked the silversmith to put some more words on it. Some of you in the back can't see the writing, but I'll pass it round. The words say, 'Sonny Allen, Independence Scholar, from ROSEHILL!'

And as the crowd clapped, he handed the cup around. A man shouted above the noise, 'Hey Sonny, how much you think we could get if we pawn that silver cup, man?' and the crowd laughed. Miss Ann told him 'Open the envelope, open the envelope Sonny. Let's see what the Prime Minister send.'

Sonny slipped the envelope open with his thumb and read the few typed lines to himself as Miss Ann watched intently. Then he crumbled the letter, shoved it into his pocket, and sat down. Willy called for three cheers for Sonny; the crowd responded, and the steelband began to play. Neighbours came forward to shake his hand, and Sonny smiled and shook hands with everybody. Miss Ann kept trying to get his attention but he refused to look at her. Finally, she went into the kitchen and returned with a plate of pelau and a glass of sweet drink.

'I take yours out first, Sonny,' she said, stepping in front of the other people who had crowded around him. 'You know these hungry people. Time you look round twice, all the food gone.' She pushed aside a woman who was reaching for Sonny. 'All you let the man eat now before the pelau get cold, nuh,' and she led him to a chair in a corner.

Sonny thanked her as he took the plate, but he pleaded, 'I really don't have any appetite, Miss Ann.'

'Is woman making you totolbay, or what?' Miss Ann asked him. 'Why you don't eat the food, eh? Up in America you think you could get pelau like this? Here, drink a shot of rum. It will open up your appetite.'

Sonny refused the rum but ate the food as Miss Ann tried to force him to consume every grain. Then she took the plate and gave him a glass of ginger beer. Sonny drank it, chatted with Reme and Tante Vivian for a while and as soon as he could, he slipped round to the back of the community centre, took the trace to the Main Road, and caught a taxi for Bagatelle.

He found Beatrice wrapped in a coverlet on the sofa.

'How'd the party go?' she asked him as he sat down next to her.

'It's still going on. What happen to you? Your voice sounds so hoarse?'

'I get wet yesterday...' Beatrice began.

'Wet? Rain didn't fall yesterday.'

'Up here it did,' she said. 'I got soaked and didn't dry my hair.'

'You want to catch pleurisy?' He touched her forehead to see if she was hot, and she pushed away his hand. 'Why you didn't send to tell me since morning? I could have gotten something from the pharmacy.'

'It will pass,' she said. 'I'm sorry I couldn't come and make the speech. Miss Ann must be vexed with me.'

'You know how Miss Ann is,' he said, 'She wanted to give the speech but Willy wouldn't let her.' He talked on about the fete but Beatrice had closed her eyes and he wasn't sure she was listening. He shook her shoulders slightly, 'Beatrice, you sleepy? You want me to go?'

'I have to mix some honey and lemon,' she said, getting off the sofa.

He followed her into the kitchen and stood watching her quietly. After a few minutes in silence he said, 'Look Beatrice, I come quite up here to see you, you could at least talk. I leaving, girl. I had to see you before I go. You act like you don't want to see me.'

'I didn't ask you to come Sonny, and besides, what I have to say?' Beatrice mixed the honey and lemon together, avoiding Sonny's eyes.

Sonny turned away angrily. 'Okay, if that's the way you want to be, I gone.' And he went out the front door leaving it wide open.

Beatrice went to the door and her mouth opened to call him back, but the words didn't come out. She sat back on the sofa, sipped the syrup, and watched the dark outside, willing Sonny to turn around.

About ten minutes later he came back. He pulled the door shut and came over to her. 'Beatrice look,' he said. 'I know that things haven't been easy these last few months with Reme being sick, and you not getting the money to go away. But why you getting vexed with me? What I do that is so bad, eh? Tell me?'

'I say you do something bad?' she asked him.

'You don't have to say it. Just the way you've been treating me ever since the announcement. You used to talk to me. For months you only giving me silence. It's as if I commit some crime.'

'You saying I jealous of you, Sonny? Is that what you think?'

'I didn't say you jealous, Beatrice. But you sure don't act as if you glad. Everybody glad I win except you.'

'What you want me to do? Jump up in a steelband? Play mass because Sonny Allen win a scholarship?' She sucked her teeth and looked away. 'What'd you come back here for, Sonny? Just go, okay.'

'I'm not going anywhere until we get this settled.' He turned her to face him. 'Look Beatrice, I promise you, when I get over there, I'll try to send for you.'

'I asked you to send for me? Not everybody in the world want to go to America, Sonny. Their streets not paved with gold, you know.'

'You used to want to go. We used to talk about going all the time. You give up on that?'

'I give up on a lot of things,' she said.

'On me too?' He moved closer and tried to put his arms around her but she pushed him away.

'I never had my mind on you, Sonny. You think I born big?'

'Well, I had my mind on you.' He tried to get her to smile. 'Ever since I meet you for the first time by the bridge. I bet you don't remember that, eh? You were about fourteen then.'

She didn't answer, and he smiled, 'You know what I liked in you right away? I liked your fresh mouth. You were a rude girl, Beatrice. And later, when we used to go down in the bamboo, you remember that? I get to like you even more.'

She shrugged and looked away, and for a few seconds they went their separate ways back to the past.

Then Sonny said sadly, 'Things could change, eh girl? One minute you think you have the whole world in your hands and the next minute it gone.'

'I don't see what you have to be sorry over, Sonny. You win the scholarship. You're the one going to America.'

'Scholarship?' he laughed. 'You want to see scholarship?' And he pulled out from his pocket the envelope the Permanent Secretary had handed to him at the fete. He threw it on her. 'Read that!'

She smoothed the crumbled paper and read:

Dear Mr. Allen:

The government of Santabella congratulates you on your high academic achievement. We regret to inform you, however, that due to circumstances entirely beyond our control that were brought on by the recent hurricane devastation to thousands of our citizens, we have had to make some adjustments in the funds available for scholarships. We will, unfortunately, be able to offer you only a one-year scholarship at the local branch of our regional University.

We deeply regret any inconvenience this causes you....

Beatrice's voice trailed off in shock.

'Big time scholarship, eh?' Sonny said. 'Two days! Two days before I have to leave.'

'I can't believe this, Sonny. Where you get this letter? Somebody must be playing a joke.'

'Is no joke!' he said grimly. 'I get that from the Permanent Secretary self. He bring it to the farewell party. Girl, I thought the man was handing me money. When I open it, I coulda drop. Miss Ann was right there trying to read it but I didn't have the heart to tell her. She work so hard to pull together the fete.' Sonny shook his head. 'This government bad, you know. I've been going down there for the past month trying to get everything arranged and they keep telling me to come back. Last Wednesday they finally say everything settle. I could

82

leave. So I book the passage. Now this!'

'You have the visa, right?' Beatrice asked him.

'Yes, Embassy give it to me for five years. And I have the acceptance letter from the University too. They tell me I have boarding and everything. I was only waiting for the government to say they had transferred the rest of the funds. Now I don't know what to do.'

'Well,' Beatrice said, 'If I was you, I would pretend I never get this letter, Sonny. I would get on that plane and take off. I would go to the university and I would show them the scholarship letter, the first one you get.'

'And then what?' Sonny asked her. 'What I going to do when they find out? This government not going to send them any money.'

'Do what everybody else do. Find a job. Work your way through.' She began to cough, and pointed to the cup with the honey and lemon.

Sonny passed it to her, and patted her back while she sipped. 'I'm sorry, girl. I'm so blasted vexed about this whole thing, I forget you not feeling well, oui. You want some water?' He got her a glass of water and held it to her lips.

'Thanks,' Beatrice said, leaning back on the sofa as the cough subsided.

Sonny knelt in front of her, 'I really just come up to see how you feeling. I wasn't going to tell you about the letter.'

'Is okay,' she told him. 'I not going to tell anybody, and you shouldn't say anything either. But you should go. Pack your grip and leave as if nothing change.'

'I don't know, nuh,' Sonny said. 'My brains all tangle up.' He rested his head tiredly in Beatrice's lap and she rubbed his neck. 'Is funny how things could change so quick,' he said. 'I had made up my mind not to go away, then this scholarship thing come through and I say okay, a way open up for me so I'll take advantage of it. Now look what happen. Is as if somebody playing a big joke on me, Beatrice.'

'I feel like that sometimes,' Beatrice told him. 'I feel as if no

83

matter what I do, I don't have any control.'

And for a while they stayed quiet, lost in their individual thoughts about the past and the fearful future, and then, as if to console each other, they hugged. Then Beatrice said her shoulders were hurting her and Sonny offered to rub it with some warmed oil, and she slipped out of her night gown. He heated a spoonful of oil over a candle, and caressed her neck and shoulder tenderly. Beatrice felt the warmth gliding through her body and she turned over, took Sonny's warm fingers, and kissed them. Then Sonny took off his clothes and Beatrice spread the coverlet on the floor. Hesitantly, shyly, they came together for the first time, releasing the desire both of them had held back for years.

Afterward, they lay together under the coverlet, whispering promises. Just before Reme came home, he kissed her goodnight and Beatrice promised to go with him to the airport when he left for America.

PART TWO

Not long after Sonny left Santabella, the dry season started. It found Rosehill still waiting for the Prime Minister to come to see what Flora had done, and the damage the Company was continuing to do to the hill and the valley. Water was still a major problem for the villagers. The main line at the bottom of the hill had not been repaired so they still depended on trucks to bring in a tank a week. Sometimes the truck came; sometimes it didn't. Willy finally bribed the driver, and after that, the truck came regularly.

Many of the houses that had blown down had been partially rebuilt. Moko, however, decided not to try to rebuild his. He had given Sonny most of his savings as a farewell present, so he moved in with Tante Vivian. Beatrice also moved back into Tante Vivian's house after Reme went to Venezuela for three months with the Ameses, and rented out her house.

Beatrice had gotten a job with the Red Cross as co-ordinator of hurricane relief for the southern part of Santabella. Night and day she travelled through the villages assessing the human damage Flora had left; finding clothes for children from boxes sent from around the world, and distributing milk and biscuits from the World Health Organisation. Late in the evening she would fall asleep in Tante Vivian's rocking chair with all her clothes on, and Tante would slip off her shoes, and throw a light cover over her. When she began to feel sick in the morning, Tante said, 'You see what I was trying to tell you? You need to rest. Hard work never dead, yuh know.' But Beatrice knew her sickness didn't have anything to do with hard work.

She had missed her periods twice. When the third month passed without her seeing it, she asked one of the doctors at the

Red Cross office to give her a test and he told her yes, she was making a baby. For a few minutes, Beatrice was happy. She thought about the last night with Sonny and how they had come together and her whole body filled up with a glad feeling. But then she remembered what she had never told anyone, what she had tried to push out of her mind: that nasty thing that would never go away no matter how hard she tried to cover it with forgetfulness, and her heart got heavy with worry. Suppose it wasn't Sonny's child... Suppose it was... No. She wouldn't think his name.

To avoid Tante's questions, she began to leave the house before anyone else got up in the morning, and to stay at work later than usual. Some nights, when the office became too hot, she would go to Black Water Beach and lie on the sand and think about Sonny, and repeat the nice words he had written in the two letters she had received from him:

'My darling Beatrice, I hope this letter reaches you safe as it leaves me fine. I miss you dou dou, up here in the cold. I think about that last night a lot, and wish you could be up here with me....' and the sound of the words would blend with the lap of the waves and the sea would console her.

One night, as she sat near the stream that came from the ravine and emptied into the sea, she heard singing and bell ringing coming through the coconut trees. A man came through with a flambeau and she could see only his shining face. He was dressed in black from head to toes. Behind him came women in white dresses, some with their heads tied in blue, some with white, and behind the women came three young women about her own age, Beatrice thought. Mother Dinah walked behind the girls, holding another flambeau.

The man in front rang his bell and said goodnight sister to Beatrice, but Mother Dinah passed as if she had not seen her. Beatrice watched them moving slowly toward the rocks that hid the jetty from the beach, and the soft singing of the women stayed in her ears. When they stopped near the rocks, she got up and moved closer.

Mother Dinah and the man moved off to the side and when she opened a book, he held the flambeau for her to read. She read softly, her words barely reaching Beatrice's ear, and every few minutes, the man rang the bell. The women had taken the other flambeau and had surrounded the three young women. One woman held long white dresses over her arm and slowly they began to dress the girls, winding seven strips of blue cloth, one at a time, around each girl's head. When the dressing was finished, each one was led to the water's edge to wait. When they were all done, the women stayed to the side, singing and clapping, while Mother Dinah and the man joined the girls. Mother Dinah wiped each young woman's face with oil and handed her over to the man. Then he led them, one by one into the water.

Beatrice, watching from the side, wondered how far he was going to take them before he stopped. When the water was waist high, the man put his hand on each girl's head and pushed her down in the sea three times. Then a woman led each girl back to Mother Dinah. Mother Dinah made the sign of the cross on each one's forehead and then the women all knelt in the wet sand as she began to pray. She prayed loudly for God to witness the virgins' coming, and to have mercy on them. Then the women rose slowly and each one hugged each girl in turn. The man's voice boomed out suddenly and they joined him in singing 'Roll Jordan Roll'. Beatrice, caught up in the spirit, came closer and sang too. Then she followed them back up the hill, singing all the way, and before they parted, one of the women invited her to share in the feast next day at Mother Dinah's church.

She went after work and ate coo-coo from boiled fig leaves and drank and prayed with the sisters and their children, and it was late when she left, but she hardly noticed the darkness. It had been days, weeks since she had felt so light, and she smiled with the memory of Sonny as she passed their favourite spots on Rosehill. When she walked into the kitchen, Tante Vivian was ironing, and Beatrice, feeling free and happy, sat down at the table and told Tante Vivian that she was making a baby.

'Is for Sonny?' Tante asked, and Beatrice nodded.

'So what you going to do, child?'

'I don't know.'

'You want to keep it?'

'I can't say, Tante. This come on me all of a sudden.'

'Well child, sometimes these things happen before we want them to happen, but if that is what God wills, what we could do? If you want to keep it, your Tante will do everything she could for you, but if you don't want it...' And she went out and picked some special bush and mixed it with a bottle of stout just in case Beatrice would need it.

She told Beatrice the medicine was under her bed and it wouldn't hurt too bad. Beatrice, curious, opened the bottle and tasted a drop. The liquid was strong and thick and bitter, and she knew she wouldn't be able to swallow it, so she corked the bottle and left it under the bed. There were other ways she had heard about, but uncertainty still kept her from making up her mind. She knew if the baby wasn't Sonny's she wouldn't want it. But what if it were Sonny's baby? She was confused, and as the days passed, she found herself drawn more and more to Mother Dinah's church.

Sonny wrote her to say he had gotten a job and had moved from Brooklyn to Harlem. He had further to go to get to school, but he was closer to the job, he said. He sent twenty dollars for Moko and five for Beatrice. Beatrice wrote back and thanked him but didn't say anything about the baby.

She didn't tell Reme either, even after her mother had come back from Venezuela and questioned her about the weight she was gaining. Finally, Tante reminded her that big belly can't hide.

'You want your mother to hear it in the road?' she asked Beatrice, and Beatrice promised to tell Reme soon. For days before Reme came on her day off, Beatrice tried to go over the conversation in her mind, worrying about what she would say, and how Reme would react. Reme would sometimes set out to humiliate her. There had been times, as Beatrice was growing up, when she would do some small thing wrong and Reme would let the whole village know. It was as if she had to make it quite clear to the villagers that she was not responsible for Beatrice's bad behaviour. So Beatrice expected her to make a lot of noise about the pregnancy, and the more she worried, the louder her mother's voice became. She could hear her shouting, making it plain she was not pleased with this news at all. The neighbours would click their tongues in sympathy because they knew Reme had expected her daughter to be different; not like the other young women on the hill. The whole of Rosehill had expected her to be different. Now they would see that she was cut from the same piece of cloth as every other young girl who had a child before a man could put a ring on her finger. Reme would exaggerate. She would tell them how she had worn one panty for a year, washing it every night, hanging it up to dry, and putting it on half wet in the morning. All to give the girl a good education. She had put her house up for rent to try to get the money to send the girl away to study. She nearly caught pneumonia so many times, working, sweating to give her anything she wanted, and all for what? This was her consolation? How she would hold her head up in public, she didn't know. She would wash her hands of Beatrice. Let her go with any Tom, Dick and Harry. She had turned out just like her father. You can't clean up bad blood. After all the years she had sweated with Kelvin, he had walked out with another woman. That nasty man. No matter how hard you try, you don't get any satisfaction from people with bad minds. Beatrice had Kelvin's dirty mind. You could take a person out of the gutter, but you can't take the gutter out of them.

Beatrice wished she could run from Rosehill.

Reme came on Sunday morning and Beatrice got up to fix her a special breakfast with fry bake, saltfish buljol, zabocca and tomatoes. While Reme ate, Beatrice told her about the job and how well she was doing, and Reme reminded her to take the civil service examination that was coming up. When Reme finished sipping her green tea, Beatrice told her, 'Ma, I have something to tell you. Don't get vexed with me, okay?'

'Is about Sonny?' Reme asked her.

'In a way, yes,' Beatrice said.

'He sending for you?'

'He say he will try, but he has to work and go to school too, so it might take some time.'

'You shouldn't put your mind on him. When these men go away, you never could tell what will happen.'

'You like Sonny, Ma?'

'I like him. He has a lot of ambition.'

'I making a baby, Ma,' Beatrice said quickly.

'What you say?'

'I making a baby,' Beatrice said softly.

'You making a baby?'

Beatrice nodded.

'For Sonny?'

Beatrice nodded again.

'How many months now?'

'Almost four,' Beatrice said.

Reme shook her head. 'Why the hell you hide this? Is too late now. Is nothing I could do.' Then she got up from the table and went into the bedroom.

As Tante Vivian told Moko later, after one time is really a next. While Beatrice sat waiting for the explosion, Reme just took her bag and without another word to Beatrice, or a good-bye to Tante, she went out the front door and back down the hill slow slow.

Moko said he didn't know why Reme was vexed because Sonny would be glad to hear about the baby, and he sat on the bridge that Sunday afternoon and told everybody who passed that Beatrice was going to make his first grandchild.

Miss Ann, when she heard, insisted that she had to be the child's godmother, and wanted to know how soon she would have to buy the christening clothes. Beatrice told her she had about five months, knowing that Miss Ann only wanted the information so she could figure out if the child could really be Sonny's.

The week before Christmas, the Prime Minister ended his tour of the island in Rosehill. Party group members had built a platform in front of Ling Chung's rum shop and a loudspeaker van went through the village reminding Rosehill that he was coming. They said refreshments would be available, and word spread through the hill that he was also bringing a truck-load of canned food to give away.

He came late in the evening, when it was too dark to visit more than one farmer's garden and that one, as people pointed out later, was in Jackson Trace, not even in Rosehill. Following the quick garden visit, he and his party gathered on the platform in front of Ling's grocery and rum shop. Most of Rosehill turned out for the event, but only a few of them clapped when the Prime Minister got up to speak.

He told the crowd that his government was doing everything in its power to alleviate the problems they were facing. 'We can't move mountains,' he told them, 'but that's not going to stop we from trying.' He said nobody, not one child, not one man, not one woman in Santabella would go hungry while he was Prime Minister.

A group of hecklers shouted WHERE THE YANKEE DOLLARS GONE! WHERE THE YANKEE DOLLARS, MISTER PM! But the PM ignored them. He said he was well aware of the special problems Rosehill people were facing and he was working with Parliament on that. However, he said, Rosehill had to accept responsibility for breaking the law in the first place. 'The law say squatting is illegal and law is law.'

Jestina, who was right under the platform, told Tante Vivian later that it was a waste of her damn time, going down there. 'I nearly get my arse lock up! After that man say we squatting, somebody pelt a big stone at him, and police charge the crowd, hitting people left and right.'

'The police wasn't picking and choosing who to hold, nuh. They grab them too. I bust away and run like hell up the hill,' Melda said.

'Police shoulda throw both of you in jail. Big women like

you,' Tante Vivian told them.

'But he promise he was going to give out food,' Jestina said. 'It was right in his Party paper. The man come up here empty-handed and then start throwing insults.'

'That man have a tongue like a razor blade,' Melda said. 'You hear how he say he nearly cry blood when he see how people suffering in this country?'

'I tell all you long time that is madness we seeing,' Miss Ann said.

'You can't blame people for pelting him. If I coulda get my hand on a big stone, I woulda pelt him too.'

Melda laughed. 'I making a calypso about him this year self. Listen, I done start it already:

> *Is licks like fire*
> *Rain down on Prime Minister*
> *They pelt him for so*
> *With shatine and topitambo*
> *Banana and yams*
> *Breadfruit and zabocca*
> *Guava, eddoes, cassava and green mango.*
> *Dey pelt down de man*
> *He had was to turn and run*
> *Den de police come*
> *Wid bootoo and plenty gun...*'

'It bound to make road march this year, girl,' Jestina laughed.

'You better don't sing that in Santabella,' Tante Vivian warned her. 'Police lock you up and throw away the key so far, we'll never find you.'

'Is true, oui,' Miss Ann said. 'When you see they lock you up in this country nowadays, nobody ent seeing you again.'

'You see how they put up tiger wire all round the fort?' Jestina asked. 'People say is another jail they making.'

'Is not jail I worrying about, nuh,' Miss Ann said. 'Look the holidays coming and I can't even scrape together money for a ham. When you see Christmas coming and I can't buy a ham, you know things bad with me in truth.'

94

The women agreed. On Rosehill, Miss Ann was always the first to buy her Christmas ham. She would make a big wood fire in the yard even though she had a stove inside, and she would fill a pitchoil tin with water and put it on to boil with cloves and spice. Just as the water started boiling she would put in the ham, and when that fragrance floated from the pot, it was like essence, and every neighbour on Rosehill had to know that Christmas was coming in truth. But this year was different.

What small amounts of money people had, they couldn't spend on Christmas. Not one wall got a fresh coat of paint; windows didn't get new curtains, not even plastic; varnish and furniture polish stayed on the shelves in the hardware shop, and Ling Chung had to call a special sale on the rum and whiskey he had stocked.

The lawyer was trying to get the government to lower the cost of the lease but no one knew how things would turn out, so they saved every cent just in case.

'Hard times is my middle name,' Melda consoled herself. 'All I and my children need is a little saltfish. Give me a glass of ginger beer to wash it down, and is like I see God's face. I not fussy at all.'

'Is not a matter of fussy,' Tante Vivian told her. 'We don't have to be in this bind. The government could reduce the cost of the leases. They putting pressure on we for a purpose.'

'They have something against Rosehill,' Jestina said. 'Ever since Sammy had his picture in the papers. Remember? We make them look small. And now they will hold us in their minds for pelting the PM. They WANT we to ketch hell.'

'Is not government alone trying to make things hard, girl,' Miss Ann told them. 'I hear is men like Doctor Chow who putting pressure on the government not to give we the land. He is one who join with the Americans to drill for oil. He trying to get this land for years.'

'He going to have to kill me first!' Jestina said. 'No Chinese man going to push me off this piece of land. I put too much sweat in it. I rather dead!'

'We just have to hold some strain,' Tante Vivian counselled. 'You never know. Sometimes, just when things looking hopeless in true, lightning could strike.'

'I wish lightning would strike in truth,' Jestina said.

'Don't wish people bad, Jestina,' Tante warned her. 'The thunderbolt could fall on you, oui. But I have faith, girl. Things bound to work out.'

And so the Rosehill women waited, hoping for improvement, and in the meanwhile, they did what they could to help themselves. Jestina began to sell fruits from a stall in the market, and Melda took in ironing. Miss Ann got tired of extending credit and put up a sign in her parlour saying, 'If You Want Credit, Come Tomorrow.'

Christmas that year was really hard for the women and for the men too. Their boats needed repairs, and their short crops in the gardens were drying up. The men heard that the government was hiring extra labourers to help rebuild offices that Flora had damaged, so they went to each project, looking in vain for a few day's work. In the evening they would sit in Ling Chung's rumshop, nurse a petit quart, and tell how it had been that day.

'They tell me I'm not in the union,' Sammy said, 'so I can't get work on the project. I'm a man struggling all my life with the land. What I know about union?'

'Government getting their cut right and left,' Roberts said. 'They getting payback from the union. Is government project and only Party people getting jobs.'

'I tell them I will join the union,' Sammy said. 'The man say is twenty dollars to join up. Now where the hell I getting twenty dollars to give this man? I tell him, well padner, take it out my first paycheck, nuh, but he say no, I have to join first.'

'And that's not all you have to pay,' Willy told them. 'Every week they taking ten dollars out of your salary.'

'Is robbery with 'V' in this country, oui,' Sammy said.

But the Village Council said, hard as it was, Rosehill's children should have some toys. The members went into town, from merchant to merchant, and collected tin cars, tops, and dollies for the Rosehill Children's Christmas Party.

Right before Christmas, the postman delivered a box from Sonny to Beatrice. She opened it and found a sweater and two pairs of socks for Moko, and a blue sleeveless blouse for herself; a blue towel and two wash cloths for Tante Vivian, and three envelopes with a post card and an American five-dollar note in each for Miss Ann, Reme, and Uncle Willy.

Yet that Christmas was so hard, even Ling Chung didn't give out almanacs. But not everybody in Santabella was suffering. Some people were eating well. On the lawns out by the pools in Eversley Park, where the government ministers lived, servants moved among the guests with trays of hams and sweet breads, chocolates and imported nuts, sliced chicken and slivered almonds, and whisky with champagne for chaser; and the Police Band in their starched white dress uniforms, with the silver buttons shining like Christmas tree lights, played until morning.

Early in the new year, Beatrice took the civil service exam and passed with high marks. She then went to work in the Ministry of Finance. Reme, pleased that her daughter had gotten such a big job, bought her a new pair of slingback shoes to wear to work the first day, and a snakeskin purse to match. The gifts broke the tension that had remained between them since the day she had found out about the baby.

'I hope you stop ketching power down by Mother Dinah,' Reme said, watching Beatrice try on the shoes. 'All that shouting and rolling on the ground not good for you or the child. And this is an important job. You can't afford to get sick.'

Beatrice took the mirror off her bureau and placed it on the floor so she could see how she looked in the shoes. 'They nice, Ma. I could wear them for a long time if my feet don't swell up.'

'I buy them a little bit too big just in case,' Reme said, and Beatrice laughed as she recalled all the shoes her mother had bought her over the years, always too big, because 'too big is a fit.'

'But you have to try to stay off your feet, Beatrice,' Reme

was saying. 'When you come home from work, rest. You don't have to keep doing all that shouting and ketching power down by Mother Dinah.'

Beatrice slipped out of the shoes, 'I have to polish it before I wear it in the street,' she said. 'Sonny used to say you should always do that with new shoes to make them last longer.'

'You never listen to anything I say, eh, Beatrice?' Reme interrupted her. 'I trying to give you some advice but you talking bout Sonny. I tired telling you, hard ears does feel.' And she went away trying hard to figure out what she could do to keep Beatrice away from Mother Dinah and the Baptists.

Beatrice had become a staunch member of Mother Dinah's church, and was getting ready for her baptism. Each evening she had to go to Mother Dinah to learn special prayers and healing techniques. She learned the meaning of the pieces of cloths she had seen being wrapped around each girl's head that night on the beach, and was surprised to find out that although Mother Dinah praised God and believed in Jesus, she had other gods she prayed to and who she considered just as powerful. 'African gods,' Mother Dinah told her. 'We people, child.'

As the weeks went by, Beatrice became more and more immersed in the religion, and soon, women in the streets began to call her sister.

When her baptism night came, Reme refused to go down to the water with them, but Tante Vivian, Melda, Jestina, and all their children came to watch.

For a time, after the baptism, Beatrice felt good, so much so that she could forgive Sonny for not writing. She had not heard from him since Christmas and when Reme or the neighbours asked her about him she had to lie and say he was doing well.

Reme looked at Beatrice's belly getting bigger and bigger and said she wanted a girl child because 'boy child does grow into man, and man bad too bad.' But Tante said the way Beatrice's belly was hanging down, she was carrying a boy for sure. Beatrice didn't know what to believe, so she bought pink booties and blue ones too, just in case. Her friend Claudette gave her a baby blanket with red rosettes embroidered around the edge, and Mister Roberts promised to make a crib.

When the bad dreams started, Reme said she knew that would happen. 'All that simmi–dimi stupidness Mother Dinah making you do bound to affect yuh mind. But you wouldn't listen to me. What I know?'

Beatrice would wake up screaming, night after night, her nightgown soaked in cold sweat. The dream always began with her in the yard playing ring around the rosy and farmer's in the dell with Jestina's children, she told Tante, and it always ended the same way. They would get to the part where she was the cat and the children would spin her around with her eyes closed, and when she opened them, the children wouldn't be there, but she would be in the middle of a snake pit and big macawells would be crawling up her legs, and she would wake up screaming.

Tante sapped her head with Limacol and checked her dream book. She told Beatrice to be careful because snakes in a dream was a sign that she had enemies. Beatrice, certain then that this was a sign that the baby wasn't Sonny's, wished she had had the courage to drink the medicine under Tante Vivian's bed. But it was too late for that.

The dream haunted her for weeks. Some nights she was so afraid to sleep, she would drink strong strong coffee to stay awake, but the coffee would only make her stomach sick, and when she fell asleep, the dream would come again. Tante gave her bitter root to drink and Reme tried to talk her into going to see Doctor Chow but she turned away from Reme. Reme told Tante Vivian that the Baptists had twisted her daughter's mind. 'Beatrice don't know what good for her. What them Baptists know?' She went up the mountain to put candles in the grotto and ask the monks to say a special novena for Beatrice, but the dream wouldn't go away.

'Somebody jealous of meh daughter, oui,' Reme told Moko. 'Some badminded person can't stand to see meh girl child in big government job. They trying to put obeah on she, but I go fix dem.' Without telling Tante Vivian anything, she went to see a man in Toco, a village at the farthest end of the north coast. The man gave her a powder for Beatrice to drink, and Reme slipped it into Beatrice's tea three mornings straight, but the dream still didn't go away. Beatrice began to look thin and frail and Miss Ann told Jestina the girl was suffering from marasme.

One night, Mother Dinah kept Beatrice in the church. The sisters bathed her with bush leaves and rubbed her down with coconut oil and soft candle, and they banned her belly with a poultice and stretched her out on a piece of pine board. Her whole body trembled as if she was suffering from ague, and she tried to get up but one sister held her arms and another one held her feet while the others sang and prayed over her. She would scream out every few minutes, but the sisters were always there to calm her down. Tante Vivian came down to the church to see what was going on and she stayed by her side all night. She and the sisters prayed over Beatrice while Mother Dinah rubbed her until her whole body was too hot to touch. Then Mother Dinah covered her roasting body with three layers of white linen sheets in between which she had placed warmed fig leaves. Then she, Tante Vivian and the sisters prayed to the African gods. Beatrice listened between fitful bouts of sleep and wake. At times she heard herself mumbling words that she didn't even understand.

When the cocks began to crow in the backyard, she finally fell into a calm sleep. And she did not dream. She woke up midday to feel the sun shining through the window onto her face, and it was as if she had gone on a long hard journey and had come back safe and sound. Tante hovered over her, trying to force her to drink ginger tea, but Beatrice wanted to get up, to stretch her legs to make sure she was as well as she felt.

She kept telling Tante over and over that she wasn't even tired although her mind was telling her that she should be. Tante went up to the house and brought her back some fresh clothes but before Beatrice could put them on, Mother Dinah made all the sisters, everyone except Tante, leave the room, and then she and Tante prayed together in the four corners of the room and over Beatrice one last time. After that, the sisters brought her warm water to bathe, and she washed, put on her clean clothes, and began to feel so light that she could hardly eat the feast the sisters had prepared. That night, Beatrice slept in her own bed and had the best sleep she had had in weeks. She never had the dream again.

After that, she couldn't stop praising Mother Dinah. She tried to encourage Reme to join the Baptists. 'Even Tante say that Mother Dinah know a lot. She could help you with the belly, Ma.' But Reme wouldn't hear of it. She said she didn't trust Mother Dinah.

'Is a lot of hypocrites saying they have power,' she said.

Tante Vivian told Beatrice not to bother trying to get Reme to change her mind. 'She believe Mother Dinah encouraged Kelvin to leave her,' Tante said. 'Kelvin is Mother Dinah's nephew, yuh know, and she never liked Reme. So is more in the mortar than the pestle, child.'

Beatrice didn't speak to Reme about the Baptists again although she wanted to. She added it to all the other things she wanted to talk to Reme about but couldn't. For years she had been wanting to ask her about Kelvin. It seemed to Beatrice that every time her mother or Tante Vivian mentioned her father's name, their words were heavy with meaning that was not clear to her, and when she asked Tante for clarification, she said it was better to let sleeping dogs lie or you could get bitten by the fleas. But Beatrice couldn't help wondering why her mother never said anything nice about her father, why even to hear his name would make her vexed, why she judged every man by a yardstick named Kelvin, and none of them measured any more than he did. She wondered what her father had done to make her mother hurt so. She wondered where he was, why he had left. All these questions she couldn't ask Reme because they would spark a bitterness in her mother that could run for days on end. And once Reme began to bad talk Kelvin, every other man she knew got his share of cussing. Even Sonny. So Beatrice held her tongue, kept the questions in her heart and hoped that one day, her mother would find peace.

101

Beatrice had the child with Reme and Tante Vivian watching over her. Tante cut the navel string, and rubbed the baby with blue so nobody with bad eyes could put maljue on him. Then Rosehill came to pay their respects, wiping their feet carefully on the mat on the front steps, and putting a silver shilling or fifty cent piece in the baby's hand for good luck.

Reme asked Beatrice how come the child's eyes so small. 'He look just like Ling Chung's little boys,' she laughed, as she patted his nose with olive oil and told Beatrice to do that every day for the boy's nose to get straight. Moko, however, said the child looked just like Sonny and he kept touching it until Reme told him he would give the baby maljue. But he didn't pay her any mind. He boasted to Rosehill about how his grandchild would be bright like Sonny, and sometimes, at night, he looked at the stars and wished they could take a message to Angelina about Sonny and about the baby. When he didn't think anybody was listening, he sang about Angelina to the boy.

Miss Ann bought a white christening dress with blue flowers on lace from the Catholic thrift shop. She told Jestina it was the most expensive one she could find in town. And on the day of the christening she borrowed Ling Chung's camera to take a picture of the baby. After the photos were developed she put one up in her parlour for Rosehill to see the nice clothes she had put on Sonny's child. Beatrice christened the child George Melvin Allen after Moko, in Mother Dinah's church. Reme didn't attend. She stayed home to make sure, she said, that nobody went into the house to touch the christening cake.

Some weeks later Beatrice took the child to the well baby clinic in Speyside. Doctor Chow was on duty. When she spotted him, she wanted to leave, but the baby had a rash and she needed a prescription. Besides, a small part of her was curious to see how he would react and how she would behave in front of him. She had never gone back to his office after that evening, having lied to Reme that the doctor had said he didn't need her to do the laundry anymore.

She watched him move about the clinic and once or twice he glanced her way and she hoped he could feel the heat of her hate across the room. She wanted him to know how much she hated him, and she was glad for the feeling because it made her unafraid. As she sat on the hard bench waiting her turn, she played with the baby's fingers and told herself she would never be afraid of Chow again; that no matter what he said, he could never hurt her again. When her turn came, she went into the small room, put the baby on the bed, and stood close to him.

Doctor Chow asked the nurse to get him a basin of water, and waited for her to leave the room before speaking to Beatrice. 'How you doing Beatrice?'

She didn't answer, and he smiled. Then he asked her to move aside so he could examine the baby. Beatrice moved to the side as he bent over the baby and placed his stethoscope on its chest.

When he was finished listening, he told Beatrice to take off the child's diaper. As she was doing so, he said, 'You didn't have to keep it, you know. Why didn't you come to me? I would have given you something. You're just like your mother, Beatrice.'

She raised her head to stare deliberately at him, through him, and he shook his head, as if to get rid of the acid glare she was spraying him with.

'So how's Sonny doing? Eh? You hear from him at all?' He was bending over the baby, examining the rash. 'I'll give you something to put on this.' He straightened up. 'You tell Sonny who the father is, eh, Beatrice? You tell him is mine?'

'You finish?' Beatrice snapped.

'You could dress him,' he moved aside so she could begin dressing the baby, and he watched her with a slight smile.

Beatrice's fingers moved swiftly, slipping the smock over the baby's head, pulling his small thick arms through the sleeves, tying up the booties, and all the while Doctor Chow watched her. Even when the nurse came back with the bowl of hot water, he couldn't take his eyes off Beatrice. He waved the nurse away as Beatrice wrapped a light blanket around the baby and lifted him off the bed. As she reached for her bag, he gripped her hand and the sound of his voice was urgent, demanding, almost desperate.

'Reme tell me this is Sonny's child, Beatrice. You tell her that? You frighten to tell her about us? Eh? You belong to me, you know. And Reme too. She ever tell you we did it, eh? But you were better. You....'

Beatrice snatched the child up and ran out of the clinic without the prescription.

All the way home his words kept hammering in her head: 'You belong to me, you belong to me.' No! No! I can't be his child. I'm Kelvin's child. Reme said so. Reme wouldn't put herself with him. But maybe she didn't have a choice. Maybe he forced her as he forced me. Oh God. No!

Beatrice wasn't sure how she got home, her mind was in such a confused state, but when she walked in Tante Vivian's house she had decided to blot out the doctor's words. He's evil, she thought. One day, one day, he's going to pay for this.

For almost a year after the *Guardian* burned, Santabella didn't have a daily newspaper. The government's paper came out every two weeks, but as Sharky said, 'All dat have in it is the PM do dis, the PM do dat, and some long long speeches. I use dat in my latrine, man.'

The editor of the *Guardian* had tried to start another paper but his license to import newsprint and ink was not renewed. The government said he owed customs too much money. The editor took all his paid bills in to show them but he still didn't get the license. He got fed up and moved to Trinidad. The market women who traded in Trinidad brought news that it looked like the editor was trying to start another down there.

'But how we going to get it?' Joseph wanted to know.

'They have ways and means, man.'

'Well, I for one will believe dat when I see it,' Sharky said. 'Dis government not letting any paper come in dis country dat criticising dem.'

'You want to bet me the paper come?' Popo, a market woman asked him. 'Put your money where your mouth is.'

Sharky put down two dollars. 'I betting you.'

They had to wait another two months, but one Friday, the *Bomb* dropped. The first copies went like hot hops bread and some people had to depend on the news second hand. The fellars on the wharf stopped working to hear Sharky who had seen a copy earlier.

'Is big big headline it have, man.' He stretched his arms wide. 'Never see a big headline so. Cover the whole front page.'

'But what it say, man? What it say?'

'Boy, it ask the same question I asking myself a long time now.'

'Sharky, you trying to sell dis news or what?'

'But how you getting vex so, man? A fellar need time to digest dese things.'

'Stop playing the arse, Sharky. What the hell is the question?'

'WHERE IS CUDJOE?'

'What you mean, where Cudjoe is? Everybody know where Cudjoe is.'

'When last you see him?'

'See him? How I could see him? Government say Cudjoe gone Cuba. Everybody know dat.'

'You see Cudjoe get on airplane?'

'I not working airport, man. Is boat I loading dese days.'

'The *Bomb* say Cudjoe not in Cuba.'

'So where de hell he gone then?'

'Dey say he never went nowhere.'

'But nobody ent see Cudjoe in months. Government say he take out passport and gone to Cuba.'

'The *Bomb* say dey know for fact, Cudjoe never leave this island.'

'So he's in hiding?'

'The *Bomb* say he not hiding.'

'So where the arse the man is, Sharky?'

'The *Bomb* say dey will tell we next week.'

Issue number two of the newspaper said Cudjoe was snatched one night on his way home in the dark, and he was beaten to death in Fort George. They took his body and dropped it in the deep sea.

'Is real mafia style down here, oui,' Joseph declared. 'I sure dey weigh down the body with cement.' And the fellars agreed that Santabella was coming more and more like an American film show.

Rosehill buzzed with the news about Cudjoe for days, and rumours spread that the government would try to stop the *Bomb* from getting into the country. When the *Scarlet Ibis* came from Trinidad the next week, squads of policemen waited on the dock. As soon as the boat dropped anchor they went up the gangplank and ordered the market women to get off, one by one. Then they told each woman to empty her bags onto the jetty. The women tried to defy them but the policemen kicked open sugar bags, flour sacks, rice bags, and cornmeal packs, and scattered the goods all over the wharf. Then they walked over everything with their heavy boots, poking and shifting, and the women could only stand aside and cuss them under their breath.

When they were finished with the goods, the policemen went back on board the boat, leaving the women scrambling to salvage what they could, fighting off the sea gulls, corbeaux, and ants that had begun to attack the food. The police searched and searched but didn't find a single copy of the *Bomb* on board the *Scarlet Ibis*. And yet, before night came down on the hill, everybody knew what the *Bomb* had to say that day.

PRIME MINISTER HAVE FAT SWISS BANK ACCOUNT BUT CHILDREN HAVE NO FOOD. PRIME MINISTER HAVE BIG SWIMMING POOL BUT CHILDREN HAVE NO SCHOOLS...

In the taxi stand the drivers talked about the news. In government offices secretaries stopped tapping typewriters to whisper it to each other; in the gullies and the valleys poor people shook their heads and said they knew that all the time, and up on Rosehill, Ling Chung listened silently while the boys argued politics. The government declared the *Bomb* contraband and ordered police to arrest anybody they found with the newspaper.

Beatrice cut out some of the articles to mail to Sonny even though she still hadn't heard from him since the year opened. In the letter she also told him that Tante Vivian had gone into the bee business with Sammy. She didn't tell him about the child. She wanted to tell him. She had even taken some pictures of the boy to send, but every time she had sat down to write the letter, something had stopped her hand from writing the words. It was as if her fingers wouldn't form the words that her own mind still doubted, that her own heart was still uncertain about. Once, Reme asked her if Sonny was sending anything for the child, and she lied. Yes, she told Reme, Sonny had sent a hundred dollars.

'He should send some clothes for the boy,' Reme said, bouncing Melvin on her lap. 'Tell him to send some blue overalls. I like to see Miss Ames' little boys in them. They look rich. And a pair of sneakers. The child's foot growing fast.'

Beatrice went to Elias's store in town and bought the most American-looking clothes she could find. She brought them home, showed them to Reme, and told her that Sonny had sent it down for his son. Reme was pleased. She boasted to her friends about how nice Sonny was treating Beatrice, and when they asked if her daughter would be going away to join him, she told them yes, as soon as the boy got a little bit older. Beatrice heard all this and felt guilty, and she tried again to write Sonny and tell him, but her hand wouldn't write the words, so she put the paper aside.

Yet, as the months passed and the boy's legs grew straight, and he made faltering steps toward her when she came home in the evening, she told herself that if he wasn't Sonny's, he ought to be; he deserved to be. Melvin had his first birthday and she brought him presents, again pretending they were from Sonny, and for her twentieth birthday that year, she bought a plain wedding band from De Lima's gold shop in town. She showed it proudly to Reme, and Reme slipped it off her finger, twisted it to see if it had a special marking, and when she saw the 14K, she smiled.

'Is real gold. I see the marking,' she said. 'Sonny ent as worthless as I thought he was. But he shoulda send one with a stone. Dat is the fashion these days, yuh know.'

The ring satisfied Reme's questions about Sonny for a while but Tante wasn't fooled. She was home every day, and she knew the postman had not brought any letters from Sonny. Her heart ached for Beatrice, but what she could do? She found an envelope from one of the early letters he had written and she folded it carefully and put it away for the day she knew she would have to write to him.

Beatrice told Claudette, though, that she had given up on Sonny. 'I ent trusting another man in this world, girl.'

'All men not bad,' Claudette told her. 'Sometimes they have to do things they don't want to do. Sonny might still love you, but you down here and he's up there. Write him one last letter and tell him how you feel. It he doesn't answer, then give up on him. It have plenty good men in Santabella, girl.'

'You marry the last one, child,' Beatrice laughed. 'They break the mold after that.' And although she promised Claudette that she would write to Sonny to find out his intentions, when she wrote all she talked about was Santabella. He did not reply and her letters didn't come back so she knew he must be receiving them. A small part of her held unto the hope that he still cared.

Rosehill, two years after hurricane Flora, was coming to life again. Poui trees blazed yellow in the hills, and pink roses grew wild in the bush. Hummingbirds and kiskedees sucked syrup from red hibiscus as little boys played marbles in dusty front yards.

The Company had started drilling in Speyside and was beginning to move closer to Rosehill, but Willy had managed to find a Minister to bribe, and the work was slowing down. The Minister had warned Willy, though, that he couldn't hold the Company off forever, so Rosehill had better try harder to get the money for the leases.

'What you think we doing?' Willy asked him. 'We ent sitting down and waiting for cock to get teeth. We hustling, man. I selling fish, I making garden. You think is two work I doing? Every manjack, every woman on Rosehill pulling together.'

Down in the gully, Sammy's bee business began to flourish. He got a commission to sell honey to a factory, and he told Tante Vivian that he would buy all of hers. He came to check on her bees regularly. 'You have to be careful, Viv,' he warned her. 'Any time you want to expand, call me. Don't do it yourself.'

Tante laughed, 'So you is expert now, eh?'

'I read book about these bees, girl. Hear what I'm telling you. These bees not sociable. You put some strangers in there with dem and is trouble for so. And don't let the little fellar play near them.'

Tante warned Moko to watch Melvin carefully whenever he played in the yard. With Beatrice working, Moko and Tante were looking after him, and Moko loved his grandchild. All day he played with him. He cut branches from the guava tree to make flutes and whistles for him, told him stories, and sometimes took a pigeon out of the coop and put it on the boy's shoulder. Then he taught him how to put his hand sideways in the coop and talk to the pigeons so they would learn to trust him. And the boy learned to love Moko.

Beatrice looked for Sonny in her son. She tried to see Sonny in his eyes, and in the way he bent his head to one side as he listened to her. She brought him story books and told him how his father liked to read, and she was glad when she found Melvin studying the pictures closely. She took him to the sea every Sunday morning and as she sat on the sand watching him roll in the shallow water, it was hard for her to believe that he could have bad blood. He had to be Sonny's child.

One day, Moko, playing in the yard with the child, left him for a few minutes to go into the kitchen to get a cup of water to drink. Melvin opened the wire netting in the bee hive and tried to pull out a piece of honeycomb. He touched a bee and it stung him, and as he pulled back his hand, he hit the hive and the box toppled over on him. He screamed and Tante Vivian and some neighbours came running, but by the time they got him to the hospital, he was dead.

The whole of Rosehill grieved with Beatrice. Roberts made a small coffin and Willy painted it white. Jestina sent her children to gather pink roses and she made a wreath shaped like a heart. Tante Vivian asked the shoemaker to whittle down her mother's silver cross and she placed in on the coffin. She held up as best she could, but on the day of the funeral she cried so much, her heart seemed to give away. She became weak and had to stay in bed. Reme and Miss Ann bathed the child and patted his face with white powder. No one could console Moko. He sat under the mango tree in the backyard refusing to eat or drink, just talking to the pigeons night and day. Beatrice told him she wasn't vexed with him, it wasn't his fault, but it was as if he could not hear her.

Everyone worried about Beatrice. They knew how she loved the boy and they couldn't understand why she didn't cry when she had heard the news. They watched her as she helped get the child ready for burial, and they saw that her face was sad, but her eyes were dry. They wanted her to cry, to break down, to scream as Reme had done, as Miss Ann had done, as any mother on Rosehill was expected to do when her child died. Tante Vivian, her forehead banned with a cloth soaked in Lima-col, squeezed Beatrice's fingers tightly and told her that she shouldn't keep things bottled up inside but Beatrice turned away silently. Reme, trying a different approach, asked her if she had heard from Sonny. 'I wonder how Sonny is taking the news?'

Beatrice shrugged her shoulders and Reme didn't know what to make of that answer. She told Tante Vivian that she was going to send a cable to Sonny because the way Beatrice was acting, she wasn't sure he knew, but when she searched Beatrice's drawer, she couldn't find any letters from Sonny, and Tante Vivian said she didn't know his address.

Beatrice didn't come home the night after the child was buried. Tante and Reme went looking for her down by the beach because some children had said they had seen her going that way, but they didn't find her. Reme started to bawl, thinking that Beatrice had killed herself, but Tante told her Beatrice would never do anything like that.

'That girl too strong. She just need to be by herself a little bit. She'll come home when she ready.'

But Reme sat up all night watching the front door. Beatrice came home early the next morning. Reme saw her come through the front gate and ran out to her shouting, but Tante limped to the front room and begged her to calm down, and after a while she left Beatrice alone.

Beatrice went into the house quietly, put on her work clothes, and went to town. In the evening, as soon as she came home, she changed her clothes and went down by the sea. Every night she did that, and as Tante watched her leave the house, she wondered what she could do to make Beatrice stop grieving.

'She need a nice man friend,' Miss Ann said one day. 'I will introduce she to meh cousin's son next time he come to visit.'

But Beatrice just smiled slightly at the man when he spoke to her. She said no thanks when he offered to take her to a theatre show, and Miss Ann, looking on, whispered to Jestina that 'Beatrice must be think she too great. She don't want no mechanic. She want a lawyer. Let she wait. Cock will get teeth first before Sonny come back for she.'

Every evening for months, Beatrice left the house, walked past Mother Dinah's church, past Miss Ann's parlour, past Ling Chung's rumshop with the fellars liming outside, past the noise down by the junction, and she crossed the road to walk down to the beach alone, to sit by the water, to listen to the waves hitting the sand, but the sea no longer gave her any comfort.

111

PART THREE

As the plane banked to the left above the Dragon's Mouth to make its final descent, Sonny leaned forward in his seat to catch a better glimpse of the hills. It was funny, he thought, how he always called them hills, never mountains or mountain ranges as the schoolbooks called them. Even as a boy, looking up at them from the Ledge, he had called them hills. Perhaps that was because he had been so close to them.

From as far back as he could remember, he had been semi-enclosed by hills. His only break had been the sea, the opening to the Dragon's Mouth. He smiled as he thought of how much those hills had defined his life and wondered, not for the first time, if it had been the same for Angelina. Was that why she had had to escape, to run away from him, to leave Moko? She must have hated the hills the way I did at times, Sonny thought. She'd had to escape before they strangled her, just as I had to leave.

And yet he remembered that there were times when he had loved the hills, when he had sought refuge in them from Moko's drunken bouts. The times when he had had no one to ask why, why my mother leave me? Why she never come back? How could she leave her own child with Moko on Rosehill? The trees, the bush, they'd had no answers, and maybe there were none, Sonny thought, that he could ever accept; none that he ever wanted to hear. But he had found comfort in them, and their presence, tall, overpowering, reaching up farther than he could see, inspired him to think of places he had never been and to dream dreams that kept him alive.

From the plane, he looked out at them and they seemed strangely different. They looked misty, bluish, and – he was almost embarrassed to think the word – well, majestic; a grand fullness rising and sloping and falling abruptly to the sea. He felt an unfamiliar sense of pride, of ownership, and he smiled. And it occurred to him then that this, this was what he had missed most: the hills.

The plane flew in over the Northern Range and deep below he saw the Oropouche River, long and brown like a lizard, slinking through the citrus groves in the Santacruz valley. Here and there, between the groves of grapefruit and orange trees, he saw a silver tin roof glinting off the afternoon sun. The Oropouche grew wide, and along its wet banks were miles of flat, empty land. He knew that in a few months vegetables would rise above the dirt and those fields would be rich with tomatoes, lettuce, and melongenes. To the south of the river he saw the swamp – rich, wet land – land for growing rice, and just above the rice fields, a green sea of sugarcane stretched broad and long. Sonny felt a silly urge, a wish, to parachute into the cane fields, to lose himself within their embrace. And yet he had that other feeling too. What was it – fear? Anticipation? He shook his head, rejecting the slight panic that had begun to rise inside him, a panic that said this was a mistake: he should not have come back, not even for Beatrice.

The passenger in the seat next to him spoke and Sonny was glad for the distraction. 'You really have to go far to see the beauty of this country,' the passenger said.

Without turning, Sonny nodded in agreement. He pressed closer to the window. Beyond the canes, another sight, one he had not seen on the land before, caught his eyes, and he turned to the man with a question.

'Oilfields,' the man confirmed. 'All over the place.'

Sonny stared at the pumps. They looked like giraffes trapped in pools of tar.

'Oil spill,' the man said, as if he had read Sonny's mind. 'Break in the line.' He pointed over Sonny's shoulder. 'See there where it running off to the side? See? Bad for the top soil,' the man shook his head.

'You live in that area?' Sonny asked him.

'I have some family near there. Monrepo. They have land up there, but government trying to take it away, man. Family live there for years. Government want it back soon as they hear it might have oil on it. Where you from?'

'Rosehill.'

'How long you away?'

'Almost three years. But it seem like I only leave yesterday.'

'A lot of things change down here, man,' the man said. 'This oil bring plenty petrodollars for some people. The other day I was up in the Holiday Hotel, you know the one on Parker Street? Well, I was holding some strain there as a waiter. This lady come in with she son and his girlfriend to celebrate engagement. Man, in no time at all these people run up a bill for seven hundred dollars! Shrimps! Three different fancy wines! I tell you, I watch them people, oui. I shake meh head. Money flowing in this country, boy. But not everybody getting a share, that's the thing. Take me now. I is a hard hard working fellar. I would do anything to make a dollar. But you think I could get work down here? I have to scramble meh arse... gawd, I sorry man, I didn't mean to cuss...'

Sonny waved away his protest, and the man continued, 'Is just that I does get hot when I think bout how it is in this country.'

'So why you not working in the oilfields?' Sonny smiled inwardly as he heard the familiar cadence of Santabella talk coming back in his voice.

'You think is two try I try? Man, it hard like crab to get job up there. Is who you know. People paying big big bribe. I say to mehself, not me, padner. Yankee man want me to pick orange, I going up. I prefer take my chances with dem.'

'But what you going to do now, man?' Sonny was beginning to feel comfortable with the old talk. I'm home, he thought. Is ole talk, is corruption, is people criticising the government. Is Santabella.

'I put away some small change, padner.' The man was

proud. 'I ent stupid, yuh know. I not like some fellars, Every time they make a penny they run women. I save the chips, man. I know how things hard in this country. Is ten dollars a pound for watermelon, yuh know.'

'So how much for rice and sugar?'

'Well, don't talk bout that!' the man said. 'Is months now we ent getting rice. We lend Guyana millions and when Burnham say he can't pay it back we tell him give we rice instead. The man promise and then turn right round and sell the rice to Cuba. You ever see things so? And don't talk bout sugar? You imagine in we own country we making the sugar and we can't even get some to buy? I tell you, you think it easy in this country?'

The stewardess interrupted them as she checked for locked seat belts, and they listened to the captain announce that they would be landing shortly. Sonny's thought flashed to the land they had flown over, the wet land that could yield so many thousands of bags of rice. What was the government doing with all its petrodollars? From what he had heard, nothing much had changed for the better.

'I buying a piece of land, yuh know,' the man told him. 'I doing just like them small island people. Buy a piece of land and plant some short crops. Tannia, cassava, eddoes, tomatoes, a lil' bargie on the side and some sorrel. Man could live off the land, oui.'

'Provided no hurricane come,' Sonny said.

'Boy, that was a real bad one we had, yuh know. Wash way everything. You was in it?' the man asked.

'Happen the year I leave,' Sonny told him. 'I just missed it.'

'One big one like that again and is pepper sauce in we tail, oui,' the man said. 'Every rainy season I frighten.'

The plane approached the airport, and the passenger nudged Sonny.

'But man, we landing jest now and I ent even introduce mehself. I is Superville. You know the Supervilles from Aripo.'

117

'I hear the name,' Sonny said, and shook the man's hand.

'I know Rosehill,' the man nodded. 'Used to have a nice dou dou darling up there when I used to drive taxi. You must be know she. Melda.'

Sonny smiled, 'She living right down from me, man.' What taxi driver didn't know Miss Melda, he wondered.

'That woman nice too bad,' the man said fondly. 'But she married now, I hear. When you see she, tell she Superville say hello, eh.'

Sonny promised to deliver the message. Then he and the man looked out of the window as the plane landed smoothly, and the passengers clapped. Superville gathered his many bags from under his and Sonny's seats, and was one of the first in the aisle, waiting for the door to open. Sonny stayed in his seat until most of the passengers had gotten off. Then he took down his flight bag, slipped on his jacket, and left the plane.

The moment he left the cool interior, hot air enveloped him and he wished he had a shirtjack as some of the passengers wore. As he walked the hot tarmac toward the terminal, he could feel perspiration gathering under his arms, and he felt sticky. Small drops of sweat began to drip down his sides. He took off his jacket and hurried into the terminal hoping that the government had modernised the building with air conditioning. Inside, however, two slow and dirty ceiling fans struggled in vain. Sonny joined one of the two long lines that had formed in front of the small booths where immigration officers were checking identities. He spotted Superville up ahead loaded down with two shoulder bags, a small cardboard box and three shopping bags. Sonny glanced around him. Every returning citizen was loaded with parcels, boxes and shopping bags, and he suddenly felt angry at himself that he hadn't brought more.

When his turn came he handed his passport to the official and the man asked to see his ticket too as he slowly turned the passport pages.

'Your passport going to expire soon,' the official said without looking up.

118

'Yes,' Sonny agreed. 'I'm going to get another one while I'm here.'

The man opened the ticket and examined it carefully. Several minutes passed as he read the ticket, then examined the passport again. Sonny felt annoyance creeping up his throat.

'Staying long?' The man finally looked up.

You've seen the return ticket, why ask a stupid question? Sonny wanted to snap, but he didn't. The man could choose to delay him for any small reason, and he had already begun to sense the irritation of the passengers behind him.

'Ah...yes,' he answered, trying to keep his tone pleasant.

The man smiled. 'Don't forget to get your ticket cashed. Wait too long you might not get any money back.' He stamped the passport and handed it to Sonny.

'Custom's that way,' he pointed, though the sign was obvious.

Sonny smiled a thank you and headed for the rows of conveyers where khaki-uniformed customs officers were checking baggage. A few yards from the baggage claim area, a glass wall separated the passengers from those who waited for them outside. He could see the children pressing their faces to the glass, and several people in the crowd waved. The faces were all strange and he turned his attention to the slowly moving baggage on the conveyer belt. He spotted Superville off to the side, busy collecting his other bags and boxes, and Sonny stared as he lifted the largest suitcase he had ever seen. Superville caught Sonny's eyes and came over to ask him to keep an eye on the luggage while he dragged each piece over to the Customs line.

'You bring back Brooklyn, boy?' Sonny laughed.

'Yuh know how it is, pardner,' Superville said shaking his shoulders. 'You can't just bring for one, yuh know. Yuh have to bring something for everybody.'

After Superville had lined up all his luggage, Sonny gathered his one small suitcase and joined the line. He watched curiously while the Customs officer chatted and smiled with the people he knew and marked their baggage without looking

119

inside. When it was his turn the officer told him to open the suitcase.

'And the briefcase,' he added.

'It has only papers.' Sonny protested.

'Open it, please,' the officer's voice was firm.

Sonny opened the suitcase. The man glanced briefly at its contents, left it open, and turned his attention to the briefcase. Sonny's pants, shirts and underwear lay exposed as the man went through the papers in his briefcase methodically. He lifted a notepad and took out the *Playboy* Sonny had picked up at the airport before boarding the place.

'We don't allow this,' he snapped and pushed the magazine under the counter.

'May I have that for a moment?' Sonny asked pleasantly.

The man grinned and raised his eyebrows. 'Want a last look, eh?' He handed Sonny the magazine.

Sonny smiled with him. And then slowly and intently, as the man watched him vexed vexed, he tore the magazine into several pieces.

'You have a garbage can?'

If man could die from cut-eye, Sonny knew he would be the first to go from the look on the man's face, but he felt a little sense of triumph as the man took the pieces of magazine and threw them into the dustbin at his side.

'Finished?' Sonny asked briskly, indicating his baggage.

The man kept his eyes on Sonny, daring him to protest, as he turned the briefcase over, dumping the contents onto the table and spreading them as if he were looking for small stones in a bowl of lantie peas. Deliberately, he went through each bit of paper while Sonny watched silently and other passengers shifted bags and boxes angrily. After several minutes, the customs man turned his attention to Sonny's clothing in the suitcase. He felt in every pants pocket; he opened every little bag; he squeezed the folded sock and the tube of toothpaste. Then he snapped, 'Close it.'

'Thank you,' Sonny said, smiling a little, and he began to

carefully replace all the items as the man watched him.

'It have other people waiting,' the customs man snapped.

'I know that, and you know that too,' Sonny smiled. He relocked both cases, and the man scratched a large X on the suitcase with yellow chalk and turned to the next person in line.

Sonny moved to the door where another officer verified the X on the suitcase, then sent him back to the conveyer to have an X placed on the briefcase. Sonny approached and told the man that he had neglected to place the required mark on the briefcase. The man told him he would have to wait his turn and sent him to the end of the line.

'Them is boss in this country, oui,' a woman whispered to Sonny as he began to protest. 'Is best not to say nothing.'

Sonny took her advice but made a note of the man's badge number.

When finally he had gone through the line and was outside, the glare of the sun forced him to put on his shades and loosen his tie. He looked around for Superville but didn't see him. Then he walked through the throng of waiting relatives and friends toward the private cars and taxis lined up at the side of the terminal. He had told Tante not to send anyone for him; not to even say he was coming because he didn't want a fuss. Knowing her, though, he thought she probably had sent somebody anyway. He was surprised, therefore, when, after ten minutes, no one except taxi drivers approached him. He finally called one over and said he wanted to go to Rosehill.

The driver put in his suitcase but kept the trunk open. 'Padner, ah hope you don't mind,' he said. 'I want to get just one more, eh.'

Sonny shrugged, and the driver hustled up to two young women approaching with two suitcases and called, 'Rosehill! Grenville! Rosehill! Grenville!' When the women ignored him, he pleaded, 'Oh gosh darlins, well lemme take you home, nuh. Is a nice taxi I have.'

'I waiting for somebody, man,' one of the women told him. And he went off in search of another passenger.

Ten minutes later he still hadn't found another one so he came back to the car. Sonny was glad. He had started to feel tired and he didn't want to engage in the talk that was inevitable when two or three Santabellans rode together in a taxi, especially on the way from the airport.

'How far up the hill you going, padner?' the driver asked him.

Sonny gave him directions and then asked how much the trip would cost.

'Depends on the currency, man,' the driver said. 'If you have some Yankee, then is a deuce and a half. If is local change, is a double treble.'

'You want to run that by me in simple English, padner?' Sonny laughed.

'Is Yankee we talking?' the driver asked, and when Sonny nodded, he said, 'Twenty plus five.'

Sonny waved him forward and settled back in the seat. As they drove out of the airport into the Main Road that led to town, the driver turned up the radio and peeked at Sonny in the rear view mirror. Sonny caught the glance, the invitation for ole talk, but turned to gaze through the window at the cane fields. The driver whistled along with a calypso on the radio and when he grew tired of the tune, he put in a tape of Aretha Franklin's 'Respect.'

In between the canefields Sonny saw the houses, some small, made with dirt and straw, some big, made from concrete and bricks. The larger, newer homes were all two-storey, and under many of them a hammock swung between two pillars. Children played in the yards and under the houses and in more than one, Indian women threshed rice, and fowls, ducks and dogs walked about the yards.

The driver had begun to speed when they entered the long stretch into town, and Sonny realised how long he had been away when his heart began to beat faster and faster as the taxi sliced down the highway. He held his heart in his hand as a lorry creased past. The taxi driver cussed loudly. Sonny asked him to slow down but he said: 'Have to beat the afternoon traffic, man. Is murderation self to get out of town after five o'clock.' Sonny had his doubts about their even reaching town. He had forgotten how narrow the streets were and the driver seemed to expect all other vehicles to yield. They sped past Quarryville, Lopinot, but slowed down at San Miguel junction to gaze at a young man lying dead by the roadside, his motorbike sprawled in the centre of the road. A woman came out of a car ahead of Sonny's taxi, and put two sheets of newspaper over the young man's face as traffic crawled past. The driver told Sonny it might be morning before an ambulance would come to pick up the body.

They came to the Labasse and Sonny saw corbeaux circling above the mounds of rubbish. Children and women ran across from the Labasse with pieces of boards and galvanize on their heads. The driver increased his speed as Sonny said a silent 'Hail Mary' that they would make it to Rosehill in one piece. The traffic was clogged in town but the driver dodged and swerved, and made it through without stopping for red lights or 'Stop' signs. In a short time they began to climb the Hill. Passing the place where Moko's house once stood, Sonny looked at the rocky land, bare except for the pomseeta tree and the old latrine, and almost unconscious of his behaviour, he straightened his tie and ran a comb through his hair. The driver slowed when they came to the first standpipe and called to a woman who was catching water.

'Oi, dou, dou. But how yuh treating meh so? Yuh leave me for a next man or what?'

The woman laughed and come over to the taxi. 'Woman can't live on love alone, yuh know. Dats all you have, Manny.' She peeped into the car.

Manny slapped her hand. 'Well, come down by me later, nuh. Is more than love I sharing tonight.'

The woman stared at Sonny as she pinched Manny's arm and smiled a promise. Sonny did not recognise her.

Manny, continuing up the Hill, said, 'That woman nice too bad, man. She come last year from St. Vincent, yuh know.

But she husband is a bad man. Beat she up. She leave him in Toco and come here. I can't let good good women like that go to waste. You know what I mean, pardner?'

'Yes man,' Sonny laughed. But he was thinking that like every other taxi driver on Santabella, Manny obviously felt that he had an open license with women.

They passed the trace that went down to the Ledge and Sonny looked out, half hoping to see Oya's house and the huge immortelle. But the only thing left was a drying stump and a yard overgrown with bush. As they neared Miss Ann's parlour, Sonny pressed back against the seat. He didn't want Miss Ann to see him yet. But he knew that news on Rosehill rode faster than a racehorse in the Savannah on Boxing Day, and before long, everybody would know Moko's boy had come back from America.

He pointed out Tante Vivian's gate, and the driver stopped. Sonny gave him twenty-five American dollars and Manny folded and tucked them smoothly behind the band on his felt hat.

'Home-boy come home,' he teased Sonny, as he helped him with the suitcase. Then he swung the car around and sped back down the hill.

Sonny climbed the steps to Tante Vivian's house and pushed open the door calling, 'Anybody home?'

Reme came through the kitchen and stared at him in utter disbelief.

'Sonny?'

'Is me self, Miss Reme.'

'My gawd!' She hugged him and drew him into the room. 'Oh my gawd, Sonny, when you come?'

Sonny laughed. He knew he could expect to hear that question over and over for the next nine days. 'Just now,' he said. 'Tante didn't tell you I was coming?' He still couldn't believe that Tante Vivian had kept his return a secret.

Reme turned him around. She touched his face, his hair. She took off his shades. 'You mean to tell me you send and tell

124

Tante? How long now?'

'About three weeks ago.'

'Well, she ent say one word to me. She tell you bout Beatrice? Come, sit down Sonny. I forgetting meh manners. Here, sit down. You must be tired from dat long plane ride.' She pulled out a chair for him.

'She send me a cable,' Sonny said. 'When I got it I called the police station and asked them to have her call me. But I haven't heard from her. The cable said urgent, so I leave everything as fast as I could to come. What happening down here, Miss Reme? Something happen to Beatrice?'

Reme sat down next to him. 'I glad to see you, oui, Sonny. Is trouble for so down here.'

'Where Tante is?'

'She in the back room, boy. Tante sick for so. Sonny... I so glad to see you. You come in good time. But I forgetting my manners, child. Don't mind me. Is a lot on my head these days. Lemme get you someting to drink.'

And despite Sonny's protests that he didn't want anything, she went into the kitchen and brought him a glass of soursop.

'I remember how you used to like soursop,' she smiled.

'Tante sleeping?' Sonny sipped the sweet drink.

Reme nodded. 'Your poor Tante sick for so, child. Stroke. One right after the other.'

'But when this happen?'

'Last week. She was coming back from Beatrice. It happen in the taxi.'

'But why you didn't put her in hospital, Miss Reme?'

'What hospital you talking bout, child? Hospital ent have no doctor, no nurse. A man get knock down in town the other day. No ambulance to pick him up. His own family had to come with taxi and take up the body. You think it easy in this country, nuh. If I take Tante in that hospital, she dead for sure.'

'I could go in and see her?' Sonny rested the glass on the table and stood up.

Reme got up too and led him to the back room where she

125

found some matches, lit a lamp and moved it closer to the bed so Sonny could see Tante Vivian's face. Her eyes were closed.

'She can't hear you too well,' Reme whispered as she folded back the patched blanket and turned Tante Vivian's face toward Sonny.

Sonny bent to touch the dry rivers in Tante's cheek. Her lips were twisted and blistered red and nothing, nothing about the dark shell on the bed reminded him of the Tante Vivian he used to tote water and wood for.

'She's like this day in day out, Sonny. I do the best I could but...' Reme raised her shoulders and dropped them.

Sonny sat on the bed and put his hand on Tante's forehead. She opened her eyes and tried to smile, to talk, but only hot air came from her lips.

'I come, Tante,' Sonny tried to smile.

'All fall down, Sonny. I tell you, everything mash up, everything,' Reme was shaking her head. 'They say when trouble hit you, it does come in threes. Well, I don't know what could happen again.' She tucked the coverlet around Tante Vivian and led Sonny back to the living room.

'How Pa doing, Miss Reme?'

'He still up there, child. You know if we coulda keep him he would still be in this house. But after the baby die....'

'What baby?'

'What you mean, what baby? Beatrice baby.'

'Beatrice? Beatrice had a baby?' The shock in Sonny voice startled Reme.

'Sonny, you making joke or what?' she said. 'What they do to you in university?'

'You telling me Beatrice had a baby?' Sonny sat down heavily. 'When this happen?'

'What you mean, when this happen? You playing a joke or what, Sonny?'

'Miss Reme, believe me, I not making any joke. I don't even know Beatrice had a baby. But what the he...' his voice trailed off in disbelief.

'But what you telling me, Sonny?' Reme shook her head as if to clear her confusion. 'You didn't know Beatrice had a baby? How you didn't know? Everybody know.'

'Beatrice never say one word to me bout no baby, Miss Reme. Why I would lie bout that?'

'I can't believe that, man,' Reme was shaking her head. 'Moko play mass in the street when the child born. Beatrice show me all the nice things you send for the child.'

'I kiss the cross, Miss Reme,' Sonny swore. 'Beatrice never tell me. And you say the child die?'

'Come,' Reme said. 'Come go in the kitchen. I have to take two aspirin now now. But what you telling me... ' and she led him into the kitchen. He sat at the table while she searched the cupboard for a bottle of aspirin.

'You want some more soursop?' she asked him as she swallowed two pills.

He waved her hand away. 'Miss Reme, tell me bout this baby.'

'Well boy, if you don't know, and you is the father, I don't know what to say,' Reme shook her head again in disbelief.

'A boy or girl?' Sonny asked her.

'A boy child,' she smiled. 'His face cut off yours, Sonny. Moko spoil that child too bad. Before sun could come up in the morning, he used to take the child up in the spring to ketch crab.'

'But what happen? How he manage to die?'

'Was an accident, oui,' Reme said sadly. 'But Moko wouldn't hear that. He say he's to blame. And what make it worse, fast Miss Ann with she big mouth come making row with the man. I tell you, that woman need some good licks in she tail. But Willy is a mamapool man... '

'Car accident?' Sonny asked.

'What car accident?'

'The child. Car hit him?'

'No. it was them bees. You know, I did tell Tante not to get involved with no bees. What she know bout bees, eh? Tell me that.'

'A bee sting the child?'

'If was one bee the child would still be here, Sonny.'

'How old he was when it happened, Miss Reme?'

'Just a little fella, Sonny. A lil child like that. You think God wasn't looking. And poor Moko mash up. I tell Beatrice we have to put him up Saint Ann's but she say she can't do that. She say she promise you she going to look after Moko, but I tell you, Sonny, that poor girl couldn't even look after sheself. If you see how margar Beatrice get. I buy all kinda Ferrol and thing for she to drink because the child done gone, what you going to do? When God ready for you, you bound to go.'

'But when all this happen?'

'Last year bout this time self. Yes. Was right when rainy season come in.'

'I remember when she wrote and tell me she had to put Moko up Saint Ann's,' Sonny said. 'But she didn't say one word about a child.'

'I really don't know what to say, Sonny. I don't know why Beatrice would do a thing like that. But I was telling you about Moko. We had to put him up there....'

'Anybody does go and look for him?' Sonny asked.

'I went up there once or twice. And before all this happen, Beatrice used to go every Saturday and stay the whole afternoon.'

'He getting any better?'

'Sometimes. Beatrice say sometimes he's just like his old self. But then again, he fall back, yuh know, and he don't recognise anybody. Is a lot of them like that in Saint Ann's.'

Sonny tried to imagine Moko as Reme described him, and he saw him stumbling up Rosehill, not recognising his own son, calling only for Angelina.

'We went Christmas time to see him,' Reme's voice broke into his thoughts. 'Tante made a sponge cake for him. He looked okay then, but it does come and go.'

Sonny forced his thoughts back to the present. 'What is this trouble Beatrice in, Miss Reme? I don't really know anything. All Tante's cable said was that I should come because Beatrice is in some big trouble.'

'I don't know where to start, child,' Reme said. 'It was right after carnival this year. The letters come, yuh know. Nearly everybody on Rosehill get one. You know, Sonny. I still can't understand why Beatrice didn't tell you about the boy. Why?'

'What letters? Why everybody get letters?'

'You know. The lease letters. Postman bring them. Registered.'

'Miss Reme, I know you think I know all this, but....'

'But Beatrice send and tell you. You don't remember? Government say we have sixty days. Sixty days! Pay the deposit on the land or tractor coming to break down every house. They threaten to sell the land from right under we. Well mamayo, was a good thing I was throwing two susu hands.'

'But they don't have a right to do that,' Sonny said. 'It's against the law.'

'Law? Is only outlaw in this country, oui. What law you talking bout? Between me and Tante we had enough for the down payment on the lease for this place but plenty people was in hot water.'

'But I'm telling you, Miss Reme,' Sonny insisted. 'I know what I'm saying. Rosehill has claim to this land. The government can't just waltz in and take it over.'

'Who going to fight them? Is robbery with violence this government doing! You shoulda see people scrambling. Five thousand dollars they have to come up with.'

'Where Rosehill would get that kinda money?' Sonny asked her.

'Even Miss Ann didn't have it,' Reme said. 'You know how she's always boasting bout she have bank account? Well boy, when the mark bust, she didn't have a cent. Is poor Beatrice they have to turn to. My daughter.'

'Because she working with the government?'

'Everybody run to she. See what you could do, Miss

129

Beatrice. Talk to the man for me, nuh. I tell you, Sonny, the girl wasn't hardly recovered from grief with the child passing and all these people coming down on she. And you know how she is. She can't refuse. She has to take on every burden.'

'So what Beatrice could do?'

'Well, she run to this Minister, that Minister. Wilfred Smalls, Padmore, everybody. She know all of them, yuh know. Was a big job she had in the Finance Ministry. Hollarun, the Minister, he take a liking to she right off. Wasn't for you, Sonny, I woulda encourage Beatrice with him, you know, but I know how she have she heart set on you.'

'And they helped?'

'Who? Them Ministers? Help what? They does only help theirself, Sonny. They tief the money and put blame on Beatrice. What today is? Thursday? Lord, my head so hot these days I don't even know what day it is.'

'So that's why Beatrice in jail, Miss Reme? The government say she tief money?'

'Yes, so they say. But you know that's not true, Sonny. Beatrice tell them over and over you send the money but they wouldn't believe her.'

'You all couldn't get anybody to stand bail for Beatrice?'

'We try, Sonny. You think is two try we try? Nobody want to take the chance. The police put a stop on she bank account until after the case. And Tante had already spent what she had on the lease.'

'Uncle Paul couldn't help?'

'Tante went to him. She asked him to hold her two gold bracelets. But you know how Paul is. He wouldn't take the bracelets. He offer to mortgage his house but he couldn't get enough for the bail. Is thousands they set it for, yuh know. Is bad mind they bad mind.'

'Where they holding her?'

'Royal Jail. Till the hearing. Then is…' Sonny could tell that she was going to break down any minute.

'It not going to come to that, Miss Reme,' he tried to

console her. 'It's too late tonight to do anything but...'

Miss Ann, her headtie crooked, pushed open the front door before Sonny could finish his sentence, stood over him, arms akimbo, and declared, 'Well is so nigger people is in truth! The child tell me is you, Sonny. He swear is you he see pass in a taxi. But I say, nah man. Sonny would never pass my house without stopping. Well, you live and learn! Is a good thing I come see for myself. But how you could treat your Tante so, Sonny?' And she folded her arms around him. 'He sweet for so, Reme!' she laughed. 'Is sweet powder and ting you putting on now Sonny?'

Sonny embraced her, and Reme, stupesing in disgust, left the room.

'Is a good thing is Tante Vivian's house,' Miss Ann laughed. 'If cut-eye could kill, I dead long time.'

'Is nice to see you, Miss Ann. You looking good as ever.'

'Is breadfruit and moco yam, oui boy. So you come see the old people? When you leaving?'

'All the people who running their mouth on my daughter go have to put salt on their tongue now,' said Reme, coming back into the room to light a candle from the lamp's wick. 'Sonny come. He come.'

'I glad to see you too bad, Sonny,' Miss Ann said, ignoring Reme. 'I went last week to see your Pa.'

'Went where?' Reme asked her. 'You ever set foot in Saint Ann's since Moko there? But this woman could lie, oui.'

'How you know my business, Reme? Don't listen to she, Sonny. She just like bitter cassava.'

'But people brass face, oui,' Reme said. 'Here the woman coming in my own house to throw words in my face. Well, look my crosses!'

'Is okay, Miss Reme,' Sonny said. 'Miss Ann only making a little joke.'

'The woman can't even take a joke,' Miss Ann said, and she folded her skirt between her thighs and sat down.

'Lemme put this candle in Tante's room, Sonny,' Reme

131

said, glaring at Miss Ann. 'Then I coming back to fix you something to eat.'

'You mean since evening the child see Sonny pass, you ent give him something to eat yet?' Miss Ann asked Reme. Then she turned to Sonny. 'Eh eh. But why you didn't come by me, Sonny?'

Reme flung a cut-eye at Miss Ann and went out with the candle.

'Is hard on she, you know,' Miss Ann whispered. 'So much things happen. I don't know how she holding up.'

'Miss Reme was always a bacchack,' Sonny said.

'But how you talking like we so, Sonny?' Miss Ann teased him. 'You didn't learn no Yankee over there? So long you gone, well talk a little Yankee nuh.'

Sonny laughed. 'I forgot all the Yankee soon as I hit Rosehill.'

'But you come at a bad time, Sonny.'

'You can't always pick and choose, Miss Ann.'

'But you should at least tell we you was coming. Clydie running taxi now. He coulda pick you up at the airport.'

'Eh heh? He doing well these days.'

'He trying, man. Since this thing with the land, you have to take what you would get and don't grumble, nuh. Even I does do a little half-day when the parlour close on Thursday.'

'It's hard all over, Miss Ann.'

'But I hear you doing well, Sonny. I always know you would do well. You didn't born with no veil on your eyes, boy. You is big time lawyer now?'

'I just start.'

'Well, is a good thing you study that, boy. Beatrice need a good good lawyer.'

'I don't know about that, Miss Ann.'

'What you mean you don't know? What they teach you in that university?'

'I was in a different kind of law. I....'

'Don't tell that woman your business,' Reme said, coming

132

back. 'Foreday morning the whole road know.'

'Is nothing to hide,' Sonny assured her. 'I was just trying to explain about my schooling.'

'I don't see why you getting so vexed.' Miss Ann told Reme.

'Look Ann,' Reme turned on her. 'The boy just come. He ent open his suitcase yet. Come back in the morning.' And she took up the broom and started to sweep.

Miss Ann stood up. 'I could see some people get their manners in the labasse,' she said. 'Sonny child, I fixing tea for you in the morning.' And without a second glance at Reme, she went down the steps vexed vexed.

'Fire brigade water the road,' Reme laughed, watching Miss Ann's hips swinging furiously, and Sonny burst out laughing.

In spite of everything, he was beginning to feel good to be home. Nothing had changed, and yet everything was different. The air smelled the same; Miss Ann was the same; but Beatrice, she was different. What had happened to her? A baby? Jail. Sonny tried to sort out his confused thoughts as Reme brought him a thick slice of roast bake plastered with butter and placed a cup of green tea in front of him. He sipped the tea and tried to eat the bake as she fussed over him. When she went in to check on Tante Vivian, and to make up a cot in the living room for him, he left most of the food on the table and went to sit on the back steps.

A cool night breeze brought the sweet scent of ladies of the night to the door and he went closer to the fence to smell the hibiscus and wild roses that were closing for the night. He picked one rose damp with dew and went back to sit on the steps, to stare out at the dark closing around him, and to wonder how he was going to be able to face Beatrice with the anger that was starting to swell up in him against her.

Reme called to him from inside the house, 'I make up the cot. Whenever yuh ready. You finish eating?' She came to the door. 'Sonny, you hardly eat anything. You don't want the tea?'

133

'No thanks, Miss Reme,' he said. 'I just want to sit here for a while, eh. Don't worry your head about me.'

She lingered in the doorway, confused, wanting to say something to Sonny but not knowing what. So she asked him if he wanted anything else to eat. Sonny shook his head and wished she would leave him alone. If she doesn't go inside soon, he thought, I'm going for a walk. But he didn't really want to do that. He was bound to meet people on the road, and he didn't feel like talking.

'You should get some rest, Miss Reme,' he begged her. 'You don't have to worry your head bout me.'

'The dew bad for you,' Reme told him. 'Remember what I tell you, Sonny. Trouble does come in threes. We ent have a dead yet but I hear jumbie bird calling last night. I don't want you getting pleurisy.'

'You forget where I just come from, Miss Reme?' Sonny laughed. 'If I didn't drop dead from winter, you think a little dew could hurt me?' He got up, pointing to a tree. 'I see the old breadfruit tree still holding strain, eh. That tree older than me, you know.' He went to stand under the tree and Reme, beginning to feel a little better about him, went back into the house.

Sonny moved from the breadfruit tree to the guava tree, checking for the marks he had placed in their trunks when he was small. They were all still there and the memories made him smile. His fingers traced the crooked arrow that he had drawn through the heart on the guava tree when he was about nine years old, and he wished he had a penknife to write something, to leave a mark in the guava bark saying he had come back. He heard music coming from the trace in the back of the house and knew it was the steelband practising for the music festival. A part of him wanted badly to jump the fence as he had done when he was young, and go down for a lime with the fellars, but another part of him resisted, and he wasn't quite sure why. He thought about it and the idea came to him that he might be feeling shame, shame that he hadn't come back for the child's funeral, shame

that his father was in the madhouse, shame to see the fellars....
But why the hell should he be ashamed. He didn't know. She
had never sent to tell him. Anger at Beatrice swelled up in him
and he tried to shake it off by walking round the house to the
front gate. The street was strangely quiet and he wondered why
until he remembered that television had come to Rosehill. Beatrice had written to tell him that Roy, Miss Melda's husband, had
won a small black and white one in a church raffle, and at night
the children crowded around it to look at 'Bonanza.' He went
back to sit on the front steps, his head bent low, his thoughts
running here to Beatrice, there to Moko, across to Tante Vivian,
back to America, until the strain on his brain became too much
and he knew he would have to take some aspirin. He started to
get up, to go into the house to see if he had brought any but
paused with his hand on the doorknob. Reme had opened the
door to look for him.

'Don't sit out there in the dew, Sonny,' she said. 'You
going to ketch cold.'

'I was just coming in,' he said.

She moved aside and he came back into the house then and
went into Tante's room again to see if she was awake. She
wasn't, and he sat down at the foot of the bed and watched her
slow, heavy breathing for a few minutes before he closed the
door quietly and went back into the front room. His head felt
heavy and he searched the small bag with his toothbrush and
toiletries hoping to find some aspirin. He found a small tin with
three left and he swallowed them without water. Then, in a
slight daze, he put his passport, ticket and wallet carefully into
his briefcase. He changed his shirt, folding the damp one neatly
and placing it on top of the closed suitcase, and slowly slipped off
his shoes. Then, his head beginning to spin, he lay down on the
cot. For several hours he lay there, staring at the celotex with its
wide brown water stains, trying to sort out the years, the events,
into patterns he could understand. Reme came in from the
kitchen to check on him twice, and he closed his eyes and
pretended he had dozed off. Just as the cocks crowed foreday

morning, he fell into a heavy sleep.

Reme had to wake him, shaking him over and over to tell him that Rosehill knew he was home, and would be coming soon to greet him. She brought him a basin of warm water and a washcloth to sap his head but he waved her away and stood on the back steps to brush his teeth and splash his face with cold rain water from the barrel as he had done every morning for years. Revived, he poured more water into a bucket and washed quickly. Then he changed his shirt, but before he could finish drinking the cup of Red Rose tea Reme had put in front of him, he heard Rosehill people coming into the front yard. Miss Ann, Jestina and their children were ahead of the band.

'But look meh crosses,' Sonny laughed. 'These children grow so tall I woulda passed them in the street,' and he let them kiss him and tell him how glad they were to see their 'uncle Sonny come home'. Sonny put quarters in their palms, and Miss Ann and Jestina sent them out in the yard to play while they settled down around him.

Willy, Roberts, and Samuel came in, and Sonny embraced them. 'Uncle Willy, man,' he laughed. 'But you ent change at all at all. Where your grey hair?'

'He using aloes every day to get rid of the grey,' Miss Ann said. 'Is young girl have he so.'

Sonny and the others laughed, and Willy said, 'Boy, a man have to try, yuh know how it is. How you doing, Miss Reme? You have a cup of tea for the old man?' And as Miss Ann stared at him with cut-eye, he gave Reme a hug while she poured him a cup of tea.

'Well, how you doing boy?' Sammy asked Sonny, and Sonny told them about America, glossing over the hard times.

'I almost finish with meh schooling,' he said.

'So you going to be a big-time lawyer, eh?' Miss Ann smiled.

'Not yet,' Sonny told her. 'I have to take some hard exams first. If I get through with them....'

'What you mean "IF" you get through,' Willy interrupted him, 'Say "WHEN" you get through, man. You bound to pass.'

Sonny nodded. He almost began to tell them about the bar exams, about how difficult they were, and how political everything was in America, but he knew they wouldn't understand, so he took his suitcase from the corner, opened it, and gave each man a shirt or a jersey. 'I wish I coulda bring more,' he apologised. 'But I come down in a rush.'

The men thanked him for the gifts, assuring him that they were nice as they tried them on in front of him.

'Well, is now Willy is saga-boy,' Roberts laughed.

'He's a Yankee, man,' Sammy laughed too as Willy took off the shirt he had on and put on the one from Sonny.

'But I wonder why dis old zandolie don't find a hole and lie down?' Miss Ann asked, as Jestina and the others praised the way Willy looked.

Sonny gave Miss Ann and Jestina a pair of earrings each, and Reme, coming into the room, told them that Sonny had to go downtown early. They left slowly, lingering to hold Sonny's hand, to ask him when he was going to see Beatrice, to assure him that Moko was doing okay, to let him know how glad they were to see him come home safe.

After they left, Sonny finished his tea and Reme told him she would go to the corner and bring a taxi up the hill because if he walked down he would have to stop at each house to say hello. When the taxi pulled up, a crowd of children were waiting for him at the gate, their parents watching not far off. Sonny gave each child a dime or a quarter, and waved hello to the mothers, and the taxi driver, realising his importance, came round the side to hold the back door open.

When Sonny told him he wanted to get to town quickly so not to pick up any more passengers, the driver said, 'Right on Brother!' in an imitation Brooklyn accent.

As the taxi sped down the hill, weaving from side to side to avoid small children and dogs, Sonny tried to relax. He had been glad for the distraction Miss Ann and Willy and the others had provided. They had kept him from thinking about Beatrice, about all that Reme had told him. In the quiet back seat of the taxi one question kept nagging him. What hadn't Beatrice told him about the child? Why? He went over in his mind what Reme had said. The child was born about nine months after he had left. It *had* to be his. That last night... but if the child was his, why hadn't Beatrice told him? The headache was returning and he caught himself rubbing his temples. When he raised his head he met the driver's curious stare in the rear view and he tried to compose his face, to force himself to think about other things.

They passed two tanker trucks and the driver said, 'Look at that. This government could do things backward, oui. They bring all them tanker trucks down here to drive on these peeny peeny road. First thing to do was build bigger road, then bring big truck, but no, eh eh. Truck taking the whole road! You see that one? You see what I mean?' And he slowed onto the edge of the road for the truck to pass.

'But is progress,' Sonny laughed, glad for the conversation to take his mind off Beatrice. 'When I was growing up here we didn't have them big truck.'

'Progress meh arse,' the driver shifted into gear and got back onto the road. 'Is the poor man suffering still to this day. All the oil, all the petrodollars, who making the money, eh? Tell me that?'

'I just come, man,' Sonny said. 'What I know?'

'How long you staying?'

'Don't know yet. I have some business to fix up.'

'You see me?' the driver said. 'When I leave this country, I not looking back, yuh know. My old mother done dead, and my two sisters fending for theyself. When I hit New York, I forgetting this country.'

'But you can't do that man,' Sonny said. 'I used to think so myself, but when you get up in the cold is a different story.'

'Talk for yourself, brother. I tell you I not looking back. Is hell for so I ketching in this country. What I looking back for?'

'You think New York so rosy?' Sonny asked him.

'I not fooling myself, you know padner,' the driver said. 'I ent saying it going to be easy, but it bound to be easier than here.'

'You know it have people living in rat holes in New York?' Sonny told him. 'You see them coming down here carnival time with sharp clothes and ten gold chains round their necks, you don't know how they living every day. Rats and roaches, man, they crawling all over them.'

'But they crawling down here too,' the driver said. 'The thing about this place is that your foot tie down, man. You can't make a move without paying some bobol and by the time you do that, what you have left?'

'Nothing change, eh?' Sonny asked.

'It change,' the driver shook his head. 'It just change for the worse. For the poor man, anyway.'

'Is the same all over, man,' Sonny said.

'But at least you have a chance in New York,' the driver said. 'If I was running taxi up there, all now I would have two or three cars for mehself. Down here, I have to run a man's taxi and pay him three-quarters what I make.'

'You can't make a loan to get your own taxi?'

'Bank not lending you money just like that. You have to have something they could hold on to. What I have? Is Indian and them with all the house and land. They own all the taxis in this country.'

'So what the government doing with all the oil dollars?' Sonny asked.

'Spreeing! Is fete for so in Government House.'

'I can't believe that, man. I hear they building a new hospital.'

'You want to go and see it? Eh?' the driver asked. 'Rust eating it away. They say money run out. I telling you, man, is bobol in the place!'

'But you sounding as if it ent have law in this country,' Sonny told him. 'You have to have checks and balances.'

'How long you gone away, man?' the driver turned to

stare at him. 'You don't know what going on in dis country or what?'

'Keep your eye on the road, nuh man,' Sonny laughed, and waited for the driver to face front again before he added, 'I used to get newspapers every once in a while. But is a long time I ent read one.'

'Well padner, is a long long story. When we hit oil, the country was rocking. Nowadays, they say the treasury empty. Locusts take big big grain ah corn and gone. You tink it easy? I just trying to get my own.'

'But that's why things will never change.' Sonny argued. 'Everybody trying to get some for theyself. How things will ever change?'

'Let the big man change first, man, then I will follow fashion,' the driver said, and he pulled up to the curb. 'Dis is it. Dis the place you want, padner?'

'Yes,' Sonny reached into his back pocket for his wallet, and the driver grinned at the American five dollar note Sonny handed him. He offered to wait but Sonny told him he wasn't sure how long he would be. 'I'll look for you in the stand,' Sonny promised.

'Name's Carl,' the man said. 'If you don't see me, hold some strain,' and he turned the car around leaving Sonny in front of a heavy wooden door locked into a high, cream-painted wall that wound around the street corner. Sonny pounded on it and it swung open. He went in and crossed a small yard to a sentry post. The sentry sent him down a long wide corridor to a reception area. Two men in khaki uniforms worked behind the counter. Otherwise, the room was empty. The men looked up inquiringly as he handed one his card.

'I'd like to see Miss Beatrice Salandy.'

The man read the card, turned it over, and flipped it over again.

'You have a picture ID?' he asked.

Sonny gave him his New York driver's license. The man read it over and over, first studying the picture, then Sonny's face. Then he passed it to his companion who examined it closely and then left the room.

Several minutes later he returned with another in the same stiff khaki uniform but with more bars and buttons on the shoulders.

'Mister Allen?' the senior officer spoke while the two turnkeys looked on.

Sonny, more than slightly irritated by the long delay, wanted to ask who else he could be, but instead he said, 'Yes.'

'We don't have a visiting request from you. You filled one out?'

'I just arrived last night.'

'I see. Well, if you'll make a request, I'm sure you'll be able to see the prisoner soon.'

'I am making a request. That's why I'm here.'

The man smiled. 'In writing, Mister Allen. You must make the request in writing.'

'Is there a form?'

'No. No form. You write a letter to the Superintendent of Prisons requesting a visit with the prisoner.'

'And then what?'

'Then we let you know.' The man smiled again.

Sonny lost his patience. 'Let me know what?'

'Whether you'll be allowed a visit. We have rules down here, you know.'

'Look!' Sonny snapped. And immediately he was sorry, knowing that getting this man angry would only make matters worse. Power, he thought, a little power in their hands, and they want to manipulate the world. He swallowed.

'Look,' he said patiently. 'I'm an attorney. I am, I believe, allowed to see Miss Salandy at any reasonable hour. That is the law.'

He caught the glance that passed between the two guards. The senior officer had not stopped smiling but the smile was only on his lips, not in his eyes. He addressed Sonny as if he were talking to a small boy. 'This is not New York, Mister Allen.'

141

'I'm talking about local law.'

'Ah… How long have you been away, Mister Allen?'

'I really don't see where that matters. But if you need to know, I've been away two years, almost three.'

'Three years is a long time, Mister Allen. Laws does change, yuh know.'

Sonny looked at the man's hard, smiling face and realised that an argument on the grounds of legality was pointless. He asked for the Superintendent's name.

The senior officer turned to one of the lower officers, 'Give Mister Allen the name and address, Corporal,' and having dropped Sonny's card and license on the counter, he turned smartly on his heel and left the room.

Sonny took a yellow legal pad from his briefcase and wrote out a brief request, folded the page and handed it to the corporal.

The man shook his head. 'You have to post it.'

'But it is to come to this address. Why do…?'

'I don't make the rules,' the man shrugged.

The other guard behind the counter had said nothing during the whole episode. Now he took the letter from Sonny. He and the corporal stared at each other for a moment, and then the corporal shrugged his shoulders again and turned away.

'Thank you,' Sonny said.

The man put the page into an envelope and placed it in front of Sonny. 'Write the address.'

Sonny scribbled quickly, and the man tore a stamp from a sheet and pasted it on the envelope.

'I'd be glad to pay for the stamp.' Sonny said.

The man waved him off. 'Come back tomorrow. Afternoon, not morning. Should know something by then.'

Sonny thanked him again and left.

He walked quickly away from the prison, his head down, hardly heeding the heavy traffic as he crossed the streets, forcing drivers to slow down and beep their horns at him. He headed down Palm Street toward the taxi stand, moving from sidewalk to street, street to sidewalk to avoid the rubbish that was piled up

142

in front every building. He found Carl in the middle of a game of cards and waited until they had pulled away from the stand and into the street before he said, 'Mental Hospital.'

Carl turned to look at him, 'Royal Jail, Mental Hospital. Who is *you*, man? Inspector?'

Sonny smiled.

'Well okay then,' Carl said. 'Some passengers like to talk, some don't like to talk. I meet all kinds. You don't mind a little music, eh?'

'No,' Sonny said. 'But keep it low, okay?'

'Sure thing, brother!' Carl responded in his Brooklyn accent as he punched in a James Brown tape. After a few minutes he asked Sonny, 'You want me wait for you this time. Is not too easy getting a taxi from up there, you know.'

'Yes,' Sonny told him. 'I think you should wait.'

The Mental Hospital had been, in the old days, the stately home of an English earl who had said that he wanted to recreate in this lush, primitive, island setting a symbol of British aristocracy. He took a thousand men and women, it was said, to build his royal castle on the top of the Maraval Hills, overlooking the Gulf, and he worked them through days that were so hot, people said the devil must by playing with his fire. Even when it rained, he had the people working. Some days too much water fell. They said Shango was crying because he was seeing too much badness.

The earl died before the castle was completed. He was out for a walk among the hills, and all of a sudden boulders began to rain down on him. It was many days before they would find him, his head crushed, his fingers grasping a small stone. The building lay neglected for years, and in time, the government turned the ruins into a mental asylum.

A guard waved the taxi through the steel gates and Carl pulled up in front of a red and white building with a veranda. Several men and women, old and young, in flowered and striped pajamas, sat quietly on old school benches, looking toward the road.

143

'They put them out to get a little sun,' Carl whispered, as he parked the car and walked toward the front door with Sonny. He sat down next to one of the old women and Sonny went into the asylum.

An orderly led him to a courtyard where Moko was getting his hair cut under a mango tree. The orderly motioned for the barber to leave and Sonny looked down at his father's face. Moko's head was tilted back, his eyes closed, a half-smile on his mouth as if he were holding a little secret to himself. He didn't shift when the barber moved and Sonny bent and touched his bony hands.

'Pa? Pa? Is Sonny.'

Moko didn't open his eyes.

'Wake up, nuh man,' Sonny shook Moko's shoulders.

Moko's head tilted slowly forward, as if he were waking up from a dream, and he opened his eyes slightly, and Sonny wasn't sure if it was because of the glare or if Moko just couldn't open them any further. Sonny dragged a chair over and sat down in front of Moko.

'So you can't say hello to your son, Pa?' he took up Moko's hands again.

Moko's lips parted and he said in a weak voice, 'Meh son. You see my Sonny?'

'Sometimes they'll recognise you, sometimes...' the orderly said, but Sonny shooed him away. The man went to lean against a post not far off as if he were afraid to leave Sonny and Moko alone.

Sonny took a handkerchief from his pocket and wiped the blots of yampee that had gathered in the corners of Moko's eyes. 'Open yuh eyes, nuh man,' he said, keeping his voice light. And Moko strained to open them but the lids trembled and remained half-closed.

'He have cataracts,' the orderly called out.

'Pa,' Sonny said, squeezing Moko's hands, 'I see the pigeons, man. You take good care of them.'

'Sonny pigeons... Sonny pigeons...' the words came out in

144

a croak as Moko tried to curl his fingers around Sonny's. 'Sonny pigeons...Sonny pigeons...' his body rocked forward, backward, forward, backward as he said the words over and over and over again. Water began to form in his eyes but he held on to Sonny, and Sonny wanted to take his hand away, to get out his kerchief, to wipe the water, but he couldn't, so he sat there holding on, rubbing Moko's fingers, squeezing his hands, wanting to give him a little life, but Moko was in another place and after a while Sonny wished he would stop saying the words, stop rocking, stop the water from dripping down his face into his open mouth, stop smiling a stupid smile.... A lump rose up in Sonny and he dropped Moko's hands and pushed his chair away. The orderly came over quick quick and Sonny asked him where the toilet was. Inside the filthy room, piss-soaked newspapers rotting on the wet floor, Sonny threw up. He splashed water on his face, but he didn't feel any better. When he came back out, the barber had gone back to cutting Moko's hair. Moko was silent.

The orderly wiped Moko's face. 'We doing the best we can for him, Mister Allen.'

'Is there anything I could get for him?' Sonny asked. 'Pajamas... toothpaste... some things to eat...'

'They get all those things, yuh know,' the orderly said. 'But if you ask me, what they need most they don't get. Family, nuh. People does just drop them here and don't come back.'

Sonny nodded. He stood there for another minute looking at Moko, at the barber clipping, at the orderly dusting hair from Moko's face, and he felt helpless. He turned abruptly and left without a backward glance.

In the front, he found Carl sitting near one of the women, chatting. He came over to Sonny and said, 'Some of these people have a lot of sense, man. That woman I was talking with? She was telling me bout her children and her husband. She was talking sane sane, man.'

'Let's go,' Sonny said.

'It have a... hey man, what happen to you in there?'

'Just let's go, man.' Sonny hurried and was in the car before Carl.

When they were out of the gate, Carl asked, 'So where to now?'

'You know a tailor name Paul in town?'

'Paul, Paul, he had a shop on Nelson Street?'

'Yes. What you mean "had"? Since when he moved?'

'If is the same Paul I know, his shop moved. That building on Nelson Street burn down last year. Wipe him out. Fire is big thing in this country now, you know. Insurance, nuh.'

'You telling me people burning down their place to collect insurance?'

'Dat is the talk. Money hard hard to come by, so them owners paying arsonists to torch their buildings, then they collect the insurance. But is not only dat, man. Whereas long time, if you and a fellar get in a little fight, he cut you with a knife and dat is dat, nowadays, he burning down yuh house. If fire in yuh wire, oui.'

'You have any idea where Paul might have reopened?'

'I think he opened up on St. Vincent Street. We could ask.'

They found Paul's shop in an alley behind the Rialto Cinema, choked between a roti shop and a used bicycle store. Sonny told Carl he would see him later as Paul came to the doorway.

'Is Sonny I seeing?' Paul laughed. 'When you come, man? When you come?' He hugged Sonny and pumped his hand and called to a young woman in the back to come and see how grown his godson was.

The woman, small, brownskinned and shy, came in softly, smiled and asked Sonny if he wanted some juice. Sonny said yes, and she went quickly back to the yard.

Sonny raised his eyebrows and Paul laughed. 'Thelma. Finally find a good woman, boy. They scarce like gold these days. But how you, man? Come, sit down, sit down.'

He took some material from a chair and Sonny sat down.

'But you looking good, Sonny. You see Moko yet?

146

A..a..man. I glad to see meh boy come home.' Paul pushed aside some more material, gathered up some pins, dumped them in a tray, all the while talking, rattling off questions, hardly giving Sonny time to answer. 'I was sorry to hear bout the child, man. I went to the christening, you know. Nice-looking little boy. You see Beatrice yet?'

Thelma came back with the juice, and Sonny thanked her. She left them alone.

'I just come from seeing Moko,' Sonny took a sip of the sweet lime juice and held the ice in his mouth. 'I don't think he even know I was there.'

'Is so he is sometimes,' Paul shook his head sadly... 'Twice I went up there and he looked me right in the face. I can't bear to see him like dat.'

'Is hard to see him so,' Sonny agreed, swallowing the rest of the juice.

'So how long you staying, man? You want another glass? Thelma, bring some more juice for Sonny. And a glass for me too.'

'I can't stay too long,' Sonny handed Thelma his glass for a refill. 'Thanks. I just take up a new job so I have to get back soon. But Tante ask me to come. This Beatrice thing, nuh.'

'Boy, dat's trouble fader, yuh know,' Paul took his glass from Thelma and sipped. 'Is a good thing you come. Is likely only you could help Beatrice.'

'But what I going to do, man?' Sonny said. 'Beatrice say I send that money but between you and me, where I would get that kinda money?'

'You didn't win the lottery?'

'I don't even buy lottery tickets,' Sonny said. 'You know how I always like Beatrice, and if is anything I could do, I would do it, but I didn't send her no big set of money.'

'So who have to know dat, Sonny? The thing done already. She was doing a good for Rosehill, man. Is hell for so they ketching these days. You up there in New York, you don't know. If she really take dat money, and I not saying she take it,

147

but if she really take it, it was only in desperation, man. Government want Rosehill. They have a lot of big businessmen pushing them. Chow and all them boys. Is they who running this country, you know.'

'But how Beatrice expect to get away with it?' Sonny asked. 'She was handling the money in the Ministry. They bound to suspect her.'

'I ask her the same thing, man,' Paul said. 'She insist she didn't take the money. She say you send the money. But I think what happen is, she decide to take the chance because she know the Minister self was stealing money. The *Bomb* says he buy up a set of houses in Miami, right on the beach, man. Where he get money for dat? And since January he gone from the country and ent come back yet. Money missing, Rosehill people boasting about how Beatrice give them money to buy lease, so the government put two and two together and they arrest her.'

'I really don't know what to do,' Sonny said. 'All last night I was racking my brain about what to do.'

'Tell them you send the money, man.' Paul advised.

'I going to be a lawyer, Uncle Paul.'

'Eh heh. So what? You want Beatrice to rot in jail? And what bout Rosehill. If they convict Beatrice, Rosehill gone, oui. Is not only Beatrice in this, you know. A lot of Rosehill people will have to give up their land.'

'You think it will really come down to that?'

'Man, you don't know what going on in this country. Poor people ketching hell for so. Is scramble people have to scramble. Take Rosehill. Where they getting money to buy land? God send Beatrice in time. I self was trying to help them out. I even went to see Chow and explain the situation but dat man heart like rock stone. And to think he grow up on the hill. When I tell Beatrice I went to him she get mad for so. She really have a hate for him. The *Bomb* say Chow and them fellars have oil fever. They grabbing land left and right and they don't care who they have to throw off to get it.'

'But most Rosehill people on the land over twenty-five

148

years,' Sonny said. 'According to law, they have first claim.'

'Law? What law?' Paul asked him. 'Money is the only law in this country. Black people don't stand a chance, nuh. We thought when we get we own people in power things would change. Change what? Is the same old pappyshow.'

'Is true, oui,' Sonny sighed, and drank the last of the juice.

'So what you going to do, Sonny? Here, let me take the glass.' Paul took the glass and rested it on his sewing machine.

'Me? What I could do?'

'But you is big time lawyer now, man. You staying up dere in the cold?'

'I'm not a real lawyer yet, and besides, I is only one man, Uncle Paul. Is like standing on the stage in Queens Hall playing the tenor pan alone. You sounding sweet sweet but you not a steelband. You have to have a lot a pan to make some noise.'

'Well, do what them other fellars do,' Paul said. 'Form a party. Come back home man. We need new blood.'

'You think this government allowing any opposition?' Sonny asked him. 'What they do with Cudjoe? Beatrice write and tell me they never find his body.'

'Cudjoe and them was big joke, man. This government tricky too bad. You have to be more tricky to outsmart them. Besides, them fellars didn't have your education.'

'You think education is all? I don't like no politics, man.'

'Well, you know your own mind. But I wish Beatrice didn't get sheself in all this trouble. We was thinking bout putting her up for County Council, you know. Against Wilfred Smalls.'

'She liked that sort of thing,' Sonny smiled, remembering all the arguments he and Beatrice used to have.

'But we have to get she out first,' Paul said.

Thelma came in to take the empty glasses away, and she asked Sonny if he wanted some food. Sonny said yes, and she came back with two plates of red fish and rice. As Sonny and Paul began to eat, a taxi pulled up outside and Carl came in. Thelma brought him a plate too and the three men sat and ate

149

and talked politics. When the food was done, Sonny thanked Thelma again, gave Paul an American twenty dollar note and Thelma a ten, and he and Carl drove back to Rosehill.

At the junction, Sonny got out of the taxi and walked the rest of the way up the hill. Every few yards he stopped to talk to a neighbour, to chat about what he had been doing in New York, to ask about this son and that daughter, and to promise to do what he could to help Beatrice. By the time he reached Tante Vivian's house an hour later, he was tired, and his head was beginning to hurt him. He went in to check on Tante. Reme had propped her up in the bed. She turned her face slowly to the door as he came through, and he smiled. He told her he had gone to see Moko, and he thought he saw her nod. Her lips formed a 'B' and he said yes, he was going to see Beatrice the following morning.

Reme came in from the back yard and offered him supper but he told her he had eaten. She insisted on him drinking something and he followed her into the kitchen for a glass of mauby. Then he slumped down in the rocking chair in the front room and went to sleep.

The next day Sonny got to the jail early, and after two hours' wait was told he could see Beatrice for fifteen minutes. A turnkey took him into a room with a high ceiling and no windows, and told him to wait at the table. Sonny sat down on one of the two chairs facing the glass door. After more than an hour, the turnkey brought Beatrice. She wore a bright orange prison dress that was two sizes too large for her slim, tall frame, and the slippers on her feet were tied with string. The turnkey left the door open and stood just outside. Sonny got up as Beatrice entered and stood at the end of the table, her arms folded across her chest. They stared at each other, Sonny trying to force a smile, Beatrice looking serious serious, tension in the air. Sonny pointed to the chair next to her.

'Sit down, nuh girl,' he said, sitting down, trying to keep his voice light.

Beatrice remained standing. 'What you doing here, Sonny?' she snapped.

Sonny put his briefcase on the table between himself and Beatrice.

'I come to see you.'

He felt embarrassment and anger coming over him at once and he tried hard to check both.

'I ask you to come? Who the hell ask you to come here?' Beatrice's voice dripped with hate.

Sonny opened the briefcase and shuffled papers. 'Look. We only have fifteen minutes. Okay? We could spend them arguing, or you could tell me what's going on here.' He took out a pen and a note pad, and pushed the briefcase aside.

'I don't have anything to say to you,' Beatrice said, turning her back on him.

Sonny decided to try a different tack. He got up and came round the table. He smiled. 'You looking good, you know that, Beatrice?'

She sucked her teeth and looked past him.

'All right.' He threw up his hands. 'Tante send for me. She say you in some kinda trouble. So I drop everything and fly down here.'

'You could fly right back,' Beatrice said.

'O...kay...' he pulled his chair around the table so that it was near to her. 'You could be stubborn if you want to, but I promise your mother I would do what I can.' He sat down, pointing to the other chair. 'Why you don't sit down, Beatrice? I didn't come here to fight with you. Is nearly three years I haven't seen you. You think I want to fight?'

'I already tell you I have nothing to say. You could just leave right now.'

Sonny leaned back in the chair. 'You know, you standing there vexed. You ent the only one who could get vexed.'

'What the hell you have to get vexed bout? I send for you? I ask you to come here? When I ever ask you to do anything for me, Sonny?' She pulled out the chair mad mad and sat down.

151

He bent forward and tried to touch her hands. She pulled away. He reached for the notepad and pen. 'Where you get the money for the leases, Beatrice?'

'Is none of your damn business.'

'Eh heh? That's not what everybody on Rosehill saying.'

'I say is none of your business.'

'Like the baby, eh? That wasn't my business either?'

She got up but he grabbed her hand and forced her to sit. 'What the hell going on with you?' he hissed. 'A child? You make a boy child for me and ent say nothing? Beatrice, you's a criminal, yuh know.'

'Let go my hand, Sonny.' He let her go and she folded her hands across her chest. 'Yes! I make a child, and I didn't tell you.'

'Why? Why? It was my child. I didn't have a right to know?'

'Right? What right you have with me? How much letters you write to me, Sonny? Eh? I write you for years. How much letters you write? The onliest time we hear from you is Christmas. I owe you something?' She sucked her teeth.

The turnkey knocked on the door and showed eight fingers.

'That still didn't give you the right to withhold information....'

Beatrice laughed shortly, 'Withhold information? Where the hell you think you is, Sonny? This ent no New York courtroom.'

Sonny shook his head, 'It was my son, Beatrice. I had a right to know.'

'Who say it was your son? Eh? I make child for you?'

'What you mean "who say is my son"? The whole of Rosehill know.'

'Know? What they know? They know something?'

'So if it wasn't mine, whose was it?'

'That's none of your business, Sonny.'

'*You* make it my business. Who you make a child for?'

'Make? You make it sound as if I wanted to have child. I

152

wanted to go to New York too, Sonny. You remember? You think I so stupid to put myself with anybody to make child? I take the exam. I take it same time as you. You didn't know that, eh? I wanted to go away to study.'

'You take the exam? You never tell me....'

'I don't *have* to tell you everything, Sonny.'

'Beatrice,' he reached for her hands again and this time she didn't pull away. 'Just tell me if the child was mine, okay? I have to know.'

'It wasn't,' she said quietly. 'It wasn't yours.'

He dropped her hands and got up from the table. 'You make a child for another man? I can't believe.... Beatrice, if anybody did tell me this, I wouldn't believe them. You? You and me....'

'You and me what, Sonny?'

'That last night. The night when we had the farewell party.... You and me.... We.... Beatrice, after that, how you could go with somebody else?'

'You don't listen, Sonny. You never listen to me. I didn't go with nobody. The man rape....'

'Rape? Who man.... Oh God, Beatrice. What you saying?'

'You want to know, Sonny? You want me rehash the details for you?' She got up and stood over him, glaring down in his face. 'It was Chow, Sonny. Chow. The biggest doctor in Santabella! Respected! Admired! Chow! He is the one who rape me. Now you know!'

Sonny put his head down on the table and groaned.

'You don't want to hear it now, eh?' Beatrice hissed. 'You can't bear to hear it. You wanted to know.'

The turnkey rapped on the door again, and pushed it open. Beatrice turned toward him, her back to Sonny. Sonny raised his head, but seemed unable to get up. 'Visiting time over,' the turnkey said, and when Sonny still didn't move, he asked, 'You okay, man?'

'He's okay,' Beatrice said.

'Yes, yes,' Sonny said. He gathered up his pen and notepad, pushed them in the briefcase, snapped it shut, and stood up. He followed the turnkey and Beatrice out of the room and into the corridor. The turnkey pointed him toward the reception room and he left without looking at Beatrice again.

Outside the walls, he leaned against a lamp post for a few minutes to steady himself. He wanted to scream, to run down Frederick Street to Chow's office, to dig his fingernails into Chow, to smash his head in. A lady, passing by, stopped and asked him if he was okay. 'Yes,' he said. 'I'll be okay.' When he had gotten control of himself, he stopped a taxi and asked the driver to take him to Paul's tailor shop.

At the tailor shop he and Paul talked for a while, and then they went down to the courthouse area to find a lawyer to take Beatrice's case. By afternoon, they had found one, an Indian just come back from England. Sonny gave him the details and paid him a deposit. Then, weary, he left Paul to go back to Rosehill.

Sonny spent most of that week at the town hall poring over land registration documents and old law books and making pages and pages of notes. In the evenings, he went from house to house on Rosehill, asking questions, and after a late lime with the boys by the corner, he would burn the lamp half the night, writing. He wrote several letters to America and despite Miss Ann's offer to hold them for the postman, he took them to town and mailed them himself.

He told Reme he was preparing the background for a case against the government's claim on the land. But even as he worked, rumours were spreading that the Company would be sending tractors to Rosehill soon and some people on Rosehill were in a panic. The sixty days they had been given to clear off the land were gone, and with Beatrice in jail, their last hope of getting money for the leases was also gone. Sonny found out that about fifteen families still had no legal claim to the land and he promised to help them but, as he told Reme, he wasn't having it easy, especially with the Land and Surveyors office. He had been trying to get documents from them but they had been putting

154

him off, putting him off. In the meantime, Rosehill people came every day to beg him. Reme got vexed after a while and told them to give the man a chance.

'I glad you helping Rosehill, Sonny,' she told him. 'But what about Beatrice? You made-up with she about the child?'

'I'm not vexed with Beatrice, Reme,' he told her. 'I hired a lawyer.'

'But why you can't defend Beatrice? You trust them In- dian?'

'He is admitted to the bar,' Sonny explained. 'I wouldn't be able to stand before a magistrate on Beatrice's behalf.'

'So all that education you get was for nothing?'

Sonny tried to be patient, 'Reme, it's just that I would have to apply for a license and take a special exam here. But don't worry. Ali knows what he's doing. We used to go to school together down here.'

But Reme was not convinced. 'I not like you, Sonny. I can't trust my daughter to them Indians, nuh. I going down and talk to him mehself.'

So Sonny took her down town to meet Ali. After the meeting she told Sonny, 'He's not pure Indian, you know. He's a dougla.'

Sonny laughed, 'It have pure Indian with curly hair too, you know.'

'I tell you the man has some Negro blood in him, man,' Reme insisted. 'I could tell.' And she went home satisfied.

When, a few days later, Ali got Beatrice's case postponed and the bail reduced, Reme shook his hand.

'His uncle is a magistrate,' Sonny told her.

'God knows when to work wonders, you know,' Reme said.

'But I thought you said God has coke-eye?' Sonny laughed.

'Even if he was blind he could see my daughter not guilty,' she said.

To pay the bail, Reme had pawned Tante's gold bracelets

and Paul gave them what he could. Sonny threw in the rest.

Beatrice came home quietly, but of course, everybody on Rosehill knew the minute she walked into Tante Vivian's house and they came all day to console and encourage her. Mother Dinah wanted to have a feast but Beatrice asked her to hold off until after the case was called. Reme went up to Mount St. Benedict to ask the monks to say special prayers and she left enough money with them for candles and incense to be burned for nine days. Then she went to see a man in Guapo who had been to Haiti and was working some wonders for people. He had been helping her with the big stomach, and it was going down gradually. She was confident that he would also help her with Beatrice so she took him a fowl and a bottle of sweet oil, and an American ten-dollar note that Sonny had given her. The man gave her things to rub on her belly and to put on Beatrice.

On the first night Beatrice was home she didn't talk a lot to Sonny. He had been back to see her once in jail, and although that visit hadn't been as tense as his first, there was still strain between them. Reme, trying to smooth out matters, told her how hard Sonny had been working, and Beatrice thanked him kindly. Sonny tried to act natural, to pretend that he wasn't grinding inside but Beatrice could see he was fighting the tension. He cracked his knuckles every few minutes without even realising he was doing it, and he often sat on the back steps for hours, his chin resting in his palm, propping sorrow, and staring off at nothing. Reme tried to make him as comfortable as she could to apologise for the unhappiness she felt Beatrice had brought upon him. Then too, she was pleased, proud really, that Sonny, whom everybody looked upon as her son-in-law, had come back to help her daughter. His presence alone, she felt, vindicated Beatrice, and she went about Rosehill with her head held so high that Miss Ann laughed and told Jestina Reme would stump her toe on a big stone.

Beatrice was uncomfortable around Sonny. The first few days after she came home from the jail, she tried her best to avoid

156

him. On the days that Reme was in the house to look after Tante Vivian, Beatrice woke up early, went downtown to the library, and came home when she thought Sonny would be out of the house, perhaps liming with the boys, or talking to Willy and the other men at the community centre. This went on for about a week and a half. Then Sonny trapped her one morning as she was coming out of the bathroom in the yard.

'How long you expect to keep this up, Beatrice?' he blocked the door into the kitchen.

'The water was cold, Sonny,' she said. 'Let me by.'

'You can't keep running from me, Beatrice. We have to talk about all this some time.'

'I don't have anything to say. I tell you everything. What you want to know?'

'Let's talk tonight,' Sonny pleaded. 'I'll wait for you down by the corner. We could go for a walk... ' She pushed him out of the way, went inside, dressed fast, and left without saying another word to him.

That evening, when she got off the bus at the Rosehill junction, he was waiting for her. He gripped her arm, and despite her protests, steered her toward the ravine down behind the bridge. There, with frogs croaking in the low grass and candleflies darting from bush to bush, he sat her down on a big rock and told her he couldn't stand the tension any more.

'I want to kill him, Beatrice. I want to go into his office and put my hands on his throat, and I want to tell him this is for Beatrice. I could kill him, Beatrice, for what he do to you.'

'You can't hate him more that me, Sonny. But I try not to think about it. I don't want to talk about it to you either.'

'But how you was so sure, Beatrice?' Sonny asked her. 'The child could have been mine. How you was so sure it was his?'

'At first I wasn't sure, Sonny. At least I didn't want to believe he was the father. The baby looked a little bit you. Moko used to say Melvin looked like Angelina's side of the family. She had Chinese in her, Sonny, you know that, so you have some in

157

you too. Your eyes slant a little and you have these cheek-bones.... Well, I look for you in Melvin and I find it. But I know I was only fooling myself. Melvin started to resemble him, Sonny. No. Melvin was his own. The poor child had to suffer for that.'

'You still love me, Beatrice?' Sonny asked her. 'You still love me a lil' bit?'

She turned her face away from him.

'Answer me, Beatrice. Please.'

'I love you for a long time, Sonny,' she whispered.

He touched her cheek and forced her to look at him. 'I still love you, Beatrice.' And she let him hold her and kiss her, willing herself not to feel anything, but that night, Reme was happy to see Sonny go into Beatrice's room and lock the door.

The days flew away, and before Sonny knew it, he had been back in Santabella over a month. He had managed to get information on two previous cases similar to Rosehill's and had turned the information over to Ali, who had agreed to represent them in the land dispute too. Ali was a busy man, and Sonny, to reduce costs, tried to get much of the background work done for him. He was in town doing that the morning the first tractor came up the hill behind the water truck. Children ran behind the tractor trying to hop a ride and forgetting to collect water from the truck. Women in their yards heard the commotion and came out in the road to shout 'Where all you going?' to the two men riding the tractor, but they got no answer. The men stopped the tractor near Roberts' house, right above the Ledge, and they got down, leaned against the tyres, smoking and waiting, ignoring the women's questions. Roberts came out and stood in his front yard with his machete and dared them to cross his fence but the men just waited, saying nothing. Miss Roberts watched nervously from her gallery as Rosehill gathered around.

About fifteen minutes later, a car came up the hill and Doctor Chow and another man got out, pushed through the crowd and went toward Roberts.

'You was supposed to move out days ago,' Chow told him. 'You had your notice.'

'Who is you to give notice?' Miss Roberts demanded. 'Who the hell you think you is? Make one move to break this house and you dead!' The villagers shouted their support.

Chow ignored her and turned to Roberts. 'Why you all don't stop all this foolishness? I trying my best to do what is right. I let all you hang on here for months, years even. Everybody had a chance to raise the money for the leases. How much patience you expect me to have? Eh? You think I is father Christmas?'

'You grow up on Rosehill, Chow.' Roberts approached him. 'Is true your family sell out to Ling Chung and all you more for higher now. But we still take you for a Rosehill man. Your father come up here and open shop and we support him. Your father was a good man. He always treat Rosehill fair. But you. Look at you. Is money make man turn beast so? Look at you now. You ready to wipe out the hill so you could profit from the oil. When you come back from studying to be big time doctor, who was the first patients you had? Rosehill people support you. We make you what you is. We build up your practice, and I tell you it hurt me to see how you turn out to be a zandolie. After one time is really a next.'

'I didn't come up here for ole talk,' Chow said. 'I always treat Rosehill good. Who you come to every Christmas for presents for the children? Eh? Who give Reme job? Who treat your children when they sick for free? If anybody owe anybody anything, is Rosehill owe me, not the other way around. You behaving as if is I who want the land. I only acting as the agent here. Is the government all you have to deal with, not me. I doing my job.'

'The man is a manicou!' Jestina shouted.

The man with Chow tilted his head and the two of them moved away from the crowd.

'This is pointless,' the man spoke with an American accent. 'We're wasting time and money. My men are ready to work on

159

this hill but you've got to do something about these people. We can't afford to have them pay off any more leases. We have to get this land.'

'My stake in this is as large as yours,' Chow reminded him. 'Even larger. Everything depends on us getting them off. How was I to know that the girl would get money to help some of them? I did my part with the government. And as for these people, we'll have to find other ways.'

Chow left him and went back to tell Roberts, 'You could make all the noise you want, but when I come back up this hill, you better not be here. I giving you and your family two hours. After that, I'm not responsible.'

'You can't move we off this hill. Not you and ten tractors,' Miss Ann had come through the crowd to stand with Roberts, and arms akimbo, she spat defiance at Chow.

'What all you getting so hot for?' Willy tried to calm her down. 'No tractor breaking this house,' he said quietly. 'Let the man talk, nuh. He not frightening anybody.'

'You all looking for real trouble here, you know,' Chow said. 'Willy, you're a sensible man. Tell these people to clear the way. I don't want anybody to get hurt.'

'Let me handle this,' the stranger with the doctor said, and he put his hand on the gate.

'Come in this yard! You put one foot in this yard!' Roberts took his machete from his belt and held it up.

The man stopped and turned to Chow. 'I told you we should have brought the police. You said you know these people.'

Chow took his arm and together they pushed through the crowd back to the car. The people shouted as the men entered the car but did not drive off. Rosehill watched them talking, arguing, the windows up, and then the stranger got out and went over to the two men on the tractor, pushing away the little children who had clambered up on the huge tyres to get a better view of the show. He told the two men to wait with the tractor until he came back, then he got back into the car with the doctor and they sped away.

Willy took Mr. Roberts and some of the other men round to the back of the house to talk quietly as some of the women went reluctantly back to their houses to check on food they had left on the fire, or to hang clothes on the line to catch the sun while it was still high in the sky. Miss Ann and a few others stayed with Miss Roberts, consoling her. The two fellars on the tractor were getting nervous and tried to talk friendly to a couple of the young girls in an attempt to persuade Rosehill that they were just the tractor drivers doing their job, so no antagonism should be directed toward them, but the steelband boys would have none of it. They chased the girls away, and warned the tractor men to leave the hill if they knew what was good for them.

Beatrice had been bathing Tante when all the commotion began in front of Mr. Roberts' house and although she was curious, she couldn't leave before she had dried Tante off, put a clean nightgown on her, and helped her back to bed. She came in time to see the back of the car as it went flying down the hill. She joined Miss Ann, Jestina and Melda on the Roberts' front steps.

'You just miss them,' Miss Ann told her. 'Chow and an American big pappy. They bring them two tractors to break down Roberts' house.'

'They not breaking down my house, Beatrice. Not when I put so much sweat in here, girl. I not taking it so,' Miss Roberts pounded the concrete in rage.

'I feel so sorry, Miss Roberts,' Beatrice said. 'I have enough in the bank to pay for your lease too, but the government wouldn't let me touch it.'

'But Sonny come and tell them he send you the money,' Melda told Beatrice. 'So why they have to put hold on it? They don't believe Sonny or what?'

'Is not a matter of believing Sonny,' Beatrice explained. 'The government still have their case against me. They still say I thief their money from the Ministry, so that case have to go through the court no matter what Sonny tell them.'

161

'But once Sonny testify in court that is he who send you the money, what case the government will have?' Jestina asked.

'Is up to the magistrate to believe Sonny,' Beatrice told them. 'We have to wait for the case to call.'

'And in the meanwhile, Chow and them trying to get as many of we off the land as possible,' Miss Ann said. 'But they going to have a hard hard time. Don't worry, Roberts girl. If they touch this place, they have to touch all of we. We ent fraid them.'

'Reme tell me the other day that Sonny would never let this happen, Beatrice. She promise me that he working on it night and day. Where Sonny is now they come to break meh house. Eh? Tell me that?'

Beatrice couldn't stand the despair in Miss Roberts' voice. She was never a strong woman, having suffered with TB for years, and Beatrice knew she was summoning up all her strength to deal with the situation.

'He working on it, Miss Roberts, really,' Beatrice tried to reassure her. 'When he leave this morning he told me he was going down to the town hall to file some petition on behalf of Rosehill. But you know how things does move slow slow in this country. If you don't have money to bribe somebody, crapaud smoke your pipe.'

'But Sonny have money,' Miss Ann said. 'All that money he win in the lottery in America. He didn't send you all of it, Beatrice. You could bet he have plenty left.'

Tante always say you should never lie, because when you tell one lie, you have to tell another one to cover it up, and another one to cover that one up and... the thoughts flew through Beatrice's mind and she had to make an effort to shove them aside so she could talk to Miss Ann. 'You know Sonny will never bribe anybody,' she said.

'Sonny was always too damn good to be true,' Miss Ann said. 'You can't depend on people like that when the river start overflowing, nuh. You need somebody who don't mind getting dirty.'

'Chow can't break down this house,' Beatrice said. 'If he touch one piece of galvanize, is trouble. I promise all you that.'

'You do enough, Beatrice girl,' Jestina said. 'If it wasn't for you, I would be in Miss Roberts' position. What more you could do? Chow is a powerful man.'

'Yes,' Beatrice said quietly, 'he's a powerful man. He think he could do anything to anybody. He think he could take whatever he want from anybody.'

Miss Ann looked across at Jestina in wonder. They had never heard Beatrice talk like that and they could sense that her words meant more than they knew.

Beatrice touched Miss Roberts' shoulder. 'Don't worry,' she said again. 'This is one time Chow not going to get what he want.'

'You right,' Jestina agreed, getting up. 'Let we send the children home before they come back. Then we could form a barricade. They can't get through.'

'You don't have to do that,' Beatrice told them. 'You don't even have to do that.'

'Don't do anything foolish, Beatrice,' Melda said. 'Chow have friends high up. They could hurt your case.'

'That man can't hurt me any more than he already hurt me,' Beatrice told them. 'You all think you know how bad he is? You don't know the half of it. You don't know how evil he really is. I know. I know.'

'I did hear some bad things about him a while ago,' Miss Ann said, trying to encourage Beatrice to reveal something, 'but you never know if people lying or what, and I is not one to go around repeating bad things about people.'

'Since when?' Jestina asked her. 'Since when you could hold your tongue, Ann?'

'I don't know what you hear, Miss Ann,' Beatrice said. 'But whatever it is, it is probably true. I don't have to tell all you what he do, but believe me, he have evil in him.'

'When you see you get big and powerful in this country,' Melda said, 'you could get away with rape, oui.'

'Yes,' Beatrice said. 'You could get away with it. But one day one day congotay. Right Miss Ann? No matter how bad you bad, your day will come.'

Willy, Mister Roberts and the other men came from the backyard, and the women demanded to know what they planned to do when Chow and the American came back up the hill.

'Why all you women don't go home, eh?' Willy told them. 'Leave this to we. We have everything under control.'

'Leave everything to you?' Miss Ann rolled her eyes to the sky. 'Well is now we dogs dead in truth.'

'One of these day, Ann,' Willy pointed his finger at her, 'you going to turn round and find me gone with a deputy. You don't appreciate me, girl.'

The women laughed. Willy had been threatening to leave Miss Ann from the day they got married but everyone knew he had nowhere to go.

'I going to have a word with the fellars on the tractor,' Mister Roberts said, and he and the other men went out the gate. Miss Ann left to check on her parlour, Jestina went to check on her children, and Beatrice left to make sure Tante Vivian was still sleeping. Melda and Miss Roberts stayed on the steps waiting.

Beatrice looked in on Tante Vivian and Tante seemed fast asleep, so she went through to the kitchen, reached behind the broom closet, and took out a bottle that she had seen Tante hide months before. She set the bottle on the table in front of her, and noted that it was almost full. Then she got an aluminium bucket from under the counter and placed it on the table near to the bottle. She sat there for a while, staring at the bottle and the bucket, and for the first time in years, Beatrice cried. And with the tears came the memories of all that she had hidden in her heart for too long.

'Melvin,' she whispered. 'I did really love you, child. You was an innocent child. Why? Why you had to suffer for that evil man? A little child like you.' She dried her eyes with the hem of her skirt but the tears still came. 'He going to pay,' she swore. 'He going to pay for what he do to me, and he going to suffer for

164

what happened to you, Melvin, and to Moko. Somebody have to stop him.' And Beatrice's body racked with pain as she remembered how he had forced her to the floor and jammed his penis inside of her. 'I hate him,' she whispered. 'I hate him.... I hate him....'

As soon as the white car left the Main Road and began to climb the hill, Rosehill knew, and they came together to form a wall in front of the Roberts' house. Willy sent the curious children home. 'This is big people's business,' he told them, as Chow and a constable jumped out of the car.

'All you have to move,' the constable told Miss Ann, coming towards her waving his boottoo. 'The man has official papers. Papers say he own the land. I telling all yuh to move out of the way.'

'You move we!' Melda shouted. 'You come and move we if you name man!'

'I telling all you,' the constable warned, 'the Yankee man gone downtown for inspector. They not making joke, yuh know. Miss Ann, I appealing to you.'

'You think is joke we making?' Jestina shouted. 'Let one manjack try to break down this house. Let them come. Even you, constable. Come let me throw pee in your face.'

'Look Beatrice coming,' Melda pointed up the road, and they watched as Beatrice paused some distance from the crowd. She stood quietly waiting, a bucket at her feet, as the constable went up to her.

'Miss Beatrice,' the constable tried to talk to her politely, 'look, I don't want no trouble. I trying to tell Miss Ann and them to move, but they don't want to listen to me. I tried to talk to Willy, but is the same thing. The doctor have papers that authorise him to break down the house. My hands tied. People could get hurt.'

'Your sister still living just down the hill,' Miss Ann shouted to the constable. 'What you going to do when the tractor man want to break her house? You going to let them?

Eh?'

'Yes, you from up here,' Jestina shouted. 'You siding with these manicou?'

'Is only my job I doing, Miss Beatrice,' the constable tried to ignore the other women as he pleaded with Beatrice. 'You think I like this? I under orders. Talk to these people, nuh. I appealing to you.'

Beatrice shrugged her shoulders.

'Well, I try,' the constable shook his head. 'I try meh best. All you don't blame me when thing happen, eh. If all you don't want to move, I have to get reinforcements.' And nodding to Chow, he went back down the hill.

The doctor went over to Beatrice.

'You playing bad john?' he asked her. 'You playing with me Beatrice? You forget who I am?'

'You is the big bad john in this country,' Beatrice faced him without flinching, and she spoke quietly. 'I know you. You have so much power, you could do anything you want with anybody in this country. How I could forget you? I know exactly who you is.'

'I own this land,' Chow's arm swept the hillside. 'I own Rosehill, girl. Don't play with me. You make yourself a leader up here. Buying up leases for people. You playing with me?'

'Is long time now you trying to steal this land,' Miss Ann called out, wanting desperately to move closer so she could hear what the doctor and Beatrice were saying, but she couldn't break the human fence she and the others had made in front of the gate. 'Ever since you used to work in your father's shop, I know you have your mind set on this land. Now you is doctor you think you could move we? You and who?'

'I don't have to stand here and argue with you people,' Chow said. 'I own this property. Tell Roberts to get off or....'

'Or what?' Beatrice asked quietly. 'What you could do?'

'I trying hard to be reasonable with all you. I....'

'Reasonable! You calling yourself reasonable? A man like you!'

166

'I didn't come here for no argument,' Chow took a step back to avoid the spit flying from Beatrice's angry mouth. 'I telling you for the last time tell these people to move.'

'You come. You move we if you name man!' Melda shouted. 'You come and move we!'

'You going to suffer the consequences,' Chow turned back to face the women.

'But hear this manicou, nuh?' Jestina laughed. 'But he brass face too bad, oui. Look me tremble, look me!' And she shook her body as Rosehill laughed.

Chow turned away and called to the men on the tractor. They got off the tractor but couldn't move further because the steelband boys had surrounded them and the tractor. Chow swung around and was face to face with Beatrice again.

'You have power now?' she laughed shortly. 'Make them come. Make them come like you.'

'I see is trouble you want in this place!' he hissed.

The steelband boys began to beat on the tractor, jamming the men against the metal. One of them suddenly saw an opening, dashed for it, and the other followed him down the hill. Rosehill let them run.

'That house coming down today if I have to move it myself,' Chow, shaking with anger, spat the words at Beatrice, and pushing her out of the way, he tried to step past her.

'Don't you ever put your nasty hand in my face again!' Beatrice hissed, and the words were hardly out of her mouth before she had raised the bucket. Willy and Valmon lifted their sticks. Beatrice shouted, 'Stay back, Uncle Willy,' and before they could move, Beatrice, in one swift movement, flung the bucket of liquid in the doctor's face. The doctor screamed as liquid spattered on to his clothes, dripped to the earth, and singed it. Beatrice raised the bucket again and hit him on the head, and she raised it again to hit him again but Willy grabbed her arm and held her down as Valmon and the other men kept the women back.

Only once before could Rosehill remember hearing such a

scream of agony. It was the time Melda had heard that her oldest son, Tyrone, had been murdered. Her scream had cut across the hill and dogs had barked for hours and even the trees had started shaking. And now they heard it again. It rose from Chow's throat as he clutched his face and tried to pull it off.

'Come nuh! Come take advantage! You son of a bitch! Come!' Beatrice was like a wild woman. She swung the bucket again but Willy and Sammy grabbed her and held her back.

Chow was on his knees scratching the ground for dirt to put on his burning face. Rosehill's mouth was open, stunned into silence at the violence of Beatrice's act.

Willy and Sammy pulled Beatrice away and told Miss Ann and Jestina to take her home and wash her off because some of the liquid might have gotten on her shoes while Valmon and Roberts held back the crowd that had begun to press forward, closing around the doctor.

'Hold back! Hold back nuh man,' Sammy shouted. 'Melda, all you women don't come near. This thing burning. Stay back!'

With Beatrice safely in Miss Ann's hands, some of the other men parted the crowd, dragged the doctor away from in front of the yard, and left him by the tractor. Then Willy shouted for everybody to calm down. 'We going to the community centre,' he shouted. 'Everybody follow me.'

'We leaving him here?' Roberts asked.

'Yes,' Willy said. 'Leave him by the tractor. We can't do nothing for him anyway.' And he led the way to the community centre. There, he talked to them about what had happened. 'Beatrice is one of us,' he reminded them. 'What she do, she do for all of us, for Rosehill. We can't let her down. When the police come, we tell them nothing. We didn't see, we didn't hear, we don't know anything. All you hear me? I want everybody's word on this. And keep the children in the yards.'

Miss Ann sent Jestina running to the phone box by the Main Road to try to reach Reme at Miss Ames' house, while she tried to get Beatrice to calm down. But it took her and Mother

Dinah a while before they could get Beatrice to stop fighting them off.

'Leave me alone,' Beatrice begged them. 'Miss Ann, just go home. Okay. Go home.'

'How you expect me to leave you like this?' Miss Ann asked her. 'You have to get control of yourself before the police come to ask questions, girl.'

'I don't care,' Beatrice said. 'I telling them the truth.'

'And make Rosehill out to be liars?' Mother Dinah asked her. 'Chile, you will not say one word to the police when they come. I will talk to them, you hear?'

'Listen to Mother Dinah,' Miss Ann told Beatrice. 'You just stay quiet and everything going to be okay,' and she left reluctantly to go back to check on her parlour.

Mother Dinah stroked Beatrice's head and forced her to sip some bush tea and refused to leave until Beatrice had promised to say nothing to the police. By the time Reme came up the hill, Beatrice had washed her face and was sitting quietly on the couch with her head in her hands, propping sorrow. She glanced at her mother and could tell she was trying to control her temper. Reme touched her head to see if she was hot with fever and Beatrice pushed her hand gently away.

'Nothing ent wrong with me, Ma,' she said quietly. 'You didn't need to leave work.'

'Nothing ent wrong with you?' Reme asked her. 'How nothing ent wrong with you? You can't tell me something ent wrong with you because is only mad people does behave like this. Why Beatrice? Tell me why, eh? Why you had was to go and do something like this? You like jail, eh? You ent spend enough time in there? You want to go back?'

'I had to do it,' Beatrice said quietly, and Reme felt that she was talking more to herself than in answer to the question.

'You had to do it,' Reme screamed. 'You had to do it? Tell me, Beatrice. Just once, come straight with me. Tell me why.'

'I had to stop him. And don't make so much noise, Ma. Tante sleeping.'

169

'Look,' Reme sat down on the couch and Beatrice felt that any moment she was going to start crying. 'I raise you good, Beatrice. I try my best to give you everything, but what you care about me. You always doing something for somebody else. You take all that money Sonny send for you and pay off leases for these Rosehill people. You think about me and my sickness. Eh? No, no, you shut up. I want to have my say now.'

'I will send you to America to see the specialist as soon as the case over, Ma, you know that.'

'As soon as the case over,' Reme cried. 'What you talking about? You not out of one trouble yet, you gone and put yourself in another one. For what? Who benefiting from this, Beatrice? Who you do this for?'

'I do it for me, Ma. And for you. I do it for....'

'For me?' Reme was outraged. 'For me? Who de arse ask you to throw acid in the man's face? When I tell you to do that?'

'I know he raped you, Ma. He tell me. He laugh about it. He... '

Beatrice's mouth closed on the last words as she saw the stunned look on Reme's face. Then, as Beatrice watched, Reme seemed to age twenty more years; her face turned grey and her shoulders sagged, and she reached for the pillow on which Beatrice had been resting her head, and buried her face in it.

Beatrice drew close and touched her mother's shoulders and for the first time in years, Reme rose up and hugged her and the two of them cried in each other's arms. Then Beatrice told her what the doctor had done, and what he had said that day in the clinic.

'Tell me, Ma. Tell me he lie. He's not my father.'

'No,' Reme shook her head. 'Kelvin is your father. But he hear that I was friending with Chow and he leave me. After he went away, I stop seeing Chow, but he wouldn't take no for an answer. He do that to you out of spite, Beatrice. I tell him I didn't want to have anything more to do with him. Tante used to warn me that he was spiteful and wicked. He do that to you to punish me.'

'Well, this is the last time he going to hurt anybody,' Beatrice said. 'The last time.'

'He might die.' The fear in Reme made her tremble.

'Let him die!' Beatrice lashed out. 'Let him die! He shoulda dead long time for what he do to me.'

'Well, if there's a God,' Reme said sadly, 'I hope he understand. I hope he understand child, because I don't know what I will do if they put you back in jail.' She touched Beatrice's head. 'You're my only child, Beatrice. What I will do without you, eh?'

'Nothing going to happen, Ma.' Beatrice promised. 'Nothing going to happen.'

Reme, after a while, looked at her watch and said, 'I just run away when Jestina call me. I'll come back later,' and she left Beatrice to go back to the job.

Beatrice watched her leave and then went into the kitchen. A calmness that she had not felt in a long time came over her, and she began to sing one of Tante's favourite hymns as she prepared some soup for supper.

Rosehill was calm that afternoon. A sea breeze came up from the Gulf and clothes on the lines dried quickly. Jestina sprinkled hers so they would be soft later when she was ready to iron, and then she put some rouge on her cheeks and went down by the docks to see Sharky and the boys. Willy told Miss Ann to take the children out for a while so she closed her parlour and took her children and Jestina's to the botanical gardens to see the new lilies in the pond. Sammy and Roberts went down in the gully to plant cassava and sorrel, and the steelband boys gathered in their shed for a game of whappie. Willy, Uncle Clive and Valmon went back to mend fishing nets on the beach.

When the constable came back up the hill a short while later with the inspector and the American who had come earlier, they found Chow in the high grass near the tractor, unconscious, pieces of skin from his face lying on the ground beside him. The inspector sent the constable running back down the hill to call an ambulance, and after it had come and taken Chow away, he and three other policemen went from house to house asking Rosehill to tell them who had thrown acid in the doctor's face.

'What acid?' Rosehill asked the police.

'You mean to say nobody on this hill see who throw acid in the man's face?' the police asked again.

And the people said no, they hadn't seen anybody throw acid in the doctor's face.

Late in the afternoon, Sonny came back. The house was quiet when he walked in and he went to Tante's room. He found Beatrice sitting by Tante's bed, holding her hand. Beatrice didn't raise her head when he came in, and Sonny went over, took one look at Tante and touched her cheek. It was cold.

'When it happen?' he asked.

'Round one o'clock,' Beatrice's voice was hardly a whisper.

'And you stayed in here by yourself all this time?'

'The dead can't frighten you, Sonny.'

He put his hand on Beatrice's shoulder, not quite knowing what to say. 'She live a long time.'

'She see too much trouble,' Beatrice shook her head, angrily. 'What is the point in living a long time if is only trouble you have to see,' and Sonny saw water forming in her eyes.

'Is true,' he agreed, rubbing her neck and shoulders.

'Is that what we born for? To ketch hell until we die?'

'But Tante was a happy woman,' Sonny tried to console her. 'She was strong. She used to say one day one day congotay. She really believe things would change.'

'But look what it come to,' Beatrice said. 'What is the use of coming into this world helping people, doing good. In the end, you alone are dancing.'

'You were never one to give up, Beatrice,' Sonny rubbed her head. 'Come on, stop all this talk. You can't sit here all night.'

'I just want to stay with Tante. You know, I wanted to tell

her, Sonny. I wanted to tell her about Chow. I wanted to tell her that I make him pay for what he did, but by the time I come in here she was....'

'You shouldn't have been here by yourself. I thought Miss Ann would be with you.'

'She was here for a while,' Beatrice said. 'But we thought Tante was just sleeping. Is only after she left that I come in here and see Tante wasn't breathing. She die so quiet, Sonny. In the middle of all the commotion she die quiet quiet.'

Sonny lifted her up from the chair and took her out to the kitchen and tried to find something cheerful to say. 'One thing happened good today. I get a magistrate to sign the order to prevent them from taking the land until we settle it in court.'

'Mister Roberts will be glad to hear that.' Beatrice tried to sound happy but Sonny heard the weariness in her voice, as if she didn't care any more.

'I already tell him when I was coming up, and he tell me what happened today.'

'You don't have to get tangle up in all this, Sonny. I only do what I had to do.'

'He might die, Beatrice. Roberts say the police inspector tell him Chow might not live through the night.'

'I wish he could suffer longer,' Beatrice said softly. 'I wish he could suffer for months.'

'He's unconscious. He can't tell them who do it.' Sonny looked at her closely, gauging her reaction.

'I'll tell them,' Beatrice shrugged. 'I'll tell them I do it. And I glad, Sonny.'

'No, you can't,' Sonny said. 'Promise me, Beatrice. Promise me you not going to say one word to them. Don't say you had anything to do with this.'

'Everybody know I do it, Sonny.'

'Yes, but nobody will say so, and you shouldn't. Do this for me, Beatrice. Keep this secret for me. You remember what you tell me when the government withdraw the scholarship? Remember how you ask me to go away still and not to tell

173

anybody? I was frightened, but I listened to you and I went without saying a word. It worked, Beatrice. And this will work out too. Rosehill care about you. Nobody will say one word to the police. Don't dig your own grave, Beatrice. Promise me, please.'

'You sorry you come back, Sonny?' Beatrice touched his cheek, smiling a little.

'No, girl.' He put his arms around her. 'What I have to be sorry for.'

'You don't have to stay, you know. Ali is a good lawyer.'

'I have to go back soon because I just dropped everything and came down,' he said.

'You going to stay for the funeral?'

'You know I can't leave before. Tante was like a mother to me.'

'I'm glad she get to see you before she die.'

'What you going to do, Beatrice? You promise me you not going to say anything to the police?'

'I promise,' she said.

'Okay,' Sonny smiled. 'What you should be concentrating on is a plan.'

'About what?'

'Well, Tante's gone. You might not get back your job at the Ministry....'

'That's not the only job in the country.'

'You don't want to go away?'

'What's over there for me, Sonny?' she asked him, and she was looking up at him and he felt she was waiting, wanting him to say something, but he couldn't.

'I could stay here with Tante,' he said instead. 'You go and get somebody from the clinic, and ask Willy or one of the men to report her death to the station. What about the funeral home? Who you want to bury Tante?'

Beatrice shook her head and a slight half smile came to her lips. 'Well,' she said. 'I guess that is that.' She moved away from him and filled a cup with water and leaned against the kitchen

174

counter sipping it, watching him carefully. Sonny looked in her eyes and knew that she had not heard him, knew that she had not heard what she wanted to hear, and he knew then that everything would change between them.

He felt uncomfortable. 'You want me to go and get the doctor?'

'Yes,' she said quietly, watching him. 'You go down. And tell the funeral home too. I just want to stay here with Tante.'

She put down the cup, and leaving him standing in the kitchen, went past him into Tante Vivian's room. Sonny stood in the kitchen for a while, wondering if he should go in and try to explain things to her. There was so much he needed to tell her, but how could he add another blow on top of all that she had suffered that day? Would she understand that he'd had to get legal? That he had had to marry an American woman? And would she understand that somehow he had stayed in the marriage, that the woman had his son? Could he make her know that although he had a wife and child in America he still felt love for her? Wasn't his very presence proof that he still cared? No. He couldn't tell her. Not now.

There was a time, in Santabella, when the death of a woman like Tante Vivian would bring people from all over the country, from Toco and Manzanilla, Cedros and Fyzabad, Maraval and Point Cumana. The women would bring packs of salt biscuits and blocks of yellow cheese, and the men would bring the rum, Old Oak and Vat 19. The people at the death house would make huge pots of coffee and the dead would lie in the centre of the living room where all the pictures and mirrors on the wall were turned around. The Maraval fellars would come ready to meet the men from Toco in a stick fight and as the dancers parried like game cocks in a ring, and the drums beat faster and louder, old women who had seen it all so many times would sing hymns softly around the coffin.

The wake could last up to three days and the dancers never got tired as long as the rum and coffee flowed. But stickfighting

..ad died out except deep in the country, and the only time most Santabellans saw it was on Carnival Sunday night when the Carnival Development Committee put on a big show in the savannah for tourists.

Still, some old fellars in the country liked to hit the sticks now and then, and people still called them by their old dancer days names like Spree, Bachack, Wattap, Spirit and Flash. Flash was an Indian fellar they used to call Boysie. One time, at a big wake in Marabella, he jumped in and started parrying with the fellars. He moved like lightning and the fellars couldn't touch him at all. They decided to call him Flash. People asked, but where that Indian learn to dance so? And he told them he had learned the dance in Arima.

Flash and the other fellars were doing day work on the road gangs and when they met they exchanged news about wakes.

'I hear it having a big one in Rosehill, man.' Flash said. 'Obeah woman. They say the rum going to flow. All you going?'

'I did hear bout that in true,' Spree said. 'But I can't make it, man. I promise to take the madam to fete Friday night.'

'You giving up the stick for fete, man?' Flash asked him, astonished.

'The madam say if I don't take she to dance with Despers, she leaving me, man,' Spree laughed.

'Woman have all you hook up tight,' Flash said. 'Not me, man. No woman could rule me. It ent have a pussy God make so sweet, nuh!'

The men laughed.

'But hear this man talk,' Spirit said. 'It wasn't he who cry blood when Rosalie leave him? Months! Months, I tell you! How much wake you went to then, man?'

'Me! You don't mean me, man!' Flash swore. 'No woman could ever make water come in my eye!'

'It was bawl you was bawling,' Spree laughed. 'I remember it, man. I say well boy, meh friend gone. We have to hold a wake for him.'

'All you drink sore-foot water, oui,' Flash said. 'That woman gone about she business. I is my own man.'

The fellars continued to heckle Flash about his woman and he took it all in good humour. As the laughter died down Spree asked what time they would leave for the wake.

'We go have to take off half-day, man,' Flash told him. 'Bachack driving.'

About eleven o'clock the next day the fellars signed in on the job and then took off in Bachack's old Renault to go to Tante Vivian's wake. Spree was with them.

'What the madam say?' Flash asked him.

'Say? What she going to say, man?' Spree asked him. 'I tell she I going and she stupes.'

'You want to bet she put your clothes on the step when you come back?' Flash said.

'You lucky if she don't burn them up,' Spirit told him. 'Woman bad too bad these days, man. You can't go nowhere without them. They getting mad mad mad and burning up your clothes.'

'I tell she we going for a sea bath, man,' Spree spoke with assurance. But Flash knew better. He said, 'You mean she still waiting for you to come back and take she to the fete? Well, your ass in trouble, oui.'

'To tell the truth,' Spree confessed, 'I glad if she leave, man. I have meh eye on a Indian girl in Talparo long time now.'

'I don't play that way, boy,' Spirit said. 'Indian girl's father cut off your head in a minute, oui. They don't play with their girl children, nuh.'

'Father? Father what?' Bachack said. 'Not even tiger wire could hold back them Indian girls these day.'

'The girl want me bad, man,' Spree boasted.

And so the ole talk continued about the ins and outs of involvement with Indian girls as Bachack sped through Beausejeau, past La Romain, across the bridge in Mon Repo and onto the long stretch to Erin where they stopped at a beer garden for a couple pints apiece.

It was making dark when they pulled up to Ling Chung's rum shop at the Rosehill junction to ask directions to Tante Vivian's wake. Ling Chung told them to follow the candles that lit both sides of the road from the Ledge to Tante's gate, and Bachack put the Renault in second shift and it climbed slowly up the hill.

Rain had been threatening to fall all afternoon so Willy and Sonny, expecting a large turnout for the wake, had borrowed Miss Ann's tarpaulin and had thrown up a tent in Tante's yard. When Spree and the fellars arrived, they shook hands all around and Sonny gave them a bottle of Old Oak and left them under the tent. Bachack opened the bottle and poured some for the spirits, and after he and the others had taken their first drink, they set the bottle on a concrete brick and went into the house to pay their respects to the dead.

Tante was dressed in her cream dress with the crochet-work around the neck and sleeves. Melda had combed her hair with a bang on her forehead and put white powder on her cheeks. As Miss Ann said later, Sonny and Beatrice and Reme really put Tante away in style. The casket was pure mahogany, and it was lined with purple velvet.

The fellars offered Beatrice their sympathies, noted how young Tante's face looked, and went back to the tent in the yard.

In the kitchen, Jestina and Melda were boiling coffee and Reme was cutting up cheese. Beatrice had given Miss Ann ten dollars for biscuits and Miss Ann brought all the packs she had in the parlour. She began to count them out but Beatrice told her she didn't have to do that. 'I could see you not thiefing me, Miss Ann,' she smiled, and refused to take the two shillings change Miss Ann offered.

Ling Chung came up early and brought two bottles of rum. His wife came with him and Jestina invited her to stay and help them. Ling Chung's wife smiled, shook her head, and followed her husband back down to the rum shop.

'That man have that woman totolbay,' Melda said.

'Don't let her quietness fool you, girl,' Jestina said.

'You mean she's underhand?' Melda asked.

'When you have a man like Ling Chung, you have to be underhand, girl,' Jestina said. 'I know things about that woman that nobody else know.'

'I always suspect she wasn't as stupidie as she look,' Melda acknowledged.

'Take it from me,' Jestina said knowingly, 'it have more in that mortar than the pestle.'

'So your mouth stick down with laglie?' Melda was itching to hear the bacchanal about Ling Chung's wife.

'She have a sweet man,' Jestina winked. 'I can't say who it is. Is confidential, nuh. But she have a deputy from right here on Rosehill too.' And with that, she turned her back on Melda, poured two tins of milk into the pot of coffee, stirred it, and took several cups out to the men in the yard. She stayed there with them listening to their mamaguy and picong, and promised to dance the stick fight with them before the night was out.

Left to herself in the kitchen, Melda thought hard about who Ling Chung's wife could be friending with. Sammy? Nah. Sammy was too quiet. Mister Roberts? Nah. Roberts had too much problem on his head. Valmon? Could be. He was fine looking and he was always hanging about in the rumshop. But Valmon was engaged to Miss Ann's oldest daughter. Nah. Willy? Willy? No, not Willy...

Miss Ann came into the kitchen and Melda looked at her as if she were seeing her for the first time. She saw Miss Ann's thick arms, her broad shoulders, her head tied with a flowered cloth, her half slip showing, and she pictured Willy, tall, thin, a nice dresser, a sweet talker, a drinker, a man for whom she herself had felt a little something before she had met Roy, and she told herself, yes. It was highly possible that Willy was the man friending with Ling Chung's wife. Melda patted Miss Ann on her back and offered her a cup of strong coffee.

By the time dark came down on the hill, Tante Vivian's house and yard were packed and people were liming out in the road. Some fellars started a card game in the backyard, playing first for cigarettes. But when Sharky and the boys from the docks came, the game got hot and people started shelling out coins.

Beatrice lit more candles and put them around the yard and Mister Roberts ran two extension cords over the fence from his kitchen to the tent so they could have more light to dance, and when the bottle of rum was three-quarters done, Spree began to beat the drum, flicking it lightly with the tips of his fingers, remembering the way his uncle Zaca had showed him. Mister Roberts took up an empty rum bottle and began to hit it with a rusty nail in time with the drum beat. Sammy ran back down the gully to get his drum and when he came back he put it between his thighs and danced the beat to the four corners of the tent like a tassa man. Spree took up the challenge and matched Sammy lick for lick and Bachack and Spirit and Flash came out into the centre and started spinning and kicking low down on the ground with only the palms of their hands for support. Wattap took the drum from Spree without missing a beat and he and Sammy beat the bongo hot hot like bird peppers as the fellars grabbed their sticks.

Wattap! Tap! Break away! Bend down low! Hit meh dey! Step high! Step low! Rain de blow! The fellars sang and the sticks answered.

Inside the house, the old women turned away from their hymn books to look out the windows at the way the fellars' old bones could still move.

'When the spirit in you,' one of them said, shaking her head, 'it in you till you dead.' And the others nodded their heads in affirmation.

The dance went on and on until each man had fallen to the ground in exhaustion. Then rum, coffee, biscuits and cheese made the rounds until the cock in Mister Roberts' yard began to crow. Some of the younger fellars and the women went home, but several older heads, used to three and four nights' wakes, held on. Beatrice made one more pot of coffee and took it to the tent for Sharky and the fellars who were still playing cards. Then she said goodnight to Tante Vivian, closed the coffin, and fell asleep in a chair in the living room. Sonny stayed up with the fellars in the yard until morning came up the hill.

On the Saturday Tante was to be buried, the sun came out, but by twelve o'clock dark clouds tried to hide it, and a drizzle began to fall. Melda said the damn devil and his wife were fighting over a ham bone and she went in search of her parasol. By two, however, when the hearse arrived, the sun was out again in a blaze.

Every man, woman and child on Rosehill who could walk turned out for the funeral. Even Ling Chung came with his oldest son. Jestina pointed them out to Melda and the women laughed at how odd Ling Chung looked in a suit that was obviously too small for him. 'He come over in that, boy,' Melda laughed. She and the older women were dressed up in black or grey, the younger ones in lily-white, and the men came sporting black suits and felt hats.

The people lined up in threes behind the hearse and the family car provided by the funeral home in which Beatrice, Reme and Sonny sat. Behind them came the officers of the Village Council, then the ladies from Tante Vivian's lodge. Willy made sure everything was in order before he waved to the man driving the hearse to begin Tante Vivian's last trip down Rosehill.

The funeral procession was so long, it blocked traffic for two hours on the Main Road and police had to re-route traffic. Three hours passed before they had made their way from the church to the burial ground.

In Laparouse Cemetery the women sang 'Nearer my God to Thee,' while the men put Tante down in the hole. Then Willy and Mister Roberts swung all Jestina's small children over the grave so they wouldn't have bad dreams, and Beatrice sprinkled a handful of dirt on Tante to say farewell. 'I will really miss you, Tante,' she said softly as tears formed in her eyes, and Sonny led her away from the edge of the grave. Reme had begun to bawl in the church so Sammy kept her in the car where she continued to cry inconsolably. Miss Ann, Melda, Mother Dinah, Jestina, all of them sprinkled dirt on the coffin before the men lowered it deep into the grave.

Before they left the grave side, Sonny gave Beatrice the silver cross from Tante's casket. Then he held her arm and they walked out of the cemetery together. Before they could reach the gate, however, Miss Ann came running up to them, pulled Sonny aside, and told him he had better have somebody watch the grave for a few nights because she had heard that some of the funeral homes were sending people to steal back the caskets.

Sonny took Beatrice home and then he joined the Rosehill men who had stopped off at the rum shop. Ling Chung welcomed them and offered Sonny a beer.

'Glad to see you, Sonny,' he said. 'You do well. You do well. Make Ling proud,' and he pumped Sonny's hand. Sonny stayed and chatted with Ling and the fellars for a while, and then he went up to the house. He and Beatrice hadn't had time to talk much in the days right after Tante's death, and he wanted to tell her he had booked his passage to leave. She was sitting in the gallery by herself when he arrived, and he sat down on the step.

'I see your grip done pack,' she said. 'I didn't know you leaving so soon.'

'Monday morning early,' he said.

'I hope you have a good flight,' she told him, looking away.

'Beatrice, I'm not going forever, yuh know. We talked about this.'

'You coming back, right?'

'Like you don't believe me or what?'

'I would never put my head on a block and say you would do anything, Sonny.'

'You mean after all I do for you, you still don't trust me, girl? You know I have to go back. I just dropped everything and come when Tante asked me. I can't leave everything like that, I have business to take care of.'

'I never expected you to stay anyway,' Beatrice said.

'You never expected me to come either!'

'I know you, Sonny,' Beatrice said softly.

'You know, you always saying that. But you think you really know me? What you know?'

'You change?' She stupesed and looked away. 'You is the same selfish Sonny.'

He stood up and came to lean over her. 'Beatrice, you're an ungrateful woman, you know that? I dropped every blasted thing and come! I wouldn't do that for no other woman.'

'So now you want me to kiss your foot?'

'Shit!' he turned away from her. 'What the hell I talking to you for?'

'So Sonny come,' Beatrice mocked him. 'That is a big deal too?'

'I came to help you, Beatrice! I lie for you! Remember that. I don't know what you want me to say! I tell you I can't stay. I have to go, but I'll come back. Why you can't believe that?'

She got up without answering him and went into the house. Later, when he went to her room, he found the door locked, and she refused to open it for him. That night, and for the two nights before he was to leave, he slept in the living room alone.

Sonny left that Monday morning for the airport. He rode down the hill with Willy in Clyde's taxi and he looked back once, hoping to see Beatrice waving from in front the house, but she wasn't there. He had knocked on her door and told her he was ready to go but she had not answered.

'She's only playing she's sleeping,' Willy had said, and he had knocked harder but she had still refused to open the door.

'I told her I'm coming back,' Sonny told Reme. 'She think I will forget about her case?'

'You better go before you miss your plane,' Reme told him. 'Don't worry about Beatrice. You know how she's stubborn.'

They got to the airport early, and after Sonny had checked his suitcase, he and Willy went up to the balcony to get a cold drink. Willy ordered mauby and Sonny had a peanut punch and they sat together looking out at the plane on the tarmac.

'Beatrice treat me bad, man,' Sonny said.

'Some women does show it in a strange way,' Willy told him.

'Show what? What's she showing, eh?'

'You have coke-e-eye or what, Sonny?' Willy teased him.

'But how she could love me and treat me so?' Sonny asked.

'All that book learning turn you stupidie, Sonny?'

'But I tell she I coming back?'

Willy laughed. 'You know what you shoulda do?' he said. 'You should engage the girl!'

'Tante just bury, man.'

'Just put the ring on she finger! You didn't have to have fete. Now you leave she high and dry, what she going to think?'

'But is so she has to behave?'

'I tell you is so some women does be, man.' Willy said. 'They love you but they have a strange way of showing it. Some of them does just fuss and fuss. That's how they show their love. Women hard to understand, yuh know. But I know them good.'

'Beatrice never had any trouble speaking her mind to me.'

'I telling you the woman want you,' Willy insisted. 'Snake does eat crapaud?'

'So you think I should send she a ring?' Sonny asked.

'Ring what?' Willy laughed, 'You should send for the girl, man. Take she up to New York. What she staying down here for? The police say they stop investigating Chow's case, but you never know in this country. That could open up again at any time. The day she get off this money case, she should board a plane to meet you in New York.'

'I asked her if she still want to go away.' Sonny said. 'She act as if she don't want to go.'

'Is how you asked her, man,' Willy told him. 'If you didn't make it sound sincere, she would say no.'

'I really want to marry her, you know,' Sonny said, 'but I have to get myself settled first. I just finish school. I have a lot of responsibilities.'

'You and Beatrice go through a lot, man,' Willy reminded him.

'I'm not forgetting, Uncle Willy.'

'You have to do more than that, Sonny.'

'You talking as if I write a letter,' Sonny said. 'I never wrote no letter. I never promise Reme or Tante or anybody I would marry Beatrice.'

'Nobody holding a cutlass to your neck, man,' Willy told him. 'But right is right.'

'Is three whole years I gone, Willy!'

'So what you saying? You get tie up in New York?'

'I wasn't in no seminary. And sometimes people have to do things they don't really want to do.'

'So you have a lady up there? If that is the case, you shoulda tell Beatrice up front.'

'I didn't say that was the case. But a man must have....'

'Tell Beatrice, man! Don't leave she hanging!' Willy cut him off.

A female voice called the flight number and Sonny picked up his bag with the two bottles of pepper sauce and the jar of mango chutney Reme had made for him and followed Willy downstairs. 'I had to marry an American woman, Willy,' Sonny spoke fast, as if he had to rush the words out or they would stick in his throat. 'I had to try to get permanent so I could work. You all don't know how it is up there. Life ent easy, nuh. And this government never send me a red cent.'

Willy stopped him on the steps. 'I can't fault you for what you had to do, Sonny. But is not fair to Beatrice to have her holding strain. Level with the girl. Tell she you had to get married. Beatrice is a smart woman. She love you. She'll understand.'

'I'll write her, okay? But tell her for me, Willy,' Sonny pleaded.

'That's your job, man,' Willy told him. 'You have to be a man.'

They went toward the final exit before the tarmac, and Sonny showed the immigration inspector his passport and ticket. The man waved him through. He turned, expecting Willy to follow, but the inspector shook his head.

'Only passengers,' he told Willy, and Sonny rested his bags on a chair and came back out to shake Willy's hand.

'Don't play crab and hide you head in a hole,' Willy laughed.

Sonny smiled and hugged him. 'Look out for Moko, okay? Do what you could do'

'I have Moko in the palm of meh hand, man,' Willy assured him.

Sonny went back into the departure lounge, picked up his bags, and walked out toward the plane, turning every few minutes to wave at Willy until he could no longer see him.

Willy waited until he saw Sonny climb the steps and enter the plane, then he went outside to join Clyde. They leaned against the fence around the parking lot and waited until Sonny's plane took off over the hills.

'You think he coming back?' Clyde asked Willy as the plane rose higher and turned north.

'Boy, no matter where you roam, home is still home. He bound to come back,' Willy told him, and they went back to the taxi and headed for Rosehill.

The last of the heavy rains that year fell in late October and Santabellans were relieved that another wet season had passed without a hurricane. Not all the other islands had been so lucky, though. Up the chain, a few of the small, flat ones had been hit hard and Santabellans contributed what little they could to ease the strain on their neighbours despite the difficult times they themselves were seeing.

Since September most of the large industry workers had been on strike. Workers on the sugar cane estates had struck first for better wages and then the oilfield workers' trade union, unable to reach agreement with the company, had also gone on strike. When contract negotiations between soap factory officials and the workers failed, two hundred pickets paraded in front of the factory and Santabellans ran out of soap to wash their clothes. Within weeks, a strike plague had hit the island. The teachers' union struck, and by the time the dry season came, more than three-quarters of Santabella's government workers were out on strike.

In a desperate move, the Government passed an emergency destabilization bill to try to make the strikes illegal, and when that failed to force the workers back, they sent squads of police in cork hats to drive the strikers away from factory gates, and to stop them from parading with placards in front of government offices. Within a month the general shutdown had begun to wreck Santabella's already crippled economy. Ships left the harbour empty, and Sharky and the other dock workers, frustrated because they couldn't get paid, emptied warehouses, smashed crates and poured anything they couldn't sell, or give away, into the sea.

All over Santabella shop shelves were empty and people from the towns headed to the country districts to find relatives who could give them a hand of green figs, some cassavas, one or two breadfruits, a handful of bodie, or anything to replace the rice, flour, sugar, oil and butter that shopkeepers were rationing.

Rosehill wasn't suffering as badly as some other parts of Santabella because the villagers could make out with the crops from their gardens and fish from the sea. Willy, Roberts, Sammy, and even Ling Chung were used to a plate of boiled yams with sweet potatoes, or corn meal dumplings and salt fish in the afternoons. A cup of tea with a piece of roast bake took them through the day. The women also managed to do with the little they had. Since they couldn't get soap, Miss Ann and the other women went back to hitting their clothes on rocks in the ravine and placing the whites in the sun to be bleached. They scrubbed their children clean with bush leaves and washed their hair with grated aloes. For butter, they used mashed zabocca with salt and pepper, and traded peas and tomatoes for rice from the Indians in Barrackpore. The rice, still unshelled, had to be pounded and the women often gathered in Miss Ann's yard to use her large mortar and pestle.

'I betting anybody Jesus was a black man,' Miss Ann declared one afternoon as she sifted the rice grains in a piece of clean merino. 'I could put my head on a block for that.'

'Every picture I ever see have him painted white,' Melda said.

'Is who draw them pictures?' Miss Ann asked her. 'I telling you, Jesus black. Don't doubt me.'

'Why you say so?' Jestina asked.

'Your eyes blind?' Miss Ann said. 'Look round you. Who you see bearing cross every day? White people or black people? Is we on Calvary every day. Nobody could tell me that Jesus was a white man. Eh eh. I quicker believe cock have teeth.'

'I don't mind all the trouble,' Jestina said. 'I is a bachack. I could take it, but is the children I worried for. Every day the sun come up I begging God for them but I getting fed up. I tell Sharky to tell me when the next boat come from Venezuela. I going down the Main.'

'How you paying the boat fare?' Melda asked her.

'Who say anything about pay?'

'You mean you going to stow away?'

'I taking meh chances.'

'And what you going to do with the children?' Miss Ann wanted to know.

'I taking them with me. By the time the captain find we, the boat will be too far out to turn back, and he can't drop we in the sea.'

Miss Ann stopped shelling peas to look at Jestina. 'Jestina, sometimes I does wonder if you have fowl brains. You can't stow away with no children.'

'Well, I ent leaving them here to suffer. Better they die with me in the sea.'

'I does listen to all you young people talk and laugh, oui,' Miss Roberts said. 'All you think this is hell you ketching? This ent no hell! My great grandmother coulda tell you about hell! Huh! This is joke!'

'Is why I say Jesus had to be black,' Miss Ann said. 'No white man ever suffer so!'

'So is how long we belly have to grip?'

'I staying right here and stand my grind, girl,' Melda told them. 'It ent easy but at least I have food to eat.'

'You does only think bout your belly,' Jestina argued. 'Is not just food I want for meh children! What about education? You think I want them dancing in clubs like me? You think I want them going down on the wharf to beg Sharky and them for a shilling? I want better for them!'

'The government promise free education.' Melda said.

'Promise my arse,' Jestina shouted. 'Is how much months now they promising to fix up the school? Water falling down on the children! Now dry season come you think they going to fix what they didn't fix in rainy season? They don't even want to pay the teachers! The children not learning anything. Lilly's in second standard and she still reading "Dan is de Man in de Van!" Don't get meh vexed here!'

'What you getting so hot for?' Miss Ann asked Jestina. 'Is better we try to help we self and not wait on this government. I was telling Beatrice that same thing the other day. The children not learning a damn thing in that government school. I tell she is best we start we own school up here.'

'Is I who tell you that long time,' Melda said. 'What Beatrice answer?'

'You know how Beatrice is. She say she have to think bout it. But I going to tackle she again before long. Don't worry. Beatrice doing anything I tell she to do.'

'We could fix up the community centre,' Melda said. She had always wanted to be a teacher and her thoughts began to whirl with possibilities.

'Me and Jestina could take the small children and Beatrice

189

could take the bigger ones. Yes, is a good plan,' and in her mind she could see Rosehill's children walking one behind the other into the new school to take dictation from her. 'Yes,' she said again, 'is a good plan.'

'Is not as easy as you think,' Miss Ann cautioned. 'Books and slates and all that cost money, yuh know. And we go have to give Beatrice a little something.'

'You think Beatrice have time with any school,' Jestina said. 'The girl head hot with worries bout the land case. How she could teach any children?'

'It might be just the thing to take her mind off the case,' Miss Roberts said.

'I don't think is just the case on her mind,' Melda told them. 'The girl quail up like soucouyant sucking she. I think she grieving for Sonny.'

'She take Tante's death hard,' Jestina shook her head sadly. 'And she probably never get over the child's death. Two deaths in so short a time. And then come the case, and on top of that she still have the business with Dr. Chow. I tell you, if I was Beatrice, I woulda be going mad mad. Is enough to bust open anybody's head.'

'Beatrice shouldn't worry bout the case.' Miss Ann called her chickens and flung some rice grains toward them. 'That case mighten call till next year. Government head hot for so with all the strikes. You think they have time with Beatrice?'

'And she hands would be so full with the children she wouldn't have time to think bout the case,' Melda agreed. 'Ann, you want me to talk to she?'

Miss Ann said no, she would do it, after all, she reminded them, she was the secretary of the Village Council, and as such, she was responsible for all these kind of official matters.

'So you want to be a one man delegation?' Jestina smiled. 'When Beatrice turn you down, don't come running back to me.'

By the following Sunday, Miss Ann had planned her strategy and she went into operation. Right after church, she took a bowl of callaloo and crab, a plate of busupshot and curried

190

breadfruit, and a cold glass of mauby to Beatrice.

Beatrice let her into the tidy living room and Miss Ann looked around approvingly.

'I see you put up new curtains, girl,' she said, examining the quality closely. 'They nice. Sonny send them down?'

'Tante had them in a box under the bed,' Beatrice shook her head lightly at Miss Ann's fastness. 'You know how she used to hide up her good things.'

'Is best you use them up, child,' Miss Ann turned to sit down. 'Tante was probably saving them for the wedding, eh, but now Sonny gone back....' And she shrugged her shoulders in resignation.

'Thanks for the callaloo,' Beatrice said, refusing to take the bait. 'I can't say the last day I had some. Reme can't make it as good as Tante used to, so she doesn't even try. And too besides, she say she have to be careful about what she eat these days. You see how the belly going down?'

'I see her passing the parlour,' Miss Ann said. 'She looking good these days. The man in Guapo helping her with the belly?'

'I don't know about any man in Guapo, Miss Ann,' Beatrice said, 'but Ma say she have to try to take care of herself better. If everything go okay, we might go up to Canada.'

'Kelvin up there, you know. So Reme want to look like young girl again to get she man back, eh. She ent know Kelvin must be married some white woman long time. She wasting she time.'

Beatrice's cheeks burned at the way Miss Ann talked about her mother, but she knew better than to get into an argument. She ate quietly and Miss Ann asked, 'You hear anything from Sonny these days?'

For a second Beatrice wanted to say 'yes,' to let Miss Ann wonder when and how the postman could have delivered a letter from Sonny that she didn't know about. But she sipped the mauby and said, 'You know the postman coming only once in a blue moon these days. Sonny's letters must be tied-up down in that post office.'

191

'You shouldn't study too much about Sonny, you know, Beatrice.' Miss Ann told her. 'With these men, you never know. Once they go away, you don't have a hold on them any more. Look at you. You had child for Sonny, and he still...'

'Who say I studying Sonny, Miss Ann?' Beatrice snapped. 'Sonny is the least of my worries.'

Miss Ann, realising that she was beginning to irritate Beatrice, tried a different tack. 'So you hear from Ali bout the case?'

'I went down there yesterday. He say I should expect it to call after the Christmas holidays. I just praying for it to be done with so I could go away.'

'To meet Sonny?'

'No, Miss Ann,' Beatrice tried to be patient. 'My life's not wrapped up with Sonny's. I thinking bout going to Canada to study nursing.'

'Is a nice place,' Miss Ann nodded, 'but it cold, girl. And this lady tell me that in winter, people does walk around as if they is dragons blowing smoke all over the place. So when you will leave if you do go?'

'After the cold pass.'

'What you going to do in the meantime, Beatrice? You can't just sit in the house all day wasting your time? You could be teaching the children something. I was telling Miss Roberts and them about it. We ready to back you with the school.'

'I really don't want to start anything and then have to drop it, Miss Ann.'

'Don't worry yuh head bout that, girl. By the time you get ready to leave, we could get another teacher. Melda already eager eager, you know *she*. And besides, I tell Miss Roberts and them you say yes. I only come to finalise the plans.'

'Miss Ann!' Beatrice protested, 'I only say I was going to think about it! How you could tell tales so?'

Miss Ann laughed, 'I know your mind better than you, Beatrice. Come teach the children. You know how education important.'

'I don't want to teach, Miss Ann,' Beatrice told her.

'You don't want to be around little children. Is that it, Beatrice?' Miss Ann asked bluntly. 'You never cry when my godchild die, but I know how you was hurting inside. Tante tell me how you used to cry in the night, and how you used to go down by the sea all the time. But after one time is a next, Beatrice. You have to get over that. You can't wallow in sorrow. You is a young woman. Look at yourself. Don't let hard time get you down so.'

In the end, Beatrice, beaten down, agreed, and Miss Ann passed the word to the women as she went back down the hill.

Shortly after, Rosehill men began to paint and repair the community centre with material the villagers donated. Knowing that the schoolmaster at the Rosehill government school would refuse their requests for chalk, slates, or any other school supplies, Miss Ann had a quiet talk with her son Clyde and a few of the steelband fellars.

When the centre was ready, the fellars began to move benches, books, blackboards, pencils and erasers from the school at night, and after they had taken all they needed, they poured pitch oil around the rotten base boards and set the place afire. From the Ledge, Rosehill looked down on the blaze as it swept quickly through the government school, leaving only the concrete drinking pipes standing dry in the yard.

In town, the trade unions were putting pressure on the government to settle the disputes before Christmas. Hundreds of workers marched through the streets every day but the carnival atmosphere that had carried the bands in the early days of the shutdown had turned sour. As the days grew into months, tempers got hot and violence broke out on several occasions when the strikers threw bottles and stones at the few workers who dared to cross the lines.

The *Bomb*, still being printed in Trinidad, urged the workers to continue the fight, but many Santabellans were getting fed up. With Christmas just around the corner, the people would have settled for the few concessions the companies and the government were willing to make, but the trade union leaders viewed the fight as a political as well as an economic one, and said they intended to go as far as possible to break the government's power. They demanded general elections. The government accused them of obscuring the issues and threatened to jail them for inciting people to riot.

Soon, rumours spread throughout Santabella that the unions and the army were going to topple the government.

'What I say about this place?' Willy asked the fellars in Ling Chung's rumshop. 'Did I say this place is like an American film show?'

'I hear they say they going to cut the head off the snake,' Valmon told them.

'After that, the whole government going to fall.'

'I don't care who in charge,' Roberts declared. 'Is same old khaki pants. Nothing ent changing.'

And the men agreed that he was right.

A few days before Christmas, a man came up to Rosehill asking for Beatrice Salandy. He stopped by Miss Ann's parlour to ask directions and she sent her daughter to show him the house, telling the child quietly to 'stay and see what the man want from Miss Beatrice.' The child reported that the man was from New York and that Sonny had sent a box with ham and sweet biscuits and a lot of nice clothes for Beatrice. Miss Ann closed down the shop and went to investigate.

'You mean Sonny didn't send a little for his Tante?' she asked Beatrice, peeping into the box.

Beatrice laughed, 'Is two hams he send, Miss Ann. Look! He mark your name big big. "This is for Miss Ann." And he send a watch for Uncle Willy.'

Miss Ann took the gifts and hugged them, 'I really thought my mouth wouldn't taste ham this year, girl. You see what I does always say? What goes round must come back round.'

'Sonny would never forget Rosehill, Miss Ann,' Beatrice agreed.

'I always say that, child. Look how he send all that money for we to get the leases. How many people would do that?'

'You think I should give my ham to Jestina?' Beatrice tried to avoid a discussion of the money and the leases. 'She didn't even have one last year. Miss Melda neither.'

'Is a sorry day when Christmas come and you can't put a piece of ham in your mouth,' Miss Ann shook her head. 'I tell you, this country gone to the dogs in true.'

'We could boil down the two hams together and share it around,' Beatrice suggested. 'Mister Roberts killing a pig and with that and these hams everybody could get a piece for Christmas.'

Miss Ann reluctantly agreed, and later the women got together and boiled the hams in her yard. They also baked butter bread, and made ginger beer and sorrel but Miss Ann waited until they had left before she put a little sponge cake in the oven.

All in all, Christmas didn't pass Rosehill too bad that year. True, nobody could repaint their whole house, but they varnished chairs, and bought new curtains, and made the children sweep the yards so clean, you could eat off the dirt.

Ling Chung gave out almanacs with sweeping vistas of the sea and the hills, and the Village Council held its annual Children's Christmas party. Valmon made up a parang group and they went from house to house on Christmas Eve mopping rum and filling their bellies with ham and sweet bread. Miss Ann even had a bottle of chow-chow to eat with her ham.

On Christmas morning, Beatrice handed out the sweet biscuits Sonny had sent to the children who had come to wish her happy Christmas, and she set a table in the living room with coconut sweetbread, butter bread from Melda, sponge cake and fruit cake Reme had made, and ham, sorrel and ginger beer for visitors. She had hung new plastic curtains at the windows and tacked a Santa Claus she had cut from Sonny's postcard onto the front door. When the steelband came up the hill playing a Christmas calypso, she gave them thick slices of bread with ham and hot pepper, and then joined the children jumping in the band all through the village. Rosehill was glad to see her happy.

In town, the government put on a fireworks display in front of the Prime Minister's house, and while everybody was looking up at the pretty sparks in the sky, two men entered the house from the back and choked the Prime Minister to death.

'The head of the snake has been cut off,' the trade union leaders declared over the radio, and according to reports reaching Rosehill early the following morning, many government ministers were running for their lives.

'Airport full,' Jestina told Beatrice. 'All them bad john ministers running like mongoose. Is a revolution, girl. The trade unions, the army, everybody turning against the government.'

'Is time,' Beatrice agreed. 'Is time people make a stand. I wish Tante did live to see it.'

'I for one have to wait and see how this revolution going to work out,' Miss Ann declared. 'It might be the same ole khaki pants.'

Melda shook her head. 'All you really think this going to make any difference? How life going to change for we? Tell me that. We still have to eat the bread the devil knead.'

'We just have to wait and see,' Beatrice told her. 'That is all we could do. The deeper the darkness, the nearer the dawn.'

And Miss Ann told Jestina that Beatrice was sounding just like Tante Vivian.

On Boxing Day, in the afternoon, Beatrice went to see Moko and dressed him in the shirt and tie Sonny had sent. She could tell by his eyes that he recognised her. He tried to nod as she spoke to him, to show that he was understanding, but he couldn't talk. The orderly told her that he had suffered a slight stroke a few days before. Beatrice thought about Tante dying and wondered how long poor Moko would hang on, but she tried to smile and be cheerful for him. She told him about Sonny's presents, and about Mister Roberts killing the pig, and about Melda's new baby, and about how the school was going, and through it all Moko smiled. Later, she took a bowl of water away from the orderly and sponged off Moko's face, and for the rest of that afternoon she sat outside in the sun with him and rubbed his fingers, telling him stories until it was time to leave.

Late one night, just as he was getting ready to close the rumshop, someone dropped ten copies of the *Bomb* on Ling Chung's counter. Ling Chung sent his son running to get Willy.

'Why you have paper to drop here?' Ling Chung demanded. 'You want police close down Ling Chung? I no want trouble with police, Willy. *Bomb* big trouble,' and he shoved the papers into Willy's hands and slammed the door on him.

'You want we to drink your rum but you don't want to join the party, eh Ling?' Willy shouted, but Ling Chung, busy bolting his doors and windows, didn't answer.

Willy distributed the papers but kept one to read with Beatrice. He went up to the house and found that she had already put on her nightgown, but she came out and sat with him in the living room to look over the paper.

'Let me see what bacchanal they have, girl,' Willy laughed.

'You couldn't wait till morning, Uncle Willy?' Beatrice asked him, yawning, but there was a laugh in her voice because she too was curious to see what the *Bomb* had to say.

Willy unfolded the paper carefully and pointed to a picture of a large house with a flower garden and swimming pool that took up three-quarters of the front page. The bold headline read: THE HOUSE THAT BOBOL MONEY BUILT.

The story on the following page said Beatrice's former boss, the Minister of Finance, lived in the house in Coral Gables, an exclusive section of Miami. The Minister had built the house, the *Bomb* claimed, with money he had stolen from the government, and the government, embarrassed about the loss of hundreds of thousands of dollars, was putting the blame on an innocent young woman from Rosehill, a school teacher who had taken on the task of teaching young children when the government had failed to do so. A picture of Beatrice surrounded by waving children was featured with quotes from Melda and Jestina and Miss Ann highlighting the page.

MUST THE INNOCENT PAY? the *Bomb* asked, and in a related story on page three, it displayed a man with a hood over his head who had told the reporter that he knew for a fact that the Minister had stolen the money because he had helped to take the money out of the country. He had asked the *Bomb* not to reveal his identity because he was afraid he would be killed. 'You think it easy in dis country?' the man said. 'It ent easy, nuh. Police could find me dead in a drain for dis.' The paper demanded that the case against Beatrice Salandy be dropped.

'Matters fix, girl,' Willy laughed.

'What you mean?' Beatrice asked him. 'Just because newspaper say something, magistrate don't have to believe it. I wish it was so easy in truth.'

'If you lose, we all lose, girl,' Willy said. 'Where else we going to get money for the other leases? Things getting from bad to worse every day. The new leaders say the treasury empty. What is revolution without money? Eh? At least these new fellars in the government not so quick to give we land to the Yankees. The *Bomb* say they halting all negotiations about oil leases.' But Willy, despite his confident manner, was really worried. He knew that Beatrice's money was their only real hope, that if she was found guilty, the signed leases would be nullified, and Rosehill would belong to the Company. And on top of that, he knew Beatrice had stolen the money. Not for one minute did he believe that Sonny had sent it to her even though Sonny had not told him the truth. As he tried to console Beatrice, his heart was heavy with worry, and he wished he could go down to the rumshop and get stoned drunk, but it was closed. He turned away from Beatrice so she wouldn't see the anxious look on his face and after a few minutes he asked her if she had Sonny's telephone number. Beatrice went into her room and brought back a little piece of paper with a number written on it.

'I never called him so I can't say is a real number,' she laughed.

Willy folded the paper carefully and placed it in his fob. Then he smiled and patted Beatrice's hand.

'Don't worry yuh head, girl. I'll talk to Ali bout things. But I sure he and Sonny done fix up before Sonny went back. Don't worry.'

'You sound like you have more faith than the Pope, Uncle Willy,' Beatrice said, 'but if you know the amount of time I get disappointed, you would understand why I have to be sceptical.' And long after Willy left that night, she stayed up wondering what would happen in court next day.

Reme came in late and found Beatrice dozing in the chair, and she shook her awake. Beatrice went to her bed but couldn't sleep. She could feel herself dozing off but would awake suddenly as if somebody, something, had frightened her. During one of these fits of sleep, she dreamed about Doctor Chow. His face blistered, burnt, came up out of the dirt and his hands, thick with mud, tried to pull her down. She thought she heard herself scream but when she sat up in the bed and Reme didn't come running into the room, she wondered if she had really screamed at all. She got out of the bed and decided to try one of Tante Vivian's remedies.

As the water boiled, something drew her to the cabinet where an old copy of the *Bomb* lay folded under some paper bags. She took out the paper and read the front page story about the doctor's funeral. The report said the police had no clues but were working on a theory that the doctor had had a falling out with certain foreign individuals over a land scheme, and that those individuals had had him murdered. The *Bomb* showed a picture of several prominent people who had attended the funeral, and Beatrice, in a moment of hysteria, burst out laughing, for the sight of the doctor, his pants down around his knees, his hands tight around his penis and sperm dripping from it, had flashed across her mind, and she balled up the paper viciously and flung it into the trash bin. She lit a match then and burnt the paper until only ashes were left in the bottom of the bin. She watched the ashes as if she were in a trance, and it was only the singing of the kettle that brought her back to reality. Then she mixed a teaspoon of honey, two drops of vinegar, and a dash of bitters into a hot glass of water, drank it and went back to bed.

Rosehill turned up in full force for Beatrice's case. They came early and waited with great expectations. So great were their numbers that they took up all the room in the courthouse and the upper balcony and spilled down into the yard. Inside the jam-packed, hot room, Beatrice, Reme and Willy waited anxiously up front for Ali who came hurrying in a moment before the case was called and told Beatrice sorry, but he had been handling another case downstairs. 'Murder, nuh. Have to keep the fellar from getting hang.'

'We paying you good money,' Reme told him, and mumbled that if Beatrice was Indian, Ali would have been in the court since foreday morning.

'Don't excite yourself,' he assured her. 'Two three minutes and we out of here,' and he snapped his fingers to emphasise his confidence.

'I always tell you not to trust Sonny,' Reme grumbled. 'Man? You think you could trust any man in this world?' and she stupesed long and hard.

The bailiff announced the case and Ali took Beatrice by the hand and led her away from Reme and the others to stand with him before the magistrate. The prosecutor came in and stood on the other side. He nodded to Ali. The magistrate asked if all parties were in court and ready, and somebody in the room shouted 'We here, man. Start de case, nuh.'

The magistrate banged his gavel and called for order in the court.

Ali said he and his client were ready, and the prosecutor asked if he could come to the bench. The magistrate motioned him and he went forward to whisper to the magistrate. The magistrate nodded; the prosecutor went back to his place, and then the magistrate told Ali to proceed.

Ali made a motion for dismissal.

'On what grounds, Mister Ali?' the magistrate sounded weary as he wiped his wet forehead with a half-dirty handkerchief.

200

'On the grounds that the government has no evidence, Sir,' Ali said. 'We have provided the court with a signed and notarised affidavit from Sonny Allen testifying that he did indeed provide the defendant with certain sums of money with which she was to purchase certain lands in the village of Rosehill. Mister Allen would have come down to testify, Your Honour, but he himself is preparing to take the Bar exams in New York, and had to return. As you know, this case has been delayed and delayed by the government as they tried every political man....'

The magistrate interrupted him. 'Mr. Ali, you not in the House of Lords. Get on with the facts of the case, okay man?'

'Look what he doing, look what he doing. He getting the magistrate vexed,' Reme whispered. 'Why he doing that? Lord, is now Beatrice in trouble. I did tell Sonny not to trust no Indian. The government probably bribe him off...'

Willy shushed her as Ali continued.

'I presented earlier to the court several documents, Your Honour....' and the bailiff passed some papers to the magistrate. He turned the pages over and read. Then he told Ali to continue.

'The fact that the defendant was at that time employed in government service, and that certain sums were found to be missing from her place of employment at and about the same time as the defendant received the aforementioned sums from Mister Sonny Allen, should in no way prejudice this court against her, Your Honour. The government bases its case against Miss Salandy on mere coincidence. They have no proof!'

Ali seemed to be enjoying himself, waving his arms, turning to address the courtroom instead of the magistrate. The magistrate shook his head but did not stop the performance.

Ali continued, 'They have provided no proof, Your Honour. The Minister himself, the person making the original charge against my client, is not even present in the courtroom.' Ali paused and looked around expectantly as if he expected the Minister in question to appear at the door dramatically.

'He in Miami!' someone shouted, and the magistrate called for order 'one last time.'

Ali faced the magistrate again, 'He is, according to the newspapers, Your Honour, languishing in a condominium in Miami.... (laughter from the courtroom) ...built, it is said, with questionable funds... (applause from the courtroom. The magistrate called for order again). I therefore ask this court to drop these false charges against the defendant and allow her to get on with the good work she is doing with the children in Rosehill.'

Rosehill clapped loudly and told each other, 'That man is a master, oui. Hear how he talking, man. Is de Queen's English, yuh know.'

'Miss Ann, Miss Ann,' Melda patted her on the shoulder, trying to get her attention.

Miss Ann shushed her but Melda persisted. 'Suppose Beatrice get off. What we going to do bout the school? She say anything to you bout going to Canada again?'

Miss Ann waved her hand confidently. 'Just leave Beatrice up to me.'

But Reme, sitting in front of them, turned around and said, 'All you want my daughter to spend she life working for all you? Well, just wait. When this case closed, I putting she right on a plane for Toronto.'

The magistrate banged again for order and said he would clear the courtroom if the noise continued. He motioned for Ali and the prosecutor to come closer. They went up to him together, and the magistrate talked to them for a few minutes.

'What he saying? What he saying?' Rosehill asked each other.

Then, with the prosecutor shrugging his shoulders and Ali beaming, the magistrate announced: 'Case dismissed!'

Pandemonium broke out. Rosehill started clapping, some rushed up to Ali and Beatrice, some shook each other's hands, but a few of them, especially those who had not been able to get into the courtroom, grumbled. One man said he had come to see a big show and all he had gotten was a pappyshow. 'That was case too? I glad the girl get off but why they have to finish so quick?' And he went away vexed vexed.

Willy pumped Ali's hand. 'You rule the court, man.'

'And I tell all you not to worry, man?' Ali laughed. 'The government know they couldn't win this one long time.'

'So what going to happen to Beatrice's bank account?' Reme had pushed her way through to Ali. 'What bout all the money, eh? Government can't keep it. Is my daughter's money. Sonny send that money....'

'You ask a question. You going to give me a chance to answer?' Ali asked her. 'Calm down, nuh. The magistrate will sign the order to release the money.' He turned to Willy, 'Now all you don't go having big fete and forget my fee, eh.'

Willy and Beatrice assured him that his money would be in his hands as soon as the account was free, and Ali laughed as he shook Beatrice's hand.

'Sonny tell me to fix up with the leases too,' he said. 'But we could talk bout that later.' He left them then to hurry off to see about another case.

Beatrice, in a slight daze, allowed Reme, Miss Ann and Willy to take her out of the courtroom, down the steps, and into a Chinese restaurant across the street to celebrate. But she couldn't eat. She excused herself when the food came, saying that she had to wash her hands and went to the back. Miss Ann followed her to the toilet.

'I don't want to bother yuh head with this now, girl, but everybody want to know bout the children, Beatrice. You not going to leave them now, eh? I tell everybody you would never do a thing like that. I say, "Me? I know Beatrice like a 'T'. She would never go away and leave the children stranded." '

'You talking for me again, eh,' Beatrice laughed. 'You know my mind before I know it. You working obeah, Miss Ann?'

Miss Ann laughed, 'I could see a lot of things, girl. It wasn't Tante alone who know how to do thing, you know. Too besides, I know you since you small, Beatrice. I watch you grow. I watch you have child. Girl, I know you inside out. I ever steer wrong? Eh? Tell me that?'

'No, you never steer me wrong,' Beatrice agreed patiently. 'And I already make up my mind.'

'You staying?' Miss Ann began to smile.

'I will tell you later,' Beatrice laughed.

'But what you going away to do, Beatrice? Sonny done married...' she stopped, her mouth staying open in surprise as she saw Beatrice's face in the mirror over the sink.

'Who tell you Sonny married, Miss Ann?' Beatrice demanded. 'You know everybody's business, right?'

'Beatrice, I sorry, girl. I thought Willy tell you. Sonny is the one who tell him. I say you know. But is only so he could get permanent. You know how you have to do these things to get to stay in the white man's country. I was telling Jestina the other day that these Yankees could come down here and take we land, and nobody asking them for visa. But we? Let we try to go to their country. Is paper here, paper there...'

But Beatrice was no longer listening. She had slammed the washroom door and was out of the restaurant before Miss Ann could finish her sentence.

So what now, she asked herself as she went down to the bus station. Sonny was married. No wonder. No wonder he couldn't tell her what she had wanted him to say that day when Tante died. And yet he had come back. Why? Because Tante had asked him? Because he still felt something for her? Did he ever love her? She doubted it. Sonny loved only himself. Reme had always known it and she had warned her. What she would do now? She had money in the bank. She would send Reme away to see a specialist about her belly. And she. What she would do?

An old woman passed her and she thought suddenly of Tante Vivian and wished she could run to her, put her head in her lap, and be comforted. But Tante gone, Beatrice whispered. Tante gone, and in the end, you alone are dancing.

She crossed the street and got on a bus without even realising that it was headed to Carenage. The seats were filled with school children and Beatrice listened to their chatter, deliberately shutting out the confusion that fought to control her mind. She rang the bell, got off at the beach road and walked through the narrow track to the edge of the water still not fully aware of what she was doing or why. Not another soul was on the beach, and then, for a reason that she herself did not know, she took off all her clothes, dropped them on the sand, and went into the water. She dove down, stayed under, and for first time in many months, the sea consoled her. She felt a calmness come over her and her spirits lifted, and she knew, even before she turned her back on the ocean to walk back to the sand, that she would stay.